DESOLATION CANYON

ALSO BY P. J. TRACY

Deep into the Dark

THE MONKEEWRENCH SERIES

Ice Cold Heart
The Guilty Dead
Nothing Stays Buried
The Sixth Idea
Off the Grid
Shoot to Thrill
Snow Blind
Dead Run
Live Bait
Monkeewrench

Return of the Magi

DESOLATION CANYON

P. J. TRACY

MINOTAUR BOOKS
NEW YORK

First published in the United States by Minotaur Books, an imprint of St. Martin's Publishing Group

DESOLATION CANYON. Copyright © 2021 by Traci Lambrecht. All rights reserved. Printed in the United States of America. For information, address St. Martin's Publishing Group, 120 Broadway, New York, NY 10271.

www.minotaurbooks.com

Designed by Devan Norman

Library of Congress Cataloging-in-Publication Data

Names: Tracy, P. J., author.
Title: Desolation canyon / P.J. Tracy.
Description: First Edition. | New York : Minotaur Books, 2022.
Identifiers: LCCN 2021037833 | ISBN 978-1-250-75495-0
    (hardcover) | ISBN 978-1-250-83019-7 (ebook)
Subjects: GSAFD: Mystery fiction.
Classification: LCC PS3620.R33 D47 2022 | DDC 813/.6—dc23
LC record available at https://lccn.loc.gov/2021037833

Our books may be purchased in bulk for promotional, educational, or business use. Please contact your local bookseller or the Macmillan Corporate and Premium Sales Department at 1-800-221-7945, extension 5442, or by email at MacmillanSpecialMarkets@macmillan.com.

First Edition: 2022

10 9 8 7 6 5 4 3 2 1

To the brave men and women, past and present, who have sacrificed so much— sometimes everything—to serve our country.

The Russian soul is a dark place.
—*Fyodor Dostoyevsky*

DESOLATION CANYON

Chapter One

A PERFECT LOS ANGELES MORNING: A cloudless sky so devastatingly blue, you'd swear God had Photoshopped it; a hint of sea in the air that embraced you in a balmy hug; palm fronds waving laconically in a gentle breeze. Beautiful people strolled Santa Monica sidewalks and disappeared into polished storefronts that enticed capacious wallets to open wide.

It wasn't the kind of morning that evoked thoughts of death in normal people. But Margaret Nolan wasn't normal.

It's surreal, Maggie, like your life gets split in half the minute you hear the news: before and after, that's all there is. Part of me wishes I didn't know, but it's too late for that, there's no going back. I have a killer inside and there's nothing they can do about it.

Sophie had died of brain cancer five years ago, at the age of twenty-seven, and there *was* no going back—not for her, not for her family, not for the other people who'd loved her. These unbidden memories of a perfectly sunny, perfectly tragic day with her best friend slinked into Nolan's mind as she drove down Montana Avenue toward Palisades Park and the ocean.

She wasn't carrying a terminal diagnosis, but she understood before and after in a different context: before you killed somebody and after you killed somebody. Loss of innocence affected every human being on the planet at one point or another, in one way or another, but the details mattered.

Her interview with the department psychologist had been desultory and unhelpful—it was just something you did after a shooting so your superiors could feel good about your mental health before they put you back on the street. Her brother, Max, would have had something profound to say on the subject of taking human life, but those words had gone to the grave with him. She was on her own.

The killer inside. No going back.

Days off were the hardest, because they gave her time to think. The empty hours stretched out before her, leaving space in her mind for a continual instant replay loop of those last deadly seconds. It was critical to fill that malevolent space with other things, so she'd devised a regimen to stay thoughtless, busy, and disciplined. It rarely varied.

Mornings consisted of biking the Strand—number one on her agenda for today—or hiking Runyon Canyon. Afterward, she'd hit the gym for weight training and stop at Sprouts on the way home to buy expensive, organic food that would invariably end up rotting in her refrigerator. Then it was laundry, house cleaning, and organizing things that had been left in disarray throughout the week.

The reward for her diligence was a bottle of wine and a dinner-sized bowl of popcorn in front of the TV while baby artichokes and grass-fed lamb languished unprepared, unwanted. At midnight, she would slide beneath the covers and sleep fitfully. Notably absent from her new schedule were visits to the gun range.

This routine of avoidance was beginning to aggravate her. Not only was it unproductive and probably detrimental, it was frighteningly analogous to her mother's recent behavior. The very behavior she loathed and railed against. Judge not lest you be judged.

The revelation was as distressing as it was motivational—today was going to be different, by God. She hadn't fired a weapon since that night in Beverly Hills two months ago, and it was time to get back to the range. Kill a silhouette instead of a real person. Face it and move on. Sophie had, confronting far worse. Make her proud.

Chapter Two

WHILE NOLAN WAS UNLOADING AT THE range, a woman who'd dropped her last name years ago—like Madonna or Rihanna—was crawling through a ragged hole cut from a rusty, metal-link fence in the desert. Marielle winced when the sharp, cut ends scored her bare arms and drew blood. Hello, tetanus, good luck getting a shot anytime soon. Stupid, stupid, stupid. In spite of the unbearable heat, she should have worn long sleeves.

Another mistake to add to the long list of them. So many bad choices, big and small. But that was all changing now. There would never be full absolution for her, but it was way past time for penance.

She found a packet of tissues in her duffel and blotted her wounds, then wiped the blood from the spines of metal that had gouged her. The sand had soaked up the fallen droplets, but she smoothed it anyway, erasing her presence here. Nobody knew this place, she was reasonably certain of that, but now was not a time to be careless. Her daughter's life depended on it, and she would protect her or die trying.

The entrance to the abandoned mine was mostly in shadow now, but there was enough light to see that the rotting timbers supporting it were canting inward under the weight of the earth above it. There were a million horrible ways to die, and being buried alive was very near the top of her list. But she'd come to realize there were worse things than death.

She tossed the duffel through the dark mouth and that slightest of concussions caused a shower of dirt to rain down on the canvas. What would happen if there was a tremor or, God forbid, a bona fide earthquake while she and Serena were in there? She knew exactly what would happen: the mine would implode and collapse on them, just like this whole plan might. But there weren't any other options. It was time to spin the wheel of fortune and let the universe decide. It was waiting for her, so said the seductive promise that had brought her to this hellhole in the first place.

Marielle dropped to her hands and knees and crept through the opening into stale, dusty blackness so complete, she felt like she'd been swallowed. She didn't believe it was remotely safe in here, but the mine provided a perfect view of the valley floor. She would be able to see the truck coming, even with the headlights off. If it didn't happen this week, when Paul was away from the compound, it might be a month before they could try again, and she didn't want to think about what could happen in a month.

You're going to be running for the rest of your life. Serena deserves better.

Serena did deserve better, but that was a problem to solve later. Right now, it was simply about survival, so she dragged the duffel deeper into the cave until a fetid smell stopped her. Until now, it hadn't occurred to her that the mine might have been repurposed by some animal, possibly a dangerous one. But the dangerous animals only lived up in the mountains. Didn't they?

With trembling hands, she fumbled for her penlight so she could scare away whatever man-eating beast might be lurking in the inky blackness beyond, or at least meet her maker before it ripped her head off. Out of darkness, let light shine.

When she finally found it and clicked it on, the corona of light landed on a lumpy, dark rock with metallic veins and speckles that reflected off the rough surface. Serena would love it and do something imaginative with it, so she stashed it in the duffel for her birthday next month.

She trained the flashlight farther into the cavern and a scream she didn't dare release almost erupted from her throat.

Animals hadn't done this. Oh, no, animals didn't arrange human bodies like strips of jerky to cure in the desert air. This was a manmade mausoleum. It was impossible to tell how long they'd been here, partially mummified as they were, and she wasn't going to examine them more closely to try and find out. Whoever these poor souls had been, they were lost to the world here. If they'd been trying to get away, things had gone terribly wrong.

Not all dangerous things lived in the mountains. She should have realized that a long time ago.

•

Serena tugged the fleece blanket tighter around her shoulders against the creeping chill of the desert night. It was strange that a place as blistering as an oven during the day could get so cold once the sun went down. She'd asked Momma about it once a long time ago, and her answer had been immediate and resolute: the desert was a place of mystery and magic and salvation, and that's why they'd moved here.

From where?

From a bad place, filled with sin.

I don't remember the bad place.

That's because I took you away when you were just a little baby. I had to save you. It's important to know when to leave places, and to be brave enough to do it.

What happened to my daddy?

Father Paul is your daddy now. He's the daddy of us all.

Serena didn't really believe that Father Paul was her daddy or anybody else's in the compound, but Momma wouldn't talk about it anymore. She wouldn't talk about the bad place, either, or explain how you knew when to leave someplace. It was so confusing, and all the missing pieces made her feel alone. Her friends didn't understand, so she didn't talk to them about it. She was content to let the desert kept her company, because it listened to her thoughts.

Finally feeling warm, she spread out her blanket and lay down on her back so she could look up at the sky. It was so beautiful, transformed from a hazy, pale daytime blue to a black velvet tapestry so thick with stars, she could feel it pressing down on her, pressing down on the world. Not in a suffocating way, but in a good, consoling way, like when she crawled into bed beneath her heavy, embroidered quilt.

The stars winked at her, like they were sharing secrets. And when she reached up into the dark, they seemed so close, like she could grab a handful of them right out of the air. What would it feel like to hold stars? And how would they look if she scattered them on the sand around her? Like the field of jewels in her favorite storybook, she decided.

Father Paul said that stars were actually the precious, shining souls of the departed, placed there by the Creator in the Heavens for all to see, reminding the faithful that there was beauty everywhere, even in death. He talked a lot about death during his sermons and how it was a gift of life everlasting, which was another thing that confused her. Why did you have to die to live? And what would happen if she somehow managed to grab a handful of stars? Would she really be grabbing a handful of souls, too? Would they be angry because she'd taken them away from their place in the sky when it wasn't time for them to leave? These were some of the many questions she wanted to ask him, but she was too scared.

Serena jumped when she heard a knock on the cabin door far behind her, shattering the perfect silence. She rolled onto her belly and scuttled back until she was concealed by a cluster of desert holly. Light filled the rectangular opening framed by the cabin door, and she saw Momma silhouetted there, then Father Paul walking inside. He'd been coming a lot lately and she didn't like to be around him, even though he was supposedly the daddy of them all. There was something about his eyes that made her feel icky inside.

If this was like the other nights he visited, they would talk about boring things like grown-ups did, so she rolled over again and stared up at the stars. She hadn't intended to fall asleep, but apparently, she had, because the next thing she remembered, Momma's whisper and touch wakened her, and she felt stiff and numb from the cold.

"Serena, you have to come inside now."

"But the stars," she mumbled groggily.

Momma enveloped her in her arms, sharing her warmth. "You feel like a Popsicle, my starry-eyed girl. Maybe I should have named you Star, you love them so much. But I didn't know that when you were a baby. Come on, I'll make us some cocoa."

Cocoa was a special thing, and there were even little marshmallows floating on top, which made it more special. The sweet liquid spread warmth all through her body, to her face and fingers, right down to her toes. The feeling was almost as good as when she watched the star souls traverse the night sky.

Momma sat down across from her at the kitchen table. She looked so pretty in her flowered dress with the pearl buttons. She wore her dark, wavy hair loose, and parts of it looked almost blue under the light from the overhead fixture. But her eyes seemed sad and shiny, as if she'd been crying. The good feelings drained away. "Momma, what's wrong? Did Father Paul make you sad?"

She took her hands and squeezed them, hard enough that it hurt, and her voice turned into a low, papery whisper. "Do you remember when I told you that it was important to know when to leave a place, and to be brave enough to do it?"

"It was a long time ago, but I remember."

"Good. We have to leave here, Serena."

"When?"

"Soon."

Chapter Three

SAM EASTON STOPPED AFTER AN HOUR of jogging in Desolation Canyon and collapsed on the rock-strewn sand with confidence that it wouldn't cook him just yet; he was equally confident that in a few more hours, it could. His thoughts suddenly conjured disturbing images of super-heated sand denaturing the proteins of his flesh. Not a good visual, but better than the visions of blood and bone and disembodied limbs he was accustomed to.

He found diversion in his sweat, which was pooling on the desiccated ground that hadn't seen rain in a year. Four mountain ranges stood between the Pacific Ocean and Death Valley, and they sucked up most of the moisture the weather systems contained before they ever arrived here. The soil didn't know what to do with anything wet. The tiny lizard testing the area with his tongue didn't know what to do with it, either.

"Hey, little buddy. You're the toughest motherfucker in the valley, aren't you?"

The lizard scampered away, leaving faint tracks in the sand, but Sam figured it would be back, so he made an offering from his last bottle of water. His pal deserved a break from life on the edge. Every living thing did, and one day he might get there himself.

He gulped the rest of the water, then stretched out on his back and took deep breaths of the blast-furnace air. According to his watch, it was already a hundred and sixteen degrees at two hundred feet below sea level. He'd just run five and a quarter miles in one of the hottest, driest, lowest places on Earth.

The sky was filmed by a milky cataract that did nothing to mitigate the punishing sun. He could just as well have been in Afghanistan as in Death Valley, except for the fact that he wasn't carrying ninety pounds of gear and people weren't trying to kill him. That was the point of being here. You had to remember before you could forget.

Sam shouted at the sky and listened to his voice reverberate against the high valley walls. The ghosts didn't answer, but he hadn't expected them to. They only came in dreams these days, and those were becoming fewer and further between.

The PTSD was gradually getting better, but he'd come to accept the fact that it would always be with him, like an arthritic joint that flared up with a change in the weather. The half of his face that had been ruined by a roadside bomb would always be with him, too— plastic surgeons had exhausted their significant reconstructive talents.

While he couldn't erase his memories or emotional and physical scars, he could continue to advance his coping skills. It had been two months since he'd started his weekly trips to Death Valley, two months since he'd blacked out or hallucinated, and that was progress.

His psychiatrist had explained that revisiting trauma in a safe environment was a critical part of working through it. Testing the limits of your physical endurance in a place that was definitely not a safe environment wasn't what Dr. Frolich had in mind. In her opinion, it was self-flagellation, borderline suicidal, another extension of survivor's guilt, and so forth. But it was his prerogative as a patient to ignore her advice—those had been her exact words—and she hadn't been able to argue with the results. And he'd been weaning himself off psychiatric care anyhow, starting to trust his own judgment more and more as he continued to reconstruct his life.

Time passed and the sun reached its brutal apex, eventually pro-
pelling him up and off the sand. He felt good and strong and thought
about pushing himself a little farther, but he hadn't thought about
killing himself for two months, either, and adding an extra mile or
two might do the job. Besides, he still had five and a quarter miles
back to his car, so he stretched out his kinks and started jogging at
an easy pace.

When he heard a rifle crack twice in the distance, he flinched reflexively, but the thought of combat didn't consume him, and neither
did his more recent encounter with a heavily armed, Beverly Hills
psychopath. But the shots troubled him in a different way, because
they didn't belong here. Maybe Death Valley National Park rangers
carried rifles, but it seemed like overkill in an ecosystem that couldn't
support a population of large, dangerous animals, if any at all.

Of course, the shots could have come from miles away and from
any direction. Sounds transmogrified in this deep, inhospitable basin
and ricocheted erratically against the valley walls. He'd ask Lenny
about it when he stopped for gas in Furnace Creek.

He started to jog again, and made it to the parking area without being ambushed by a homicidal ranger or dying of thirst. It was
a great way to start the day. There was nobody else around, so he
stripped down, stuffed his drenched clothes in a plastic bag, and
enjoyed a few minutes of nakedness in the eerily empty landscape
where undulating ripples of heat turned the distant mountains into
a murky illusion. Out here, it was easy to imagine that he was the
last man living on a post-Armageddon earth, or Adam in a scorched
Eden.

Dressed in fresh clothes, he started the car, cranked the air-
conditioning, and pulled out of the dusty lot. It still felt surreal, piloting Yuki's blue Honda. The last time he'd seen her alive, she'd been
behind the wheel, driving away from their house and their marriage.
Every time he got in, he could smell her expensive shampoo, a lingering olfactory ghost inhabiting the limbo between life and death.
It tormented him and consoled him at the same time, and as much as

he wanted to get rid of the car, he knew he never could. At least not until the scent of her shampoo was gone.

Sam pulled into the Furnace Creek gas station, filled the tank with his credit card, then went into the station and grabbed a bag of cashews, a couple bottles of water, and a quart of orange juice. He paused at the deli section, where plump hot dogs rolled under a heat lamp and trays of donuts tempted him from a glass case. He resisted his post-run junk-food cravings, knowing his system couldn't handle it just yet.

The clerk was a scrawny man with lank, sandy hair and an unfocused gaze that wandered randomly, unable to decide on a destination. He studiously avoided eye contact and his right hand was twitchy. Some kind of a disability, maybe; or if you were of a cynical bent, he existed on a steady diet of drugs and little else.

He bobbed his head at the items on the counter. "Will this be all, sir?"

He was polite enough. Sam considered a beef jerky display on the counter and grabbed a package. "This, too. Where's Lenny?" he asked, hoping to engage him as a trusted regular who knew the owner.

"He's off for a couple days."

Still no eye contact—a hopeless case, whatever the reason. "I just heard gunfire out in Desolation Canyon, seemed kind of weird to me."

His eyes kept roaming, from the refrigerated case of beer and ice cream to the candy rack to the back of the store where the restrooms were. "Nobody shoots in Desolation Canyon. Nothing to kill. Except maybe a person, and this is a good place to do it. What's left of them after the vultures get their fill would mummify in no time, and the sand would eventually bury them."

As hot as he still was, Sam felt the prickles of a sudden chill. "You've given this some thought?"

"Everyone knows what happens to bodies in the desert."

Not everyone, perhaps, but Sam did, and it was disturbing that this guy seemed to as well. He pulled out his wallet, eager to leave. "How much?"

He stared down at the jerky, the cashews, the beverages, then slowly poked on the cash register's keypad. "Sound travels around here, you know. Lots of military installations nearby."

"It was just two rifle shots; there would be a lot more if it came from a firing range."

"Probably came from Area 51, then. That's where they keep them. Maybe one tried to get away."

A picture of the clerk's mental health was filling in quickly and the prognosis wasn't good. "Aliens?"

He nodded somberly.

"Area 51 is a long way from here."

"Like I said, sound travels, and sometimes I hear their voices. Aliens are loud and they can sound like anything, even like gunshots if they want to. If one was standing right here and started to talk, our eardrums would explode and our brains would liquefy."

What an astounding gift for detailed visuals. "I didn't realize."

"Most people don't."

"Well, let's hope they don't pay us a visit."

"They won't during the day, the sun's too hot for them. I'm Mike." He finally looked at Sam and his mouth went slack as he stared unabashedly at his scars. Death-obsessed Mike definitely wasn't on any kind of spectrum that recognized socially appropriate behavior, so he didn't take it personally.

"You got hurt pretty bad, I'm sorry," he finally said. "Twenty-seven dollars and forty-two cents, please."

It was an apology he wasn't used to hearing, which was somewhat refreshing. "Twenty-seven bucks, huh? Worse than LA prices." He slid two twenties across the counter and Mike methodically picked out the change from the cash drawer, then carefully placed the items in a bag.

"That's where you're from? LA?"

"Yeah."

"Lenny has a boat there."

"I know."

"Whenever he takes time off, he goes to his boat. Are you friends with him?"

"Yeah."

"You ever see aliens in LA?"

"Every single day."

"You're having me on."

"No man, I'm not."

He scrutinized Sam's face further, then his eyes widened in revelation. "That's what happened to you. Man, you're lucky to be alive."

"That's God's truth."

Mike leaned over the counter. "How did you survive an alien attack?"

"I honestly don't remember." Sam gathered his bag, anxious for escape. "Thanks, Mike, see you around."

"What's your name?"

"Sam."

"Sam Spade?"

"You're a reader."

Mike blinked his bewilderment.

"Or a movie buff."

"I watch a lot of movies. I like movies."

"I had you pegged as more of a sci-fi fan."

His face remained blank and remote, but his body suddenly animated like a marionette with a drunk puppeteer at the strings. "Clint Eastwood! Make my day!"

Sam decided he would. "My name is Sam Easton. Pretty close to Eastwood, right?"

Mike's mouth formed an O. "Are you related?"

"Not that I know of."

Mike grabbed another package of jerky from the display and tossed it in the bag. "Extra, you might need it. Watch the sky, Sam Eastwood."

"Easton. I will." As he pushed the door open, Mike said, "The gunshots didn't come from Furnace Creek, I can tell you that."

"O-kay."

"Yob tvoyu mat."

"Is that alien for something?"

His eyes started zigzagging around the store again. "Yeah, but I don't know what it means, I was hoping you did."

"Sorry. Where did you hear it?"

"Here sometimes, when they come into the store."

"Who's they?"

"The Children of the Desert. I'm pretty sure they're connected to the aliens."

Sam decided Furnace Creek might be weirder than Area 51 and considered jogging there next week instead. "You take care, Mike, okay?" *And start taking your meds again.*

He nodded. "Have a nice day."

"You, too."

"I hope your face gets better."

"It won't, but thanks anyway."

When Sam got in the car, he turned the air-conditioning on high and pulled away from the station with all the horsepower the Honda could muster. If he'd been in his Shelby Mustang, the place would be a speck in his rearview mirror by now, but he'd never subject his cherished baby to Death Valley. He thought about calling Lenny and asking him about Mike, but decided against it. He'd hired a kid who was struggling, so what? Good for him. And it's not like there were a lot of employment opportunities in a town of less than two hundred people.

Everyone knows what happens to bodies in the desert.

It was a phrase that wouldn't let go.

Chapter Four

THE NIGHT SKY HAD CHANGED FROM star-spangled black to the granular gray of dawn an hour ago, and now the sun was hovering over the Los Angeles skyline, glittering on the glass façades. The soothing hiss of tires on pavement had finally put Serena to sleep in her lap, and that was Marielle's sole comfort in the seething crush of fear and uncertainty. Her nerves were ragged, crackling like stripped wires, and her pulse was still racing, even though the compound was two hundred miles behind them now. Still, it wasn't far enough.

Don't cry, honey. We're on a new adventure, isn't that exciting?

I'm scared.

Everything is going to be okay, trust me.

But it wasn't okay. Serena was only eight, but old enough to know that fleeing in the middle of the night with a stranger was terribly wrong; old enough to absorb her mother's anxiety like a dry sponge and wonder why she'd suddenly been ripped from her life without a convincing explanation. But telling the truth wasn't an option.

Trust. It was the only thing either of them had right now. Serena had to trust her, and she had to trust Lenny, a man she barely knew. But the calming way he'd talked to her daughter about stars and how they were a map of endless possibilities had broken down some barriers for both of them.

The trip had been mostly silent because adult discussion would have frightened Serena even more, but now it was time to speak. The colorful palette of the rising sun behind them was beginning to tint the distant Los Angeles skyline, and they couldn't keep driving forever. The ocean would stop them eventually.

"I don't know how to thank you, Lenny."

"No need for thanks, I'm just glad I could help. Where do you want to go?"

Where *did* she want to go? Where *could* she go? Definitely not to Remy Beaudreau. "Union Station."

"You don't sound too sure about that."

"I'm sure." She tried to project confidence, but her voice was weak and faltering, not up to the task.

"You don't have any friends or family here?"

"No." Marielle glanced at him. His sun-browned face was carved with an intricate pattern of wrinkles and creases, like a topographical map of the desert where he lived. The parentheses around his mouth deepened as he frowned.

"Thought maybe you'd want to go to the police."

"I can't go to the police," she blurted before she realized how terrible that sounded. "I mean, there's nothing to go to the police about. We just had to get away, that's all." She balled her fists in frustration. "It's hard to explain."

He reached for his McDonald's cup and sucked the last of his Coke through a straw. "The bruises on your arms explain enough."

Marielle realized the wrap around her bare shoulders had slid down, exposing ugly purple marks and her fleur-de-lis tattoo. She tugged it up to cover her arms again, which was a stupid, knee-jerk reaction. It was too late for that.

"Does that tattoo mean something?"

"A stupid mistake."

"I have a couple tattoos myself, and they were both stupid mistakes. Makes you wonder if anybody gets inked when they're in a solid frame of mind."

"Probably not. It always seems like a good idea until you realize you have to live with it. I could get it lasered off, but it's a reminder of things. That seems important."

"Are other folks at that place in trouble?"

Marielle thought about the bodies in the mine with an internal shudder. But Lenny couldn't be repaid for his kindness by getting drawn into her mess. That was something she had to take care of herself, in her own way. "No."

He released an anxious sigh. "I generally make it my business to stay out of other people's, but if you're afraid, I can call the police for you and leave you out of it."

"No, Lenny, please don't. You can't get involved."

"Seems like I already am."

"Just drop us off at the station, we'll be alright."

"I can tell you from experience that sometimes, the things you're running to are just as bad as the things you're running from."

"I know that." God, did she know that.

"Los Angeles isn't a place to be without a plan and a friend."

"I lived here, I know the city well enough."

"You haven't lived here in a while, and the city has changed." Lenny withdrew a packet of chewing tobacco from his shirt pocket and tucked a pinch behind his lip. "Didn't want to do this while Serena was still up, but it keeps me awake, hope you don't mind. Went off cigarettes a few years ago, but the nicotine doesn't give up so easy. This is a compromise."

Marielle thought of all the pills Father Paul had given her over the years and how hard it had been to stop them once she'd realized they were all about control—her relinquishing it, him taking it. "I understand, and I don't mind at all."

"Whenever Father Paul brought you and your friends to my store for hot dogs and ice cream, you never paid for anything yourself. Do you have any of your own money for bus or train tickets to wherever you want to go?"

"A little. And I can sell some things if I need to."

"That's not acceptable to me. You and Serena need a plan and some rest before you move on. And a better meal than McDonald's on the fly."

Despite everything, Marielle smiled. "She loved her Happy Meal. Thank you for that."

"My pleasure." He pointed out the windshield. "See that building that looks like it's on fire with the sunrise playing on it? That's the Wilshire Grand Center, the tallest skyscraper west of the Mississippi."

"I know it. It's beautiful."

"Sure it is. A beautiful building in a big city. People think it's easy to get lost in a big city, but that's not true. There are a lot of eyes on you all the time and if you stand out for any reason, those eyes get sharper. What do you think will happen when a pretty young woman with a pretty young daughter tries to sell something out of a duffel bag for fare?"

Marielle closed her eyes. God, she'd been so stupid, so fixated on escape, she hadn't thought of anything else beyond that. "We'll get noticed."

"By all the wrong people. And there are a lot of them of all stripes hanging around stations, looking to take advantage. I think you've had enough of that."

"I don't have a choice."

Lenny tapped a slow beat on the steering wheel, the kind of gesture people make when they're thinking hard about something, trying to make a decision of import. "I'd like to give you one. I have a boat in Marina del Rey. It's not much, but you can stay there until you figure out your next move. You don't have any money, and I'm guessing you don't have a phone, either, and I can help you with both those things. I'm not leaving you and your little girl to fend for yourselves."

"You've done enough already . . ."

"Listen, Marielle, you seem to think you have a bad tailwind riding you and I'm inclined to agree. I don't suppose you're real big on trust, but I'm asking you to give me a little."

Chapter Five

THE BONES IN NOLAN'S WRIST STILL felt dense and stiff after her session at the range. She hadn't lost her accuracy with the Beretta—that was good. The absence of any emotional response—that had to be bad. The experience had been one gigantic anticlimax, yielding no sense of catharsis. It had probably been wildly naïve to think that perforating a paper target would magically lead to clarity and resolution. Killing was a lot more complicated than that. At least the range hadn't been a negative experience. Maybe there was nothing to resolve.

She thought about Sam Easton and his struggle with PTSD, which made her own situation seem trivial and unworthy of consideration. He would argue with her about that and tell her trauma is trauma—you couldn't compare experiences or designate appropriate reactions based on the severity of an incident. The only thing that mattered was how an event affected each individual. It was solid reasoning, but she still felt guilty.

She found a parking spot a block away from Chez Louise and began the reluctant slog toward a brunch she was dreading, with a man who knew about killing.

Nolan was always surprised to see her father in civilian clothing, which was absurd. He was retired now, for one thing. And it wasn't like he'd run around the house in uniform all the time while she was growing up. Mostly, he'd always looked like a regular dad, in regular dad clothes, unless he was going to work or attending a military function.

She'd been an impressionable ten-year-old the first time she'd seen him in full dress, and his powerful visage had scored an immortal groove in her mind that had never stopped playing, like an old vinyl record on repeat.

To her, Colonel York Nolan would always be the imposing demigod whose chest was bedazzled by a mystifying array of medals and ribbons; whose polished shoes were like black mirrors. An intimidating specter, unreachable unless she stood up on her tiptoes and he bent down to meet her halfway. Now, at five-eleven, she was almost as tall as he was, but in many ways, he was still unreachable.

That York Nolan of her childhood memory certainly wasn't the same man who was sitting across from her at a French bistro sipping wine. This beta version of her father was loosely postured and dressed in a Tommy Bahama shirt with a repeating pattern of decorous palm trees roving across the herringbone silk fabric. Demigods didn't wear resort clothes, they didn't drink chardonnay, and they certainly didn't discuss the details of hula lessons taken during a recent trip to Hawaii.

As a homicide detective, she overanalyzed everything, and she couldn't help but imagine he was trying to distance himself from his rigid, ordered past in an attempt to work out an internal conflict. He was a loyal Army man who'd dedicated his life to the service—his identity was entirely wrapped up in it—but the military he revered had also gotten Max killed. If Daddy had been an accountant instead of a career warrior, her brother might still be alive. The road to reconciliation had to be rocky.

Or maybe she was way off the mark and he was simply relaxing into retirement, secure in the knowledge that his only son had died bravely in battle, which salved the wound with pride. In a convoluted way, it justified his existence as much as it diminished her mother's. How did you span that gap? If her parents' newly strained relationship was any indication, you didn't.

"You're awfully quiet, Margaret. Working a big case?"

"No. Sorry, just thinking about you taking hula lessons," she lied.

"Does it amuse you?"

"It's unexpected, but I think it's great. Mom didn't mention it, but she said the trip was nice." How could a month in Hawaii be anything but nice?

He lifted his gray eyes—jarring eyes, the color of wet slate. It was the single thing she'd indisputably inherited from him. They were as clear as they'd always been, but the aging flesh of his eyelids was encroaching on them, giving the impression of perpetual weariness.

"I think so, at least up until the Pearl Harbor Memorial. It was probably a foolish thing to do, taking her there. I thought maybe it would help."

"It's not foolish to try to help someone you love."

"She wanted very much to come today, but the migraines have been giving her hell."

"I know, I talked to her this morning. She said she was starting a new medication."

"A reason for optimism."

Her mother had never had a migraine before Max's death and they both knew it, but it would be counterproductive to bludgeon her father with the obvious. Diplomacy was required here. "Have you broached the topic of grief counseling yet?"

He looked at her as if she'd just proclaimed the sky was green and the Earth was flat. "She's handling her grief in her own way. She'll get through this."

Nolan diverted her eyes to the menu in front of her and studied it, hoping the dilemma between *frisée aux lardon* and *moules frites* would distract her from the grating irritation she felt. "I'll talk to her."

"She won't discuss anything to do with Max."

"Because she's running away, and we can't let her, Daddy. Did she tell you what precipitated your last-minute trip to Hawaii? No? It was pictures of Max, she unpacked them when she was helping me move.

She locked herself in the bathroom, cried for ten minutes, then fled like she'd just robbed a bank. That was the last time I saw her."

Her father drank the rest of his chardonnay and gestured to the waiter for another glass. "I didn't know. She just said she needed to get away for a while."

She'd always considered her father to be the smartest, strongest man she knew, but there was suddenly a fissure in that incontrovertible belief. Jesus Christ, they never talked about the things that mattered. Poor Max, he deserved honesty and remembrance, not denial. Apparently, Mom didn't have the market cornered on that after all, the both of them were knee-deep in it. "You and I should remind her of what she still has, but I think we remind her of what she lost, just like the Pearl Harbor Memorial did."

Her father's lips folded into a thin, bloodless line. "That's a horrible thing to say, Margaret. And ridiculous."

"That's how I see it. And I'm not blaming her, I just want to help."

"Give her some more time. She's going on a retreat and I'm hoping it will be a step in the right direction."

"She didn't say anything to me about that."

"Oh. I thought she had already."

"What kind of retreat?"

"A healing one, she says, probably a lot of yoga and spa treatments. It's in the desert."

Nolan felt her cheeks flame, vivid emotion displayed on pale skin that was genetically entangled with strawberry-blond hair. She would never be a poker player. "She has to go to the desert with strangers to get healed? What about talking to a grief counselor or her family instead?"

"That's enough, Margaret. Your mother deserves support right now, not judgment."

Time to dial it back. Colonel Nolan wouldn't tolerate any further blasphemy. This battle wouldn't be won in a day, if ever, and she knew when to withdraw. "You're right. What's the name of the place?"

"I don't remember off the top of my head. Something spiritual-sounding. I'll text it to you when I get home."

Or she could call me and tell me herself. "Mom isn't exactly the spiritual type."

"She's religious, which is by its very nature spiritual, and she needs a bigger picture, not lectures on coping."

"Therapists don't lecture, they ask questions."

"You're being pedantic, when you should be grateful that she's searching for options she thinks might work for her. She doesn't want to be miserable, you know."

It was outrageous that such a staunch doctrinaire was sermonizing about having an open mind, but they both shared a common goal. "I know that. When is she going?"

Her father didn't do chagrin, but the expression on his face was a reasonable facsimile. "Actually, she's leaving this afternoon."

That stung like the evil bastard ground wasp she'd stepped on when she was twelve. She hadn't been able to wear a shoe on her right foot for two days. God, it never ended. Emily Rose Nolan would be injuring her daughter until the day she died, and it was little consolation that all the tiny knife cuts were probably unintentional.

"Don't be hurt, Margaret. She has high hopes for this. I think maybe she wanted to come back in a different state of mind and surprise you."

"I'm definitely surprised. How long will she be gone?"

"Just two days. It's an introductory program. They have longer ones if you think it's something that will work for you."

"I'll drive her there."

"They're sending a car. It's part of the package."

"Very posh." Very posh *and* very clever. Luxury was a form of hypnosis—it made people highly suggestible. After a limo ride and some pampering, guests would be primed to devour any spiritual healing meted out to them, and then rush the box office for tickets to the next showing. Vulnerable people were easy to exploit, it was the stock and trade of criminals and con artists.

"It's not cheap. According to your mother, it's gained the attention of celebrities."

"Then I'm sure it's worth every penny." Nolan was shocked by her own bitter sarcasm and wished she'd kept her mouth shut.

His face reddened beneath his tropical tan. "Have you always been this cynical, or is it the job?"

Yes, and yes. Had he just read her mind? And since when did her mother even know or care that celebrities inhabited the same planet? "I'm just saying that amenities come with a price tag. I'm sure there's a lot of overhead in the desert."

"Oh. Yes. They do."

The ensuing silence was sour, like half-empty wineglasses the morning after a party. "What are you ordering?" she finally asked.

He gave his menu a cursory glance. "How are *you* doing, Margaret? It's something to take a life."

Yes, it was. Something big, something that could destroy you if you let it, thanks for asking. "It can be a part of the job, I knew that going in."

"True, but it was your first time."

Like losing your virginity? Once the cherry is popped, it gets easier, and suddenly you're a slut for murder? "I'm okay, Daddy."

"That's my girl." He patted her hand, then gazed out the window at the vine-covered pergola sheltering the patio, where patrons were genuinely enjoying their lunch instead of limping through it. "It's different in war, you know? There's always the expectation that you will have to kill, multiple times. You train for it. Being a cop, you understand it *could* happen, but the odds are against it, so it's more of a shock. I pray it never happens to you again."

Nolan wondered if this was some kind of warped pep talk that satisfied an unconscious need to demean her career choice outside the military. She wanted to ask her father how many people he'd killed, and if she finally had some cred with him now that she'd shed some enemy blood.

"I don't think it is different, not at all. Killing somebody is killing somebody, whether you're a cop or a soldier."

"I didn't mean that as an insult."

"How did you mean it, then?"

"Margaret, making the choice between living and dying is easy, but the fallout isn't. You didn't just kill somebody, you confronted your own mortality, and that changes you forever. Let it make you stronger, not fearful."

"I'll try. Thanks for your insight."

He searched her face for more sarcasm, which hurt Nolan's heart. Had the distance between them really become so vast?

"I wonder how Sam Easton is doing, do you know?"

"I have no idea."

"You share some trauma."

"We don't keep in touch with victims. Everybody is anxious to move on. I hope he's doing well."

"I'm sure he is. He's an extraordinary individual—a fine man and an exemplary soldier. Speaking of fine men, give my best regards to Al and his wife. Corinne, is it?"

"Yes. And I will."

"It consoles me and your mother, knowing you have such a strong, capable partner. You drew a lucky card, getting paired with him. In our lines of work, good partners make the difference between life and death."

Nolan had indeed drawn a lucky card to get partnered with Al Crawford. He wasn't just a wise, older mentor anymore, he was family. So was Corinne. A family she not only loved, but liked, which was more than she could say for her blood relatives at the moment. "I'm grateful."

He took a slice of baguette and dispiritedly smeared butter on it. Strangely, it reminded her of the time he'd molded a figurine of a dog out of Wonder Bread at the dinner table. She and Max had laughed so hard. Even her mother hadn't been able to maintain the required look of disapproval for long. The passage of time wasn't kind. Life wore people down.

"I'm getting the bouillabaisse," he finally mumbled.

Nolan decided on the frisée salad. Bitter greens seemed appropriate.

Chapter Six

EMILY NOLAN WAS STANDING IN HER closet, trying to subdue her mounting panic. She'd never been to a desert on any continent and had no idea what sort of clothing and shoes were appropriate. She didn't know if they would even venture outside during the day in Death Valley's infernal summer heat, or if they would go out at night, when deserts supposedly got chilly. Why hadn't the literature been more specific about what to pack?

She ran her fingers along the hangers that held her summer wardrobe of linen and cotton and pulled a few pieces as possibilities, then added some wraps, a few light sweaters, and a quilted vest to the growing pile on the bed. It was always best to be prepared for every contingency.

The footwear was another story altogether and stalled her modest progress. Heels were definitely out of the question, and so were open-toed sandals—there were surely poisonous things lurking everywhere. That left her with a choice of tennis shoes or driving loafers, neither of which would save her from Gila monsters, scorpions, or rattlesnakes. And they certainly wouldn't compliment any of the outfits she'd chosen. Back to the closet to reconsider.

As she rummaged through the recesses of her shoe rack, she saw the presentation box with Max's medals and let her hand hover over it before backing away. Frozen between closet and bed, she heard the downstairs door open and the thump of York's feet on the foyer tile. He was back from brunch with Margaret. Her only living child, and she hadn't been able to muster the courage to face her. What kind of a horrid mother was she, making up lies about migraines to avoid confrontation?

To avoid the truth.

"Emily?"

"Just packing, I'll be right down, dear."

Thump thump thump, up the stairs. The bedroom door opening, York's face inquisitive and concerned.

"Feeling alright, Em? You look pale."

"I'm much better."

He eyed the pile of clothes.

"I'm having trouble deciding what to bring. How is Margaret?"

"She missed you."

"I missed her, too."

"You need to call her. I blabbed about your trip and she was hurt. I thought you'd talked to her about it."

Her hands fluttered like nervous sparrows in front of her chest. "I feel terrible that I haven't, time just got away from me." She was ashamed by the feeble, pathetic excuse. There was no excuse except her own cowardice. "I'll call her just as soon as I finish packing."

"Please do."

He was disappointed, possibly even disgusted, and she didn't blame him, but she couldn't bear it. "I'm sorry, York, this is just . . . so stressful. And the packing on top of it, you know how I hate to pack. I'm not thinking clearly."

He touched her arm gently. "It'll be okay, Em. What can I do to help you?"

"Well . . . you could go to the storage room and see if you can unearth those hiking boots I bought in Germany. I'm worried about snakes."

He teased her with a smile. "I don't think they'll put their paying guests in mortal danger, but I'll take a look."

Emily watched her husband of thirty-two years execute a drill turn and march out of the room to carry out his new mission. Such a kind, good, understanding man, but she felt him slipping away; and Margaret, too. They were both worn down by frustration and probably resentment that accrued every day she wouldn't face that box in the closet. If things didn't change, she was going to lose them both.

Chapter Seven

AFTER ANOTHER LIVELY HEAD-SHRINKING SESSION WITH Dr. Frolich, Sam impulsively detoured deeper into the heart of the city so he could troll past his former place of employment. Pearl Club's façade was imbued with the kind of ultra-hipster glam that intimidated some people. *You're not cool enough to cross the threshold,* it seemed to broadcast—but once you got inside, the staff was always friendly and welcoming; especially Melody, who had run the bar like a benevolent sovereign. Everybody's money was good. But it was still a place for trendy Angelenos and, gauging by the lunch crowd visible behind the sparkling street-side windows, it hadn't lost its allure.

It had been a crazy, vibrant place to work; an intoxicating shot of exhilaration injected into his battle-weary veins at a time when he hadn't been stable enough for more serious employment in his field. Even now, feeling somewhat steady and primed for a fresh start, he was finding it difficult to envision the transition from bar back to desk jockey. How did you go from the unremitting adrenaline overload of war or the rush of Pearl Club's manic energy to electrical engineering? There was still a vast chasm to cross without a reliably sturdy bridge, but he'd get there eventually. PTSD didn't have to rule your life. Dr. Frolich had been vehement about that this morning, and he believed and trusted her.

After Yuki's death and the incident in Beverly Hills, Sam had quit Pearl and gone off the grid to escape the relentless hounding. He'd spent a couple weeks in Big Sur with Melody and had laid low ever since his return to LA. A few months had passed and the media had largely moved on, but he still got calls and the occasional ambush—the case was just too juicy for them to let it go entirely.

He didn't miss much about that black period in his life, but he did miss Pearl Club, and especially Melody. She was in Chicago now, trying out a new city. They talked and texted often, but there were times when he physically craved her presence—not in a sexual way, he constantly reminded himself—but the two of them had cheated death together and with that came a bond that could never be broken. They were the civilian equivalent of battle buddies, he supposed. His attraction to Margaret Nolan had the same roots, but it was less chaste.

He indulged his reminiscences in a no-parking zone as long as he could before getting shooed off by a truculent parking patrol. As he drove away toward home, he saw and felt the past contract until it was just a speck in his rearview mirror; a floating dust mote in his memory.

Sam was getting used to Yuki's physical absence in their humble Mar Vista home, but sometimes she seemed more present now than when she'd been alive. It was like the walls and floors, the furniture and fabrics, had absorbed and concentrated her essence like a diffuser. Random memories hit him unexpectedly and were so intense, they felt more like combat flashbacks than recollections. But they possessed none of the horror and were restorative in an odd way. Like the Honda, he knew it would be a long time before he could ever consider parting with this place.

He settled in at the kitchen table with a tablet computer and a crystal lowball of excellent, small batch Kentucky bourbon. The crystal had been a wedding gift; the bourbon a parting gift from Melody.

He'd cut back on the booze, but hadn't taken temperance as far as total sobriety. Alcohol unfailingly subdued the cadre of evil spirits residing in his psyche and for that reason and a few others, drink made him happy. He didn't have enough fingers to count the near-death experiences he'd accrued in his thirty years, and he was damn well going to enjoy every second he had left by doing whatever the hell he wanted to do. If his liver was the thing that ultimately killed him, all the better—the irony would send him out of this world laughing his ass off.

Mike's disturbing comments from yesterday were still loitering in his mind, so after catching up on emails, he did a search on Children of the Desert. Two fingers of bourbon later, he learned that it was a life-affirming spiritual group, and getting hot with the Hollywood set. None of the articles referenced aliens, no surprise there.

The home page of their website was dominated by a florid epistle-slash-mission statement and the slogan: The Universe Is Waiting for You. It was vague about the location, disclosing only that it was in the Inyo Foothills. It wasn't mentioned that those foothills were in Death Valley. No life-affirming organization would want to be associated with a moniker that conveyed such ominous finality.

The site was lean on content but heavy on proclamations of salvation for even the sickest of souls, miraculously dispensed by a "remarkable visionary" called Father Paul. There was no bio or photo of the head witch doctor, probably meant to enhance the impression of divine mystery.

Sam clicked on a tab labeled "Healing Journeys," which offered a menu of pricey retreat packages that promised hope and healing. Below that was an endless thread of glowing, five-star testimonials from former attendees whose lives had been transformed. There were more than a few celebrity endorsements and he wondered if they'd been paid.

Furthering his investigation of Mike's idiosyncratic utterances, he also learned that *yob tvoyu mat* meant "fuck your mother" in the crass Russian slang called *mat*. It was used as easily as "oh my God" by insalubrious types. Salvation and Russian profanity—an unlikely combination weird enough to pique anybody's curiosity.

Sam closed the tablet and decided to call Lenny after all, if for nothing but to satisfy his inquisitiveness. It went straight to voice mail, and a robotic message informed him the mailbox was full. Mike said he spent days off on his boat, so why not take a short drive? Sam had a standing invitation to visit the *Royal Bess*, which was moored in Marina del Rey. In return, he'd promised Lenny a ride in his grandfather's Mustang. It was a perfect day for both prowling the streets in a vintage muscle car and sipping beers on the ocean.

Chapter Eight

FAMILY DRAMA WAS A PRECURSOR CHEMICAL that catalyzed questionable decisions and actions, increasing the likelihood of reckless behavior. Life was an endless series of forks in the road, and if you didn't choose wisely, you'd end up doing something foolish, like following the pheromone fork instead of the wise and responsible fork. Calling Detective Remy Beaudreau was a classic example of a lapse in professional judgment and disregard for the consequences, but she didn't even try to resist the temptation.

"Hi, Remy."

"Maggie, good to hear your voice. Is this a work call?"

"No, just checking in to see how your vacation is going."

"I've been shamefully idle and homicide-free for almost a week now. I'm so bored, I've been thinking about killing somebody myself."

The topic of killing was inserting itself into her thoughts and conversations far too much lately. "Are you interested in a sidekick?"

"In boredom or murder?"

"I've been promising you a drink for a while."

"Yes, you have. I'd almost given up on you, Maggie."

A slight taunt, a challenge in his voice? "If you're trying to guilt-trip me, it's a really bad time to do that." She thought she heard a soft chuckle just beyond the range of his phone.

"Guilt-tripping is a repugnant, infantile effort to dominate, something I've been subjected to most of my life, which is why I never do it."

"And I never renege on a promise."

"Then it's settled, and your timing is excellent. I'm sitting in the lounge at the Hotel Bel-Air with a martini as we speak and I would enjoy your company."

"Drinking lunch at the Bel-Air doesn't sound boring to me."

"You'd be surprised. Although I do have an excellent plate of Kusshi oysters sitting in front of me, so I'm not entirely drinking lunch."

"Why are you at the Bel-Air?"

"Because there are worse places to be, but none much better. And it's within walking distance of my house. It comes in handy sometimes."

Nolan's thoughts stuttered. "You live in Bel-Air?"

"Contrary to popular belief, family money doesn't have many perks, but real estate is definitely one of them."

She wondered if his rich, guilt-tripping Louisiana family disdained his choice of career as much as hers did. "You're incredibly jaded."

"I'm worse than that. Join me."

What the hell. One drink with a colleague wasn't going to define her life or ruin it. Hopefully. "I'll be there in an hour."

•

Remy nodded to Malachai Dubnik when he entered the Bel-Air lounge. Nobody else here would know who he was, unless life circumstances had required them to engage the services of the most exclusive, expensive private investigator in the country. Still, every eye was on him. The attention wasn't directed at his notable stature and build, nor did it linger on his impeccable suit or ostentatious gold watch. Nobody noticed things like that in LA, they were timelessly de rigueur. What made him a subject of great interest was his startling absence of hair. People without eyebrows or eyelashes distinguished themselves in any crowd, even in this room liberally sprinkled with celebrities. Alopecia universalis, an autoimmune disorder that attacks the hair follicles, he'd explained once.

"Remy!" He gave him a firm shake with his smooth, hairless hand. "You look excellent."

"You're looking pretty good yourself, younger than last time I saw you. Botox or something more drastic?"

He let out a rolling chuckle. "Neither. Never underestimate the positive effects of being bald all over, it makes you look like an infant." He rubbed his smooth, shiny scalp. "If I could package my disease, I'd be a billionaire. Crazy how people don't want hair anywhere these days. The ladies, they have fake eyelashes out to here and painted-on brows, but below the belt . . . if you think about it too hard, it's perverse."

"If you think about anything too hard, you can assign a degree of perversity to it."

Malachai snorted and sank into a chair situated beneath a large Norman Seeff photograph of John Belushi. "True, true. Seriously, you look good. Well-rested. I've seen you looking like a crackhead after a weeklong jag more than once."

"I'm on vacation. It's amazing what a little sleep will do."

"What else have you been doing besides sleeping?"

"Playing with my drones."

"I never got the whole drone thing."

"Seeing things from a bird's-eye perspective is liberating. You should come out with me sometime."

"Maybe I will. I like the idea of being liberated in a wholesome way." When a waiter approached, Dubnik pointed to Remy's empty martini glass, then held up two fingers. "This is how I shut my mind off these days. Congratulations on your vacation, well-earned, my friend. Most detectives never pull a serial, let alone catch one. I have to admit, I'm a little jealous."

"Don't be. The media fanfare is too inflammatory and grotesque to bear. They're very selective about which murders they care about and they always miss the point. Dead bodies don't ever seem to factor into the narrative."

"Of course not, that's the nature of celebrity-obsessed mass culture and the press that feeds it. They tell you what to care about based on ratings, and serial killers are headlines that always seem to capture the imagination. There aren't enough of them these days. Or so it seems."

"The human race is in decline because of a lack of intellectual curiosity. Nietzsche was very prescient on the topic. It sounds like you've read him."

"No, I'm just naturally enlightened."

Remy smiled. "How are you, Mal?"

"Busy. Happy. Rich. Not as rich as you, but I'm enjoying my stake of the winnings."

"You worked for yours, which makes you the nobler man. Do you ever miss Homicide?"

"Once a year, on March fourteenth, when I told the captain to go fuck himself. Best thing I ever did. I could relive that moment every day and never get tired of it. How is that bastard?"

"Still an indolent autocrat who has issues with nonconformists."

Dubnik rubbed his hands together with relish. "But you're his golden boy now, so he has to play nice. Must drive him absolutely batshit. He hates you as much as he hated me. Maybe more."

"It's a complicated relationship." It really wasn't that complicated or besieged with the animus Dubnik envisioned and maybe hoped for, but Remy saw no harm in indulging his friend. He'd truly been screwed by the captain and the system, which had ultimately been to his great benefit, but it was still a canker in spite of his post-LAPD success. Nobody wanted to be a persona non grata—it violated the instinctive necessity of community. Humans were pack animals, even when they pretended they weren't.

The waiter delivered their martinis and Dubnik smiled at the three olives and three cocktail onions impaled on a silver skewer. "Still getting your vegetables in a glass, I see."

"There isn't a better way to eat them."

"What would happen if they didn't get it right? Like if there was an extra olive or a missing onion?"

"Armageddon."

"I never got the cocktail onions. It's weird in a martini." Dubnik considered the oysters, then helped himself. "So you asked if I missed Homicide and the truthful answer is I do sometimes. The world of privateering isn't the same, but I get some interesting cases from time to time. It's not all cheating spouses and embezzlers. I'll tell you about Minneapolis one day, it will blow your mind."

"I'd enjoy that. And my case?"

Dubnik blew out a dejected sigh. "I'm sorry, Remy, but I have a feeling this is going to be one neither of us can solve, and I'm not a negative person. I've been working it hard after you put in your own blood, sweat, and tears."

"This was never an LAPD case, so I didn't have latitude. It's never been any PD's case, which is why I called you."

"I know. But people disappear all the time, right? And if they're on somebody's shit list, they can disappear forever. There wasn't much of a trail to begin with and it was cold when you started looking. Now it's stone cold. It's been a long time."

"Enough time for complacency to set in. People on the run start to feel invincible once they've stayed off the grid for that long."

"It's also enough time to get dead and buried, and that's a possibility you have to face."

"I know that."

"I've spent enough of your money chasing down a cipher."

Remy had become inured to the disappointment, but still, the words stung. "You're quitting?"

"Are you kidding? I'll work this until it's solved or I go to the grave. It's not a job anymore, it's a mission. It really pisses me off when I can't seal the deal. What I'm saying is, I won't accept any more payments until I can deliver something."

"Forget it. You're putting in man hours I can't, so you get paid."

"If I get one more check from you, Remy, it's over for real. Deal with it." He plucked another oyster from the iced tray and slurped it down. "These are supposed to be an aphrodisiac, but I don't buy it."

"I'll ask my date about it when she gets here."

Dubnik's forehead rose on the bridge of glabrous brows. "Happy to hear you're keeping busy on vacation."

"And I'm happy to hear the oysters aren't putting amorous thoughts in your head. You're not my type."

"Listen, I get why you're doing this and why you couldn't go the official route. But do you ever ask yourself if maybe it's time to let go?"

Remy *had* asked himself that, a million times. But the pursuit had become an obsession, and obsessions were absent of rational thought; a form of mental illness. Something that ran in his family. "No."

"I thought so." Dubnik rummaged in his Hermès briefcase and placed a file on the table. "The best I've got is a mentally compromised, possibly drug-fried cashier at the Furnace Creek service station who says he's seen her. Keep in mind he also hears aliens on a regular basis."

Remy forgot his martini and daily helping of vegetables and leaned over the table. "When? When did he see her?"

"He couldn't say because he probably never saw her until I put her picture in front of him. I'm telling you, this guy is a fruitcake with extra nuts in the batter. If I'd shown him a picture of Marilyn Monroe, he'd tell me she was in the bathroom putting on a foil hat."

"What brought you to Death Valley?"

"I managed to track down an old roommate of hers in Victorville. They parted company after a few months back in 2015, but she told me Charlotte was hanging around with a group called Children of the Desert. Ever heard of them?"

"No," Remy said.

"Neither had I. I figured it was one of those sex and drugs fringe groups that pop up here and disappear almost as fast. But they had legs. It morphed into a quasi-religious spiritual group that runs a retreat center up there. Word is, it's the next big thing."

"Like a cult?"

Dubnik's eyes followed the progress of a thin, statuesque beauty as she slinked through the lounge like it was a catwalk. "I wondered, thinking it might fit, but from what I can tell, they're a legit nonprofit and not on the FBI's radar. Their main tagline is spiritual healing and growth—warm, fuzzy, commune bullshit like that. I can't speak to the value of their retreats, which they charge a fortune for, but they do community outreach and charity stuff. California Corrections is even working with them."

"How so?"

"An experimental charter program, rehabbing felons through whatever brand of mysticism they're selling. I called a guy I know, and he says it's the damnedest thing, it's been successful so far."

"Have you been there?"

"I tried, but it's fenced and gated and nobody was answering the call button. The fence is high and cast concrete, all dolled up to look like adobe, so I couldn't see anything but the nice xeriscaping out front. Cactus, rocks, and whatnot. They didn't do such a good job hiding the security cameras. I know a fake rock when I see one."

"They value their privacy."

"Or their rich clientele do. It reminded me of a posh rehab facility. I learned the hard way they don't do walk-ins, so no getting in there on the spot without a crime and a warrant. It pissed me off to leave empty-handed after making the trek—which really sucked, by the way—so I took a look at the records when I got home. The property is huge, it spans almost five miles of desert. It was purchased back in 2012 for less than a two-bedroom shack in Inglewood."

"Who bought it?"

Dubnik slid a sheet of paper across the table. "Hercules Mining. The property used to be an operating silver mine in the late nineteenth century, so my guess is they probably bought it up to try new technology and see if there was anything they could pull out, or maybe reclaim slag. It was obviously a bust, because two years after the purchase, they leased to Children of the Desert, which is as pure as the driven snow on paper. As a nonprofit working with the state, that's pretty hard to fudge."

Remy scanned the paper. "Interesting. Maybe I'll sign up for a retreat."

"If you want to pursue this angle, let me handle it, that's why you hired me. I'll take another run up there, take a look around, discreetly show Charlotte's picture around if it feels right."

"Make an appointment this time."

Dubnik smiled. "I finally got ahold of them this morning. If you give me the green light, I can head up there today."

"If you won't accept payment, you don't need my green light."

"I guess I don't."

"I appreciate this, Mal."

"No problem. A date, huh? Anybody I know?"

Remy dismissed the question with a shrug. "It's not really a date."

"If you say so." The model walked by again, recapturing his attention.

"She's too young, Mal. You'd be bored in a month."

"But what a month it would be." He finished his martini and stood. "I have another appointment, so I'll get out of your hair. Do you believe people have said that to me before?"

"Idioms are so entrenched in speech, they're entirely spontaneous. Nobody ever stops to think that they might be inappropriate."

"Always the philosopher. You take care, Remy. I'll be in touch."

For a large, eminently noticeable man, he slipped away like a wisp of smoke.

Chapter Nine

SERENA DECIDED THAT LENNY WAS THE smartest, nicest man she'd ever met—way better than creepy Father Paul. He knew a lot about stars and how sailors used them to navigate in the old days. He explained how plants and animals survived in the desert, which she'd never been able to figure out. Then he'd bought them the best breakfast in the whole wide world: blueberry pancakes topped with a huge dollop of fluffy butter that looked like ice cream, and magic eggs with pink yolks that oozed yellow when she poked them with her fork.

While she was finishing her pancakes, he told her about his boat and how it was like a toy house on the water. And it was! Everything seemed scaled to her size, from the tiny kitchen he called a galley to the closet bathroom with the folding door he called a head. You could go number one there, but you had to visit the marina building to go number two.

Even more magical was the ocean, which seemed as big as the night sky, but so bright instead of dark. The sun sparkled on the waves, and the water winked at her exactly like the stars did.

But the best part was the curved bank of padded seats by the windows where she sat now, drawing and watching the seals. Seals! She'd seen some once at Sea World a long time ago, but these were wild.

Can we feed them?

You're not supposed to, but I don't see any harm in giving them a little something.

They like fish.

Is that so? Well, when I run to get some things for us in a little bit, maybe I can pick up some bait fish. But we have to feed them when nobody's looking, okay?

Okay!

Momma was right, this was a new and *wonderful* adventure. She wasn't scared anymore and she shouldn't have been such a crybaby before. She refocused on her crayon drawing of the ocean and the seals and added a boat with Lenny standing on the front of it. He called it a bow.

"That's a fine-looking picture," he said over her shoulder.

"Thanks, Lenny. You're just a stick figure now, but I'll add more to you later."

"It's important to get the composition right before you add details."

"That's exactly what Sister Carina says in art class. How come everything has a funny name on a boat?"

"Nautical terms. Seems a little silly, having two words for the same thing, huh?"

"No, it's cool. Like a secret language."

"You think you can be happy here for a day or two?"

"Yes! I love your boat. It's the best." She put down her crayon and frowned. "But it's kind of wobbly. Momma puts things called shims under our chairs and table when they wobble. Can you put shims under a boat?"

He chuckled, and she liked the way it sounded, like the soft rumble of rain when it finally came to the desert.

"That would be nice, wouldn't it? But it's normal for a boat to feel wobbly. The water never rests and anything on top of it doesn't, either. It's just nature talking to you and you'll get used to it. You don't feel sick, do you?"

"No."

"Then you don't have seasickness. You're a born sailor."

"Is seasickness bad?"

"Only if you have it."

She giggled. "Do you think I could be an old-fashioned sailor and navigate by the stars?"

"I think you could do whatever you set your mind to. But a sailor's life isn't easy."

Serena thought about that. "Momma said life was never easy."

"Well, she's absolutely right. Speaking of your momma, I'm going to go outside and have a chat with her while you work on your masterpiece, okay?"

"Okay." She went back to her drawing, more determined than ever to make Lenny look perfect.

•

Marielle had always sequestered memories of the wild, dark days of her teen years in the periphery of her consciousness, often with the assistance of drugs: recreational or prescribed, it didn't matter. Over time, the memories had been softened by a soothing mental haze, diminished to blurry motes that were easy to ignore, like specks of dust in an ingot of sun or a floater in your eye. It was another lifetime, and one she didn't care to recall.

But sitting here on the bow of Lenny's boat, staring down at her bare toes above the water, those memories sharpened and rose to the surface, as if they'd been lurking in this harbor all along, waiting to devour her. Along with them came an amorphous emptiness; a hollow ache that throbbed deep in an inaccessible part of her psyche. She could only explain it as a deeply rooted fear of failure; of failing Serena like she'd failed herself and everybody else in her life.

As a teen, her violent emotions and consequent, reckless acts of rebellion had been dismissed as a difficult puberty at first and were punished mildly by her brain-dead parents. When the episodes escalated and she started running away regularly, a psychologist was brought in, along with mood-leveling prescriptions she tongued and flushed. Stealing the money and the car and driving to California with a man twice her age had been an abrupt shift to things more serious; a bellwether of more ill-informed decisions to come. It was difficult to muster any sympathy for her disinterested parents, the feral girl she'd been then, or the woman she was now; but none of that mattered anymore. The only thing that did was Serena.

Lenny's soft tread on the deck startled her out of the past. She forced a smile so patently false, she knew it wouldn't pass muster. "It's so beautiful here. It's like a dream. Freedom with nothing in your way." The smile may have been fake, but the sentiment wasn't.

He leaned against the railing. "That's what I first thought when I put in *Bess* here. I still think that."

"Why is she called *Royal Bess*?"

"This was my uncle's boat. He named her after a ship in his favorite Costain novel." He chuckled. "It was a pirate ship in the book, but as far as I know, my uncle didn't do any pillaging on the high seas, just a lot of drinking and fishing." He crouched down beside her. "Things are going to get better, Marielle, it's just going to take some time and patience."

She felt her throat tighten, her eyes sting with emotion. "I know they will. I thank you for giving me the chance."

"I'm going to take a run to get some groceries and supplies, but after we have dinner together, I have to run back up to Furnace Creek. I'll show you everything you need to know about living on *Bess,* and how to close her up if you decide to leave before I can get back down here."

Marielle's heart started to thump with the familiar panic of desertion. "You can't stay?"

"I'm very sorry that I can't."

Of course he couldn't stay. He had a business, a life.

"Before I leave, I'll let the folks up at the marina office know you'll be staying here. They're good people, and you can go to them anytime if you need anything. Just to make things less complicated, you're my daughter and Serena's my granddaughter."

"I like the sound of that. I wish it were true."

"I like the sound of that, too. Do you feel comfortable staying here alone until I can make it down here again?"

"This is the safest, nicest place I've known for a long time." She fumbled at the clasp of the necklace she hadn't taken off in a decade, then passed it to Lenny. "Take this."

She watched his eyes widen at the large diamond set in a gold heart.

"I can't take this, Marielle. I won't."

"Think of it as collateral. Keep it until I can return what I owe you. The money, anyhow. I can never thank you enough for your kindness."

"Kindness is one thing that doesn't require repayment."

"Please take it, hold on to it. It's not stolen, it's mine."

"I never presumed you were a thief."

"I am. Was. A long time ago. I want you to know I'll never steal from you."

Marielle watched him consider the necklace resting in his palm. The facets of the diamond shot rainbows brighter than the sunlight that brought it to life. He sighed and finally put it in his jeans pocket. "You don't know what I was a long time ago, either. I told you truthfully my uncle wasn't a pirate, but you're putting some trust in a man who might be, and I've got some booty in my pocket now."

Marielle felt a genuine smile lift her lips. "I know who you are, Lenny. So does Serena."

Chapter Ten

GLENN RAMEY WAS STILL TRYING TO square the tranquil Father Paul sitting across from him with Roger "Snake" Jackson, the man he'd done time with at High Desert State Prison. He looked different, for sure—all polished up and clean-cut, his tattoos hidden beneath the white, full-length tunic thing he was wearing. Snake in a dress? Fucking unbelievable.

He talked different, too, crazy talk, like one of those hardcore, holy rollers on Sunday-morning cable TV. Hell must have frozen over while he'd been sitting in his cell all these years.

In spite of the dramatic superficial transformation, Glenn had recognized his eyes immediately, still dead as roadkill. Snake eyes. Religion had changed his thinking, appearance, and language, but it hadn't been able to change the guts of the machine, and that's exactly what he was: a machine, and a badly broken one, worse than anybody behind bars here. At least he had been before his miraculous conversion, although Glenn wasn't convinced that morality was something you could pick up in a charity bin at a local church and slip on like a jacket. There had to be some kind of personal enrichment behind the oily, apocryphal rhetoric.

"The desert was the place where Jesus battled Satan and won," he was saying. "We are re-establishing His dominion there by restoring wounded souls and reaching out to the lost and hopeless with love and compassion . . ."

Fuck all, Snake actually seemed serious. Maybe he'd lost his mind. Or maybe he really had found a new purpose in God, but Glenn was still skeptical. "If you came here to help me find the Almighty, you're wasting your time."

"Five minutes," the prison guard interrupted sharply from his post by the door.

Snake looked up and nodded, then leaned forward and folded his hands in supplication. "The Children of the Desert need you, Glenn. God needs you. I need you."

He considered that for a moment. He didn't want anything to do with Snake and his Children of the Desert, but where there was need, there was money. "For what?"

"I've lost two of my key security people."

"So a religious guy like you needs security?"

"We all need security, Glenn. It's an unpleasant world. I may also need your help reclaiming some stolen property."

"Is that so? The Shroud of Turin? The Ark of the Covenant?" The jibe didn't wipe the solemn expression off his face, so Glenn sobered himself. "Well, Father Paul, it sounds like you have your own obedient flock, so why don't you let them handle it? Or better yet, God. He should be able to take care of things for you."

His mouth eased into a patient smile, displaying pearly new teeth. "Earthly pursuits require human tools and the flock cannot be diverted from their purpose. You would be a tool of our Lord."

"Yeah? Well, human tools need earthly paychecks, so what are you offering?"

Snake leaned back in his chair and closed his eyes, then started rocking, like he was going into some kind of a trance, and for all the things Glenn had seen and done in his life, this made his skin crawl like nothing else had.

"The greatest reward any man or woman can receive. Your soul will be saved. You will find eternal peace instead of eternal suffering, and the glory of our merciful Lord will surround and nourish you forever."

Glenn couldn't help himself—he raised his cuffed hands to the ceiling and let out a hyena laugh. "Praise Jesus! Let the good times roll up in Heaven! But I guess you forgot I don't have a soul, which means there ain't nothing to save."

"You are so wrong about that. So wrong, Glenn."

"No pay, no play, amigo. Save your breath for somebody who gives a shit."

Snake didn't break character, and remained undaunted and stalwart in his role as shepherd and prophet. "I believe in you and so does the Lord. We won't give up."

Glenn sneered. "You put on a good show, I'll give you that. But I know you and I know what you are. You can hide behind this religious bullshit all you want, but the demons are still there, they'll always be there. I can see them and I can feel them. So I'm asking you again, how much?"

The soft, beatific countenance of Father Paul hardened, and for a brief moment, he was Snake again, irrefutable confirmation that the man in front of him really hadn't shed his scales. Wasn't there some Bible verse about taking the scales from your eyes? Whatever the hell that meant.

"Twenty thousand to start," he whispered.

Glenn tried to keep his expression impassive, but the number made the black rock in his chest come back to life. When he got cut loose in a couple hours, he would have nothing. Zero. They'd set him up in a halfway house, get him a shitty job, and watch him day and night. He wouldn't be able to take a piss without somebody breathing down his neck. But if he did what Snake wanted, he might have a lot more options.

"Must be quite a job."

"It's not just a job, it's a position. It would require some commitment."

In Glenn's world, commitment meant wearing a chunk of concrete around your neck with the water always in view. He looked down at the cuffs on his wrists. How many years since he hadn't been wearing bracelets? Too many. Anything was better than this. "You know I don't just walk out of here today, there are some logistics to deal with. And I'm pretty damn sure they're not going to remand me to a former felon."

His countenance transformed fully into a nightmare mask: the worst of Snake, the terrifying Snake. "You're mistaken. I'm Father Paul, not a former felon. Do you understand?"

Glenn got it immediately. New life, new identity. Snake Jackson, sociopath and master of fraud, was dead and gone. "Roger that. Get it?" His laugh died in his throat as Snake stared him down with bloody murder in his eyes.

"Never mention it again. Don't even think it. I'm here to save your life but it wouldn't trouble me to end it."

He swallowed hard. Snake could and would if he crossed him. "Sorry."

"Never again."

"Never again."

"I'll be watching you."

Glenn let out a shaky breath. "Okay, so how does this go? Is it like work release or what?"

Father Paul, the serene preacher and teacher, reconstituted before his eyes, unruffled by his jaunt back in time. "In anticipation of your cooperation, I've already made arrangements for you to join us at the compound. Many Children of the Desert are former stray lambs and we've been extremely successful in our charter program with the California Department of Corrections and Rehabilitation. There is a zero-recidivism rate for all who've joined us and we fully comply with all post-release requirements to the satisfaction of the state."

"You're *shitting* me."

"No, Glenn, I'm not."

"So you'll just spring me and I walk away from here no problem? Sounds like a fucking con to me."

"The governor is a very enthusiastic advocate of our program. You're an excellent candidate."

Glenn grunted. "Friends in high places, huh?"

"If you agree to join us, I'll send my rehabilitation team . . ."

"Rehabilitation team?"

"They handle intake and orientation for former prisoners. I'd do it myself, but I have some pressing commitments today. Your work would start immediately."

"Well, shit, I guess that's an offer I can't refuse. You got yourself a deal."

"Time's up." The guard marched over, gestured Glenn out of his chair, and gave Snake a deferential nod. "Good seeing you again, Father Paul."

"And you as well, Brother Calvin. I hope you'll visit us again soon."

"I'm definitely planning to, Father, as soon as I save up the money."

Glenn felt his newly reanimated heart pounding hard against the wall of his chest. Bizarre as it was, maybe this visit had been the best thing that had ever happened to him. Snake was obviously hooked up, and hell, who knew? Maybe he did have some kind of a conduit to the big guy himself, if such a being existed. Or was he just a wolf in sheep's clothing? The fox was smarter, the saying went. And a snake was always a snake.

As he was being escorted out, he looked over his shoulder. "Lots of money in your line of work, Father Paul?"

"Money has never been a problem for me. Salvation has been, but I've found that, too. And so will you."

Chapter Eleven

NOLAN HAD BEEN TO THE HOTEL Bel-Air twice before: once for a suspicious death that had turned out to be the suicide of a Silicon Valley scion with deviant sexual proclivities he could no longer countenance, and once for a decadent brunch with Max the day before he'd deployed for the final time. They'd swilled mimosas like the world was ending, wandered the lush, tropical gardens, and watched the famous swans of Bel-Air glide on Swan Lake. It had been a magical morning in Elysian Fields that seemed a million miles away from the reality of the city and light-years away from Afghanistan.

On her third visit to Shangri-LA, her pet name for the Bel-Air, she found Remy at a table near the lounge fireplace. He hadn't noticed her yet, so she took the opportunity to study him, one that didn't exist when he was on the job. His dark hair was a little too long, curling against the white collar of his linen shirt; his lean frame was slouched casually in the chair, perfectly at ease in these luxe surroundings. He was a man who belonged here. He could easily be a director, a movie star, or a billionaire—anything but a homicide detective. She supposed when you grew up with money, you were naturally blasé in settings like this. Business as usual.

Oddly, he fit in just as well on the grittier side of life and something compelling must have drawn him to it. There was an explanation for this seamless adaptation buried somewhere in the ambiguity of his history before the LAPD. Did she want to know what it was? She decided she really didn't.

Remy turned around and smiled at her and she had the sinking feeling that she'd just been busted as the voyeur she was. Too late to run now.

He stood and pulled out a chair for her. "You look too lovely to be having a bad day."

"I never said I was having a bad day."

"The guilt-tripping comment gave you away, but you knew that. What are you drinking?"

Nolan weighed the palliative effect of alcohol against the negative effect on preexisting conditions like poor judgment. The decision was easy. "Your martini looks good."

"It's vodka, or would you rather have gin?"

"Vodka is great."

Remy caught the waiter's attention and apparently communicated with him telepathically, because a vodka martini appeared in front of her roughly thirty seconds later. "Here you are, ma'am."

"Thank you." She watched him scurry away, a model of efficiency and obsequiousness, then clinked glasses with Remy. "This feels really weird."

"Drinking in the afternoon with a colleague is abnormal behavior for you?"

She stuffed down a laugh. "Very. Especially at the Bel-Air."

"What inspired you to travel this aberrant and dangerous path?"

The vodka left a trail of flames down her esophagus and she imagined it starting to dissolve the lining of her stomach. Salt from the olives and the herbaceous blessing of vermouth made the pain bearable. "Lunch with my father."

"Ah. Many sensible people are driven to drink by family, myself included. He's not a tyrant or an ogre, is he?"

"No. He's actually a lovely man, we've just been butting heads lately."

Remy's pitch-dark eyes were unnerving and made her feel like a frog pinned to a dissection tray. She should have kept her mouth shut.

"Something to do with Max?"

She choked on a piece of olive. "Why would you ask that?"

"It seems logical. You said you've been butting heads *lately*. Traumatic events and grief cause strife in relationships."

"You just can't stop being a detective, even when you're on vacation."

"I imagine you have the same problem." He swirled a skewered cocktail onion in his drink and took a sip. "I met your father and mother at Max's visitation—very stoic people. But stoicism doesn't change what's happening inside, it only makes it impossible to come to terms with it."

Nolan scowled. "Let me guess: you majored in psychology and then hung it all up to become a cop because you were so frustrated with the human mind."

"No, but I know something about this. Losing a child isn't the natural order of things. The mourning process can be destructive instead of healing."

Nolan's hand was covering her mouth before she realized it had left the stem of her glass. "Oh . . ."

"No, Maggie, it's not like that. I didn't lose a child, but my parents did."

She stared at him, dumbfounded. "You lost a sibling?"

"My little brother Louis."

"I'm sorry, Remy. When?"

"A long time ago. He was seven, I was ten."

"Was he sick?"

"Car accident. My father was driving. You can imagine what that did to the family."

Nolan's heart ached for him. She understood. And she hated herself, because that wicked, suspicious part of her brain was analyzing the possible reasons why secretive, enigmatic Remy Beaudreau had just divulged a painful part of his past. The first thing that came to mind was that empathy was a primary building block of gaining trust; a way of manipulating somebody . . .

Oh, for fuck's sake, you idiot, you think he's making up a tragic story to get you into bed when he knows damn well it's going to happen anyway?

"I'm sorry," she repeated moronically.

"I told you because I understand a little about what you're dealing with."

Her wicked, selfish, groundless cynicism deflated like the bellied sails of a ship hitting dead calm. "Is that why you moved to LA?"

Remy gave her a sad, inscrutable smile. "One of the reasons. Come on, let's take a walk and look at the swans. They're eye candy that will take your mind off anything and they have very little to say about human misfortune."

"I love the swans."

"You're no stranger to this place, then."

"We have a passing acquaintance." Her phone started skittering across the table, rudely disrupting the meaningful moment of dead-sibling-swan-loving bonding.

"You're not on call, are you?"

Nolan downed the rest of her martini and grabbed her phone. "You think I'd be drinking like this otherwise?" She read a text from her father and pocketed her phone in flagrant disgust. Children of the Desert. God, could the name be any cheesier?

"Is something wrong?"

Nolan was conflicted about how to respond. Trust did not come naturally to her or to Remy, but he had bared his belly. Reciprocating would have uncertain ramifications and present new risks she could avoid, but mental gymnastics were so wearying. She had a life to live, and that wasn't going to happen if she constantly jumped at every shadow of emotional peril. Cowardice was sheltering, bravery was empowering. Shoot now and ask questions later.

"My mother is going to some stupid, New Age retreat in the desert today instead of talking to her family or going to see a grief counselor. I'm pissed about it."

The sudden intensity of his gaze made her feel hot and itchy, like she'd been in the sun too long. "What? Why are you staring?"

"A friend recently mentioned a spiritual group called Children of the Desert. Self-help, salvation, that sort of thing."

"That's the name. And a total scam, I'm sure." She frowned at him. "I don't see you keeping company with ersatz hippies or emotionally needy people."

"Thank you for the compliment."

"So why was your friend talking about Children of the Desert?"

"I have him looking into an old missing person's case and there may be a connection."

Nolan's stomach was already protesting the damage the vodka had done, but it roiled a little more. "I don't want my mother involved in a place where people disappear. Actually, I don't want her there at all."

The corner of his mouth lifted slightly. "I wish I could give you an excuse to use, but my friend said they do good things."

"Let me know if you hear anything else," she said a little more tersely than she'd intended.

"I will. Come on, let's go see the eye candy."

The elegant muses were gliding on the serene, eponymous Swan Lake—more of a pond, really—but a spectacular one. It was ringed by stacked stone and embraced by lush foliage. Rioting blooms punctuated the jungle palette, and the air was dense with the perfume of earth and flowers.

A million miles away.

Remy pointed to a gazebo partially obscured by a towering cluster of pampas grass. "That's the wedding venue."

"What a magical place to get married. But you haven't even proposed."

Remy let out a rare laugh. "There are private suites tucked away in this subtropical paradise. Places where the rich and famous have been disappearing for decades. There's the Swan Lake suite, right there."

"I don't see anything."

"That's the point. Do the swans look plump to you?"

"A little. They have a good life." Nolan watched them circle, then bat their wings against the water. They seemed agitated, but what did she know about the *Cygnus* genus? Maybe they were playing duck duck goose.

Patches of sun filtered through the trees, laying an ever-shifting blanket of jagged diamonds on the water. Even with sunglasses, it was blinding in its brightness and played tricks on the eye. Nolan kept imagining something just below the surface, within the rippled perimeter of the swans' circular route. She nudged Remy.

"Yes?"

She pointed. "Do you see something?"

His eyes followed her finger. "I believe I do. What an abrupt end to a promising day."

•

Nolan watched the uniforms defile the perimeter of Swan Lake with their ugly crime scene tape. A pair of LAPD divers was suiting up to recover the body and search for underwater evidence. Prior to any show of police presence, guests had been discreetly shepherded away from the vicinity with apologies for a *temporary situation* that in *no way* presented a public safety risk. Because of the terrible inconvenience, comps would *of course* be offered. Dom Pérignon and caviar all around.

She was genuinely impressed by the composure and efficiency of the manager and staff. They had done an admirable job minimizing the impact of a catastrophic disruption in their carefully curated, paradisiacal realm. In fact, there was no sign that any of the guests had suspected a corpse was involved. But that blissful ignorance had surely been shot to hell by now, because there was no way to conceal throngs of cops stringing crime scene tape and CSI techs in their jumpsuits and booties trampling the pristine grounds. The Bel-Air was probably already a hot topic on social media, for all the wrong reasons.

In the meantime, without bedlam and rubberneckers, the police work was easier. A win-win, high-fives all around. The swans were the only living things here that were pissed off. Who knew such splendid creatures could be so territorial?

She tried Al again, and this time he answered. A strong wind buffeted in the background, fuzzing the connection. "What's up, Mags?"

"Where are you?"

"In Malibu with Corinne, eating fish tacos."

"Sounds nice. Sorry to ruin it, but—"

"If you're calling about a dead body, forget it. It's the first off-call weekend we've had in a month."

"Hotel Bel-Air. It's ours."

"Was there a major homicide call-out I didn't hear about that bumped us to the top of the list?"

"No."

"So why is it ours?"

"Captain's orders."

"High-profile?"

Nolan squeezed her eyes shut. Her impetuous decision to meet up with Remy here was going to come back on her by a stroke of unimaginably bad luck, and she was going to have to suck it up. There was no innocent explanation for the two of them being here at the same time, at least in the minds of rapacious department gossips. The circumstances would be vastly inflated into a tawdry assignation that would become more salacious with each telling.

Remy would have to deal with the fallout, too, but he was senior, grades above her, and untouchable after he'd solved the Monster of Miracle Mile case. She was low-hanging fruit, so she'd bear the brunt of the razzing. It wasn't sexist, it was just pecking order.

"I found the body," she admitted.

Al was silent for a moment before he chuckled. "Well, you've got my mind racing now. Detective Margaret Nolan at the Bel-Air, rubbing elbows with the swells on a Saturday afternoon. Did you know Remy is a regular at the Bel-Air? Great martinis, he says."

"I recently became aware of that."

"I don't suppose Remy happens to be around?"

"Just get your smart ass over here, Al."

"Wilco. Damage control is my specialty."

Chapter Twelve

IVAN SERGEYEVICH LUKIN IN HIS HOLMBY Hills mansion, wearing a sleek Italian suit as tight as the surgically manipulated flesh of his face. In his obscenely Baroque office, fashioned after the interior of the Winter Palace. With his omnipresent vodka and lime and slobbering Caucasian shepherd of grotesque proportion, snarling at his master's Ferragamo-shod feet. The dog had killed before, and she could kill again, that was the message. It could always be a bad day when you were summoned by Ivan.

Gregory Rybakov desperately wanted to turn back the calendar pages and see Ivan languishing in his concrete bunker of an office in Lubyanka prison—just another party apparatchik, sucking the dicks of his bigger bosses in what was then called the KGB. But that had been a long time ago and Ivan had adjusted to the times and thrived like a cockroach surviving nuclear holocaust. When the Soviet Union fell, he rose, fattening himself on the carcass. With morality being no impediment, he quickly expanded his operations beyond the borders.

Now he carried the mantle of international *biznesman*—another word for a state-sponsored criminal, a uniquely Russian export. He had his feet firmly planted in both worlds now, which made him virtually indestructible. Yes, cockroach was a very suitable analogy.

"I think your beast is hungry, Ivan Sergeyevich, do you ever feed it?"

He discharged a gusty laugh. "I don't see you often enough anymore, Grisha. I miss our time together. You always cheer me up. Vodka?"

He considered Ivan's use of his diminutive name, which could be a good sign, or a very bad one. Either way, he wouldn't turn down an opportunity to drink his vodka, which was probably distilled from the piss of Lake Baikal water sprites or Buryat shamans. "Yes, thank you, but no lime."

Ivan waved a manicured hand toward the shadows at the back of the room, where his brainless, neckless, well-armed *byki* lurked. The bodyguards—literally, the bulls—were less conspicuous than the dog, but equally menacing. "Vodka for my old comrade, no lime, and some meat for Angel."

He snapped at them in Russian, which meant he was still going to the same old poisoned well for talent. He didn't trust domestic help—they weren't vicious enough. Gregory lit a cigarette and directed a stream of smoke toward the monolithic Angel, which didn't improve the dog's disposition. "Can I offer you one, Vanya?"

"I would like one very much, but I gave it up some time ago. We're not young men anymore, Grisha. We need to have concern for our health."

He knew Ivan's mention of health had nothing to do with concern—it was a warning, meant to set the tenor of the meeting. Gregory chuckled gruffly, releasing another plume of smoke that hung at eye level. "As you said, we're no longer young men. I don't worry so much about what might kill me these days. Isn't there an American saying about chewing glass while looking down into the abyss?"

Ivan brightened, almost smiled. "I've always admired your spirit. And your fearlessness." He pushed an onyx ashtray across his desk and regarded him with flat, dark eyes, exceptional only in that they possessed no dimension, no shine. "Life is good, very good in Los Angeles, wouldn't you say?"

Gregory gestured to a gleaming Fabergé egg on a gilt pedestal. "A new addition?"

"It is."

"Then life is very good and getting better." Gregory watched in morbid fascination as Ivan coaxed his bloated pink lips upward in a feral smile. Fuck your mother, had he gotten injections, too?

"International import and export is quite lucrative."

"One of Viktor's?"

"Yes."

"How did you get him to part with one of his precious eggs?" The acquisition was surely the result of blackmail, but Gregory relished asking the question.

"What's one egg out of so many? Viktor can barely keep track of his collection, it wasn't so painful for him. And what about you, how are you finding life these days?"

"Excellent."

Ivan nodded thoughtfully. "I'm happy to hear that. And we'll keep it that way, won't we, Grisha?"

So there was a problem. Gregory felt a trickle of sweat course down the hollow of his spine as a *byk* returned with vodka, no lime, and a plate of raw meat. His boss dismissed him with a nod and he retreated back into the shadows to rejoin the rest of his sociopathic brethren.

Ivan tossed a few bloody cubes of steak on what Gregory assumed was a priceless rug. "I have concerns about Pasha."

"He's done well for us."

"He has, but I fear he is getting confused about the difference between illusion and delusion, and succumbing to narcissism. That's a very hazardous place for the psyche."

Gregory almost gagged on his vodka. Ivan talking about narcissism? "Tell me how."

"It appears to me that his priorities have shifted and become very self-focused. He's getting too much notice. That is not something we value." He scowled at his tablet computer and spun it around. "Father Paul, healer and visionary? Children of the Desert retreats? He's running a fucking spa now?"

Gregory shifted in his chair. This was dangerous territory. "Of course it's not a spa. It's very ascetic. A few steps up from a gulag bunkhouse."

Ivan snorted his disbelief. "And yet people come—some of them famous—and they pay handsomely for the privilege."

"Yes. For the same mumbo jumbo he uses to attract full-time members. He's got quite a talent for persuasion. He can convince anyone that desert sand cleanses their sins and purifies their soul."

"I agree that people are unfathomably stupid, but I don't like this, Grisha. Not one bit. It exceeds the scope of what we originally discussed."

"He wanted to expand our outreach. Improve the bottom line. That has also exceeded what we originally discussed." Gregory smiled lugubriously. "Pasha is a young entrepreneur, preoccupied with money. You understand the way that kind of mind works. We all do."

Ivan's face was stormy and foul. "I should understand the mind of a man who foams at the mouth with religious fervor like an insane Dostoevsky character?"

"It's part of his craft."

He made an unpleasant sound. "He's not a fucking actor, he's an *employee*. This asinine enterprise draws too much attention and generates too much income."

"Too much money? Is the world ending? Are you feeling well?" Ivan was not amused, so Gregory continued on a more serious note. "The retreats are doing what they were designed to do, just like the government grants for the prison program. Additional income, additional opportunity to clean money. My reports show how much more."

He steepled his fingers and gazed at a distant point. "Yes, I've read your reports. Making money is all about the balance between risk and reward. But the equation is becoming unbalanced."

Gregory kept his face impassive, hoping his trepidation didn't bleed through the mask. "You said to me, 'make more fucking money.' Now you want us to stop?"

"It's raised suspicions. Mine, included."

"This whole venture has been about building a community beyond scrutiny or criticism; outside the reach of the law as a religious, non-profit entity. The retreats further enhance the impression of legitimacy; transparency. And the more money we make, the more money we can clean. It's a business model that's been a proven winner."

Ivan slammed the tablet closed. "Tell me, Grisha, you don't think this exposure is dangerous?"

"More dangerous than laundering money or defrauding the government through a bogus prison program? No, I don't. People leave happy. 'Children of the Desert is a magical place, a place of spiritual healing and growth,' they tell their friends, our pockets get filled, the rates go up. We look authentic, we look good. When you hang a lantern on something, people are less apt to look. It's one of life's greatest ironies."

Ivan caressed his chin thoughtfully. "I'm still having difficulty believing people would pay so dearly to stay in a gulag bunkhouse. It seems to me there must be an additional source of income in the desert."

"There is nothing worth a kopek in that wasteland except your business interests and the fantasy Pasha creates."

"You're a vocal advocate, so eager to defend this fantasy. Perhaps you have a personal interest in ensuring this project continues?"

Gregory swallowed the acid creeping up his throat, because he did have a personal interest. Children of the Desert hid Ivan's money and the retreats hid the money he didn't know about. "That comment was very far beneath you. You're under some pressure, I see that now. But we're old friends, so I'll forget you said that."

"You shouldn't forget anything."

Gregory didn't forget anything, and he certainly hadn't forgotten about Kaliningrad, a speck on the Russian map between Poland and

Lithuania that served as a main transit hub for smuggled goods: drugs, humans, weapons, plutonium, cesium. It would be just like those Prussian swine to descend into paranoid psychosis over a few extra dollars. In their minds, more money meant they were being cheated out of it. In Ivan's mind, too, for that matter.

Then there was the delicate issue of balancing his legitimate enterprise and position in local politics, both of which he'd managed to corrupt in glorious Soviet style. Even in America, it was *vorovskoy mir*—a thieves' world. "So this has become inconvenient for business in the broader sense."

"Ah, so you understand after all."

It was difficult for Gregory to contain his joy. Ivan the Terrible, formerly Lubyanka torturer, now criminal royalty as well as a respected international businessman, was straddling a razor. And he was desperately worried that his nut sack was about to get split in two. When that happened, those little beans of his would just plop out of his body in a rush of blood and he would be no more. He wouldn't even leave a stain in the book of human history. "You are *vor v zakonye,* a thief in law, Vanya. You shouldn't worry about a harmless desert preacher."

Ivan's patience was visibly degrading. "My concern is what separates me from you, Gregory Alexandrovich. It's always been that way. And Pasha is not harmless. I think he might just be crazy enough to destroy everything we've built in the pursuit of satisfying his ego. Power can be very corrupting."

"Yes, I've heard that somewhere."

Ivan snatched the lime from his empty glass and sucked on it as if he was draining the blood from a virgin's neck in the hopes of restoring his virility. "You really are forgetful these days, so let me remind you of another important thing: we store inventory on that property, the very same property now being used to mollify spoiled, puling Americans. We might as well put up a fucking neon sign."

Gregory let out a phlegmy, rattling cough and crushed out his second cigarette in the onyx. "It's a vast property and the warehouses are nowhere near the retreat area. The guests never come in contact with the residents. Perhaps you'd like to come visit. It might even do you some good. We could all use a little spiritual rejuvenation from time to time."

Ivan's anger suddenly became a palpable thing, heavy enough to displace the air in the room. Even the dog stopped eating. "Pasha thinks he's Rasputin now, exploiting the Romanovs. I'm not going to let an insane person ruin everything."

Gregory looked at the beautiful, golden egg in the corner, an egg commissioned by the Romanovs themselves. What an incisive analogy, and surely intentional. "What would you like me to do?"

"Our desert preacher needs a course correction and you're going to take care of that for me. No more financial compensation for our wayward friend unless I clear it personally. And no more free samples of *my* products, of which he seems so fond." He offered a smug smile. "You think I didn't know about him dipping into the drugs, the flesh? And the Lamborghini? I can't imagine how he could afford that on a preacher's salary."

"You're being very ridiculous, Ivan. His cut of the retreats is hardly a preacher's salary."

"You're a lucky man, not to have fallen prey to the same temptations, Grisha. I admire your discipline, just like I admire your fearlessness." He stood, a gesture of dismissal. "I won't keep you from your important task. Be in touch more often. And don't kill him. If it comes to that, I'd like to handle it personally."

Chapter Thirteen

NOLAN KNEW SHE WAS DISADVANTAGED BY the martini because she couldn't banish the phrase "swan dive into Swan Lake" from her mind. It was uncharacteristically flip and insensitive of her. Usually, homicides plunged her into a deep funk, but her neurons were misfiring down inappropriate avenues, and she felt like she'd lost control of her personality.

Even worse, the same stupid part of her subconscious that was cracking poor interior jokes also wanted to blame Remy for the situation, which was outrageous. *She'd* called him, *she'd* agreed to meet him, *she'd* slammed her drink. *She* needed to get her mind in the game.

Properly self-chastened and feeling very disciplined and serious now, she followed Crawford behind a hastily constructed privacy screen where they got their first close look at the corpse. His blue suit clung to the softening body of a man approaching the back side of middle age. His neatly trimmed, salt-and-pepper hair was plastered to his skull and Gucci loafers still miraculously clung to his feet. His eyes were milky and the flesh that was visible was pruned and plaster-white. No obvious signs of violence, and he wasn't yet bloated with death gas. In Nolan's estimation, he didn't look too bad, considering he was dead. She'd seen a hell of a lot worse, and she mentioned it to Crawford.

"Is this your first water body, Mags?"

"Yes."

"They're a bitch to read. Rate of decomposition in water is slower, so it screws things up. The body can sustain deceptive antemortem injuries from underwater obstacles. Evidence gets washed away." Crawford prodded the body. "He's limp, but that doesn't necessarily mean he's passed through rigor. It also doesn't mean that he's fresh. Without getting inside his body, we don't even know if he drowned or hit the water dead. But there is one thing in our favor: immersion cases get priority because the bodies start decomposing fast the minute they hit air, which can screw things up even more."

"We don't need an autopsy to tell us this didn't happen in broad daylight. Everything about the Bel-Air is designed to feel secluded, but it's not. He went in late last night or early this morning before this place woke up. Somebody would have seen the body if he'd been here any longer than that."

Crawford nodded, pleased. "Smart, Mags. You can think after a cocktail, that's an important skill to have as a homicide detective."

She crouched over the body. "Middle-aged professional, dressed for the Bel-Air, so maybe he was staying here. No outward signs of traumatic injury. If he was impaired, he could have fallen in and drowned."

"Or someone could have whacked him on the back of the head and tossed him in. We won't know that until the coroner shows up and we can flip him."

"If this was a homicide, it was risky as hell."

"Could be suicide, but there are better ways to do it than drowning yourself in a shallow lake." He patted the corpse's jacket and withdrew a set of keys with a Mercedes fob, and an ostrich-skin wallet. "No phone, but this is good." Crawford pulled out a few soggy hundred-dollar bills, some business cards, credit cards, a driver's license, and a plastic California bar card. "He's a lawyer."

"We have a motive for murder, then." More martini flippancy, rewarded by a sly smile from Crawford. He often extolled the virtues of gallows humor as another important survival skill in the job. Gold star for Margaret Nolan.

"Blake Lindgren. Lives . . . lived up in the bird streets in the West Hills. Tanager Way." He rocked back on his heels. "His name sounds familiar."

The bird streets were a bewildering network of narrow capillaries that vined along the crest of the Hollywood Hills. Prime real estate. "It doesn't sound familiar to me, but if he lived up there, he was hauling in big bucks. Maybe he had a high-profile case you remember."

He handed her one of the business cards. "Doubt it. He was general counsel for an import-export outfit called Krasnoport. Pretty dry stuff."

"Nothing else in the wallet?"

"Nope. No receipts, no dry-cleaning tickets, no condoms."

"Oh, for God's sake, Al."

"Hey, sex isn't just for the young and stupid."

She saw Remy approaching and gave him a somber, professional nod. Like she hadn't been drinking with him an hour ago. Al waved a gloved hand at him.

"Hey Remy, we got an ID. Does the name Blake Lindgren ring any bells for you?"

"No. You're wearing a suit."

"Yeah, so?"

"Maggie said you were in Malibu with your sainted wife. I expected board shorts and flip-flops."

"I learned a long time ago to keep a suit in the trunk."

"Good advice." His eyes drifted to a stout man with feathery gray hair as he approached, followed by an entourage of younger colleagues wearing windbreakers that projected in bold yellow letters that they were with the Los Angeles County coroner. "Well, the cat's definitely out of the bag now. You pulled Doc Weil, that's reason for celebration. Odd duck, but the best. I'll run Lindgren's name while you all do your thing."

"You're on vacation," Nolan protested, eager to shuffle Remy to the periphery, if not get him out of the picture altogether.

He shrugged affably. "I'm here, I might as well make myself useful. What's the middle name?"

Crawford squinted at the license. "Douglas. He's a lawyer and he lived on Tanager Way. I know that name from somewhere."

"Got it."

"Thanks, Remy." He returned his attention to the body, but remained annoyingly mute.

"I owed him a drink," Nolan finally snapped irritably.

"Hey, you don't have to explain anything to me, Mags."

•

By the time Remy finally returned, Dr. Weil and his crew had already left with the body. Crawford raised a brow at him.

"Where the hell have you been? You missed all the good stuff. Not a mark on him, front or back. Looks like an accident."

"The circumstances are so bizarre, it should be a slam-dunk. Find out why he was here and who he was with, you'll find out what happened to him. When is the autopsy?"

"Doc said later this afternoon."

"Good. Did you find a phone?"

"It wasn't on him, but we'll get his records before the day is out, same with his credit cards. What do you know?"

"Blake Douglas Lindgren came up clean—not even a parking ticket—so I did a little research for you. Al, you know his name from the kidnapping. Laguna Beach, back in 2002. His ten-year-old son Michael was taken from the home in the middle of the night while his wife, Zoe, was sleeping."

"Oh, shit, I remember that now. She'd been drinking, forgot to set the alarm. There was a fire, too. God, that was awful. Mags, you wouldn't remember, you were just a kid."

"And we were stationed overseas then. Did they ever find the boy?"

Remy shook his head. "And no ransom demands or suspects, either. The FBI got a black eye for that, probably unfairly. Stranger abductions are tough."

She thought of Remy's little brother. At least they'd had a body to bury. "It was a long time ago, but suicide might not be off the table after all, Al."

"I hear you."

"What about the wife?"

"Still living. Santa Monica, Alta Avenue. The Lindgrens relocated to LA a year after the kidnapping. They were divorced last year, and he bought the Alta house shortly after it was final. Amazing they kept it together so long after something like that."

Crawford nodded. "Thanks for the legwork, Remy, you saved us some time. Do you want a piece of this?"

"Hell no, it's all yours. The media is already swooping in and I don't want any part of that noise, but keep me in the loop and let me know if there's anything else I can do to help." He shot Nolan a brazen look. "This didn't count, Maggie. The dead body ruined everything."

The traitorous twin furnaces in her cheeks lighted, ensuring her embarrassment was in full view. What a jackass. "Dead bodies have a way of doing that."

"Occupational hazard," Crawford agreed jovially.

Remy smiled and sauntered away.

"You've got to give him credit for being a persistent son of a bitch. Plus, he's right. You definitely need a redo on the drink."

Chapter Fourteen

SAM ICED A SMALL COOLER OF Sierra Nevada and fired up the Mustang. Hearing the throaty snarl of the engine as it came to life never got old. Neither did the feel of immense horsepower vibrating beneath him, or the way the car leapt when he hit the accelerator, as if it could fly. There had been a dark time not so long ago when he'd considered ending his life by driving off a cliff on Mulholland. But the thought of destroying such a beautiful machine had seemed far worse than the thought of ending his own life.

He roared to Lenny's marina, enjoying all the heads the Shelby turned along the way. It was a cheap thrill, getting noticed for something other than his face. Beauty and the Beast.

As he pulled up to the docks, he remembered the charter he and Yuki had taken from this marina on their first anniversary. They drank too much wine and Yuki had puked over the side halfway through the cruise, but he'd still kissed her long and deep as the setting sun saturated the ocean in warm, spectral light. That night, it seemed their love and life together was as infinite as the vast Pacific. It was a good thing people couldn't see into the future.

The *Royal Bess* was an aging cabin cruiser Lenny had inherited from his uncle, a Navy man who'd been stationed on the U.S.S. *Ranger* during the Vietnam War. *Bess* was no beauty, but she looked solid and well-maintained, with fresh paint and shiny new fittings. She also looked deserted, save for a cluster of gulls hovering over the deck. They squawked and reeled away at his approach. Some people reviled them as sky carp. Others considered them sanitation engineers. Sam didn't have an opinion about them either way. They had their place on the food chain, and who was he to pass judgment on every living thing?

Being Army, he knew nothing about boats or the etiquette surrounding the culture of the water, but he was pretty sure you were supposed to get permission from the captain to board.

"Lenny? Lenny, it's Sam Easton. Are you in there?"

The only answer was the soft lapping of water against the hull and the grunts of seals sunning themselves on the marina's breakwater. By outward appearances, Lenny hadn't taken a couple days off to spend time on his boat as Mike had suggested. Even so, Sam decided to hang around for a little while in case he was on a supply run.

He opened a beer and walked down the dock a few slips, where a fine sailboat named *New York Doll* was being provisioned for a trip by a sweating, sunburned man with silver hair and a notable girth. He loaded a cooler onto the deck, then wiped his brow with a yellow bandana and waved in greeting. "Can I do something for ya?"

His speech was rapid-fire and heavily accented by one of New York City's outer boroughs. Or maybe New Jersey. Sam was no linguist. "I'm looking for Lenny Jesperson. He's a friend of mine, he owns the—"

"The *Royal Bess*! He's worked some wonders on that old dowager, right?" He squinted at Sam's face as he processed the disfigurement, but didn't comment. "That old desert rat, never could figure how he got the itch for the sea, but he's a fair sailor. Must be in his blood."

"He has a Navy background. Uncle was in 'Nam, Lenny did a tour in Desert Storm."

"I knew it! I figured him for some kind of a frogman. You, too?"

"Army."

"I see you got pretty nicked. God bless ya for your sacrifice." He reached over the rail and offered an exuberant handshake. "Frank Wiley."

"Sam Easton." He raised his bottle. "Want one?"

"Thanks, but I'll wait on happy hour until I'm out there." He waved a hand toward the open water. "I don't see Lenny around as much as I'd like, but I did run into him early this morning. He's not on his boat?"

"No. And I didn't see his truck in the parking lot."

Frank laughed heartily. "Hard to miss a beat-up, red two-ton in LA. Maybe they went to lunch or something."

"They?"

"Yeah, he's with his daughter and granddaughter. They're staying a day or two, I guess."

Sam's thoughts stumbled. Lenny had often lamented about never having kids and warned him off the same solitary path. No reason to lie about something like that. So why had he lied to Frank? "Great that he's getting some family time." He redirected to the sailboat. "*New York Doll* is a beauty."

Frank's fleshy, crimson face lifted with a besotted smile. "The love of my life. I bought her after my divorce. I thought the end of that marriage was the best part of it, but it turns out my *Dolly* was."

"Where are you headed?"

"Maybe Catalina, maybe just out to sea. I go wherever the wind takes me. The luxury of being single and retired."

"Sounds like a great life."

"It's the best. You're a young man, take my advice and get yourself a boat, she'll always be faithful. Hey, if I see Lenny, I'll let him know you were asking."

"Thanks. It was nice to meet you, Frank."

"Likewise. You and Lenny catch me another time and I'll take you both out."

"I'd like that. Safe travels. Anchors aweigh, or whatever it is I'm supposed to say."

"That's good enough for me."

Sam wandered to the end of the dock and watched a couple of seals roll around in the oily marina water. The sight depressed him, so he headed back toward the parking lot, waving a fond farewell to Frank as he pulled out of his slip.

The *Bess* was still quiet, but the gulls were back, and probably shitting all over Lenny's pristine deck. He waved them away and they fled his threatening, windmilling arms. The new angle of approach provided a different perspective, and he noticed something he hadn't before—splashes of red on the deck.

Sam's stomach clenched. He'd seen too much blood in his life to mistake it for anything else.

Chapter Fifteen

PAUL PULLED THE DRAB BROWN VAN into the Furnace Creek gas station. He hated driving it almost as much as he loved driving the Lamborghini, but that was only for trips to Los Angeles, when he took a vacation from being Father Paul.

He closed his eyes, inhaled deeply, and sought the eye of the hurricane—the peaceful place that sheltered him when the internal storm raged. And it was raging. The ultimate betrayal by a woman he'd actually thought of as his one true wife had let loose the gale and he couldn't allow himself to be battered by it. He had to stay calm, stay in control. He *was* in control.

You obviously weren't in control of her. You gave her too much freedom, you didn't hurt her enough. Bitch, bitch, bitch.

He'd selected two of his most trusted men to search the desert, secure in the knowledge that the evil, conniving harlot and his daughter—*his* daughter—couldn't have gotten far on foot. But those men had found no sign of them, and their failure had been punished accordingly by a vengeful Lord.

Paul knew he had to consider the possibility that his men had done their job with diligence; that Marielle and Serena had somehow found alternative transportation. If that's the way things had gone, then he'd killed two perfectly good men for nothing, which reignited his anger.

The necessity of recruiting an insect like Glenn Ramey was just more fuel feeding his inner conflagration. He didn't trust him, but he could control him, and he had a broad range of useful skills, including a complete lack of conscience. Even insects had redeeming qualities.

His thoughts meandered back to alternative transportation. Hitchhiking was clearly out of the question, there was no traffic. There weren't even any roads. There had been the bald man two weeks ago, but he'd walked right up to the gate and leaned on the buzzer—not the behavior of a co-conspirator bent on extraction. Besides, Marielle didn't have contact with the outside world, she hadn't for years.

Except for this gas station, during the monthly trips for gas, propane, ice cream, and hot dogs. A little gift to his faithful.

Was Lenny a Judas, running a fucking Underground Railroad out of here? He was going to find out.

Paul was disappointed but not surprised to see Mike at the register, his eyes rattling around in his empty head like pinballs. There wasn't much to be done with somebody like him, but at least he was being useful. Everybody needed a sense of purpose, even morons. "Good afternoon, Misha, how are you today, my son?"

"Hi, Father Paul. My name is Mike."

"Yes, I know, sorry about that. It's an old habit, you remind me of somebody I used to know." Mike wouldn't ever make eye contact, which made him impervious to charm and manipulation, and it really pissed Paul off. "Is Lenny here?"

"No."

"Do you know where he is?"

"No."

"Maybe he's at home?"

"He took a trip."

"Like a vacation?"

"I don't know."

Paul ground his teeth, visualizing his molars crushing his frustration. "Did he say when he'd be back?"

"Later today. In time to close."

Not a vacation.

Mike gestured awkwardly out the window, his eyes tracking across the overhead rack of cigarettes that got smaller every year as e-cigs and vaping products replaced them. "Gas?"

"Not today."

"Are you buying something? Ice cream?"

Paul tried to keep his tone calm and warm. People like this spooked easily and he needed Mike's trust. "I think I'll just get some water. Mike, I'm wondering if you've seen a woman with a little girl here, maybe last night?"

"Wasn't here last night. We close at five."

"How about this morning?"

"Uh-uh. No customers except a guy with a melted face. He bought orange juice, cashews, beef jerky, and water. He lives in LA and his name is Sam Eastwood."

"What do you mean by a melted face?"

"It was messed up. He got hurt bad. He asked about Lenny, too."

A man with a melted face, looking for Lenny. That was ominous—reminiscent of a dark prophecy or a beast in Revelations. "Is this Sam a friend of his?"

"He knew about Lenny's boat, so I guess that makes them friends."

A boat? "Yes, I remember him talking about his boat," he lied. "I don't recall what marina he docks at, though."

"LA."

"He never mentioned the name?"

"No."

Shit. There had to be dozens of marinas in greater Los Angeles. But it gave him a starting point. If Lenny had offered to help them instead of dumping them off at a bus station, a boat would be an excellent place to hide a couple fugitives. And he probably had because they were pathetic. Marielle had no money, no family, and nowhere to go—he'd made sure of that. He also knew she wouldn't go to the police.

Or would she?

Shit, shit, shit. She'd left, which had seemed unthinkable. He didn't know what was in that woman's head, and it would be foolish to think her behavior would become any less unpredictable. He couldn't trust her anymore. He also realized he couldn't wait for Glenn to handle this.

He went to the cooler, selected a bottle of sparkling water, and placed a fifty on the counter. "Keep the change, Mike."

"Thank you."

"I need to ask you a favor."

"Okay."

"Nobody can know I was in here asking about them. Not even Lenny."

"Why?"

"Well, Mike . . . because I'm hoping to surprise them with a special gift and nobody can know about it, otherwise the surprise will be ruined."

"Oh. Okay."

Paul's jaw ached from clenching his teeth. "Do I have your word you won't say anything?"

Mike nodded dully. "I can keep a secret."

"Good, that's very good. May God bless you."

He watched curiously as Father Paul pushed through the door and stomped to his van. Losing the woman and the little girl had made him really mad. The aliens were definitely behind it, they were getting bolder. He should have warned Father Paul about them. Next time.

Mike made change for the fifty and slipped it into the envelope containing the money he'd put in for Sam Eastwood's extra bag of beef jerky. In a careful, shaky hand he added a second notation on the back: *From Father Paul.*

None of it was his money to keep.

•

Paul sat in the van for a long time, his grip slimy on his phone. He knew a lack of action could be ruinous, but he did *not* want to make this call.

His hands shook as he plucked two pills from a tiny enameled box and washed them down with the sparkling water. Eventually, the knots in his shoulders loosened and his central nervous system softened like ice cream in the sun. Pressing the keypad was no longer an insurmountable task.

"Grisha, I need some assistance."

"Ah, Pasha. You must be a psychic now. Yes, you do need help. Badly."

Paul swatted a stream of sweat from his cheek. "What? What do you know?"

"I know I just left Ivan's office and he is very unhappy. We need to talk."

Fuck.

He sat up straight and smoothed his cassock along with his voice. "Yes, we'll talk about Ivan, but not now."

"Oh no, no, it *needs* to be now. But not on the phone, I'm driving up."

"Grisha, I have a *situation* down there. An urgent one, and I can't take care of it personally because I have a new group arriving." He checked his watch. Fuck. "They're already here."

Deep sigh, followed by silence.

"Grisha, did you hear me?"

"I heard you. Fuck your mother, what have you done now?"

Chapter Sixteen

AFTER TWO HOURS OF VIEWING HOTEL security footage and interviewing staff, Nolan and Crawford were no closer to finding a trace of Blake Lindgren when he'd been alive on the Bel-Air grounds. He hadn't been a hotel guest and there were no reservations under his name at any of the restaurants on the property. The bartenders and valets had never seen him before. The Mercedes registered in his name was nowhere on the premises, and the BOLO on it hadn't yielded any hits. No cab or ride share had picked him up at his home or office and neither had the private car services she'd been able to reach. It was like he'd been dropped in the lake without ever setting foot on the property.

Despite Remy's optimism, slam dunk investigations were as likely as a unicorn in a herd of mustangs. Clearing a case required arduous information gathering that would eventually form a revelatory landscape of the deceased's life and death. Dot-to-dot. Earth to earth, ashes to ashes, dust to dust.

She dialed Al as she passed through the lobby. "I'm thinking he must have gotten a ride here with a friend or colleague and we won't find that here. Where are you?"

"In my car making some calls. The scourge of the media has descended and they're crawling outside the barricades with saliva dripping from their chins. Let's get the hell out of here. Pick me up on Stone Canyon."

Nolan asked the valet to repeat himself when he told her what she owed to get her seven-year-old Toyota out of hock. Her hearing was fine. Fondling a corpse on hotel property probably didn't qualify her for free parking, so she kept her mouth shut and turned over half her week's grocery money plus a five-dollar tip. The department would reimburse her eventually, hopefully before she retired.

Her mother had called twice, and even though she was on the job, she felt guilty for not answering. Guilt was a family parasite that had enmeshed itself in the fabric of their lives like moth larvae in cashmere. Remy claimed he had gotten over his own infestation, but did you ever, really?

It was probably best that she hadn't been able to answer, because her bruised feelings and hot temper would have undoubtedly manifested in unpleasant, pointless, wounding dialogue. In the context of a dead body and her conversation with Daddy this morning, that suddenly seemed so petty; so irredeemably selfish and fucked up. She *should* be offering unconditional support and compassion instead of callous sanctimony. Her mother had absorbed the heartbreaks and disappointments of her life with silent strength and bravery, but it seemed obvious to her now that Max's death had drained her dwindling reserves. When the strong became weak, they had further to fall.

As she watched her Toyota pull into queue behind a Bentley, she sent a quick text to her mother, apologizing for being unavailable and promising to call when she could. Start small and build from there.

She picked up Crawford just outside the hotel's entrance. He was sitting on the back of his car, enjoying the shade of the hovering tree canopy while he finished the rest of his Malibu lunch. When he saw her, he crumpled the foil wrapper and tossed it through the driver's side window before he locked up and settled into her passenger's seat.

"I can't believe you just ate a fish taco that's been baking in the sun and heat for half the day."

"It tasted great."

"Food poisoning has no flavor. You'll be dead in an hour." Nolan hated the snippy, nagging sound of her voice, but it had been a snippy, nagging, intolerable kind of day. She modulated her tone. "How did you do on next of kin?"

"The only living relative I could find was a second cousin in a memory care unit in Texas. I called the ex-wife, but she isn't answering her phone. As far as I can tell, his life and his bloodline end here. Erased, just like that. At least he'll be remembered fondly by his boss. He was very upset by the news."

"'My boss remembered me fondly.' Not a great epitaph."

"Better than 'nobody remembered me.' The boss is at home, let's stop there before we hit the Tanager address. Lindgren was an employee at Krasnoport for over twenty years, so he's about as close to family as we're going to get."

"Sounds good."

"Krasnoport is a Russian-American company and the guy has an accent."

"So?"

"Don't make any cracks about Russia. Relations are bad enough as it is. The Cold War never really ended, you know."

Nolan rolled her eyes. "You're punchy."

"Must be the food poisoning. I probably don't have long to live. Do you think it will be painful?"

"I've heard it's the worst way to die. I'm sorry, Al. I'll make sure Corinne moves on."

"Thank God I have my affairs in order. It'll make it easier for the next guy."

As Nolan drove down Stone Canyon Road, she wondered if any of the grand homes they passed belonged to Remy.

Chapter Seventeen

THE PARANOIA THAT ACCOMPANIED PTSD WAS tenacious and unpredictable. Blood was one of the triggers and when a trigger got pulled, it was difficult to analyze a situation without psychological artifacts clouding judgment or spurring an overreaction.

Keep your head straight, Sam, you're not on the battlefield. It's fish blood. That's why the gulls are hanging around. They scored a meal and Lenny's deck is their picnic ground.

That was one scenario, and the most likely. But something didn't feel right, and Sam had been trained to pay attention to that sixth sense. If you didn't, you could get hurt or worse. He'd learned that the hard way.

He made a decision: fuck sea etiquette. He set his beer bottle on the dock and boarded the boat, which swayed gently under his weight. He could see that the blood had been smeared by determined beaks, but there wasn't a lot of it, which he took as a good sign. Alternately, he didn't see any fish guts, which he took as a bad one. He stood at the cabin door and listened for a moment, his palm itching for his gun—his version of a security blanket.

"Hello? Lenny, it's Sam Easton." No rustling, no voices. He tried the latch and the cabin door swung open. He couldn't imagine that

Lenny would leave it unlocked when he wasn't here. Of course, up until a few minutes ago, he couldn't imagine Lenny lying, either.

He was hit by the unmistakable smell of a watercraft that had been closed up a while—stale with undertones of mildew and sea water. The interior was gloomy with the shades drawn over the windows, but he could see enough to know the place hadn't been tossed. "Hello?"

Frank was probably right. Lenny was out to lunch with the impostor daughter and granddaughter. He'd forgotten to lock up, or maybe he hadn't believed it necessary with the activity on *New York Doll*. But his lie continued to rankle and Sam's sixth sense was persistent, tugging at the corners of his mind.

He stepped inside and called out again. Nothing. Nobody. A ghost ship. He walked to an open hatch and peered down into a sleeping berth, also empty. He took a step down the narrow staircase and noticed a small backpack—a child's backpack—with a puppy appliqué on the front. Next to it was a crayon drawing.

He suddenly felt like a contemptible intruder and backed up and out of the cabin, closing the door behind him. The gulls had returned and he shouted them away. He was beginning to form an opinion about them.

"Sam?"

He started at the sound of Lenny's voice. "Lenny! God, am I glad to see you."

He was heading down the dock with an uncertain smile, his arms laden with grocery bags. "I saw the hot Mustang in the lot and figured it had to be yours. Why are you here?"

"I missed you at the store today, and Mike said you spent days off here. I thought I might catch you for some beers and a joy ride. Sorry I boarded your boat, but I didn't feel like I had a choice."

Lenny's perplexed expression darkened. "What's wrong?"

"Hopefully nothing. Frank Wiley told me you were busy with guests, so I was heading back to the car when I noticed some blood on your deck . . ."

Lenny dropped his bags, jumped the *Bess*'s rail, and burst through the cabin door.

•

Sam never wanted anything to do with a police interview ever again, yet here he was at the Marina del Rey sheriff's station. He had nothing useful to contribute to the proceedings, and Lenny's story wasn't much more informative. The poor guy had just been trying to help a couple strangers, and the possibility that his generosity may have backfired in a bad way was hurting him—Sam could see it in his posture and in his face.

The detective was a man named Sanchez, who strongly resembled a French bulldog: small and compact with bat ears. His manner was professional, but there was nothing about his demeanor that could be misconstrued as personality. His moon face featured a caterpillar moustache that he stroked occasionally like a cherished pet. The brown eyes that sheltered beneath the promontory of his brow kept landing on Sam. Sanchez undoubtedly recognized him from the media furor of the past couple months—nobody forgot a face like his—but he stayed on track.

He made a few more notes on his computer, then regarded them both dolefully. "This is going to be a challenge. No photos, no last names, no dates of birth, no phone—"

"Marielle has that fleur-de-lis tattoo on her left arm, did you write that down, Detective?"

He gave Lenny a long-suffering look and continued. "No signs of struggle, no evidence of a crime—"

"Except for a missing woman and her daughter, and blood on my deck," Lenny interrupted again.

"Of course we're looking at everything." Sanchez consulted his computer again. "No one has been reported missing from Inyo County."

"An abuser isn't going to call Missing Persons. But he might kidnap her and her little girl and bring them back."

"It establishes that *she* didn't kidnap the girl. These things can go both ways. If we go with your scenario that they were taken, then the alleged abuser knew you were helping them, knew about your boat, and went straight there. Did you tell anyone else about your intentions?"

"Absolutely not. And offering my boat wasn't planned in advance."

"Who else knows about your boat?"

"Some friends, family, the folks at the marina. But like I told you, I know those Children of the Desert folks from the station and there's nothing else around for miles. I'm about the only person who could have helped. Not hard for somebody to put two and two together, and my boat's no secret."

Sanchez rubbed his moustache again. It seemed like a tender gesture to Sam, almost as if he was coaxing it to purr. "You said Marielle wanted to leave town. Maybe she decided to do it on her own after all."

Lenny was taut as a wire and Sam touched his arm to bring him down. "No. She wouldn't do that."

"What makes you so sure?"

"She had no money and no phone and no family to call. She was grateful for some help and a place to stay while she figured things out. Serena was happy, too, and that's what's most important to her, she told me that, and I believe her."

"If that's the case, then please be careful until we get this sorted out. Domestic violence often expands beyond the victim when there's been an intervention."

"I know that."

"Frank Wiley," Sam said. "He was around all day. He might have seen something."

Sanchez flashed him a tight, tolerant smile. "He's at the top of the list of people to question, along with marina staff. And we'll do everything we can with what we have. Because there's a child involved, we'll put out an alert with the description you gave us, Mr. Jesperson. Inyo County will take a run out to this Children of the Desert place. We'll call you as soon as we have any further information."

•

"How bad would it be if we cracked open a couple of your beers in the sheriff station's parking lot?"

Sam opened the Mustang's trunk and pulled two from the cooler. "Who cares?"

Lenny nodded absently and placed his hand on the sleek, blue skin of the car. "This is some machine, Sam. Guts and glory, the whole package."

"It is." He clinked Lenny's bottle. "Here's to Grandpa Dean, God rest his soul, for having such damn good taste in cars."

"And for passing it along." He took a pull off his bottle and squinted up at the sky. "I don't think Detective Sanchez has a whole lot of fire in his belly."

"I'm not a huge fan, either, but he's taking this seriously. Cops are methodical, they have to be. You didn't mention the necklace."

"She's not wearing it now, so it won't do the cops any good. Besides, she trusted me with it. Sam, she never would have left on her own. They're in real trouble, I can feel it."

Sam could, too, through Lenny, who'd formed a strong attachment to them during the midnight drive. The daughter and granddaughter he'd never had, maybe. And now they were gone. "Have you ever been up to Children of the Desert?"

"I've made some propane deliveries. Fancy place with a big gate and lots of fencing; nice old buildings. Before the COD people showed up there, the property was a ghost town on its last legs, but they did a good job restoring it. Even put in electric and septic."

"That must have cost a fortune."

"I'm sure it did."

"How did you get Marielle out of there?"

"I picked her up outside the property. She had it all planned, she'd spent some time working on it."

"Do you know anything about the group?"

"Same as you found out on the website and no more. It's some kind of religious community, and Father Paul is the head preacher, or whatever you want to call him."

"Is he American?"

Lenny looked puzzled. "As baseball and apple pie, why?"

"Nothing. Never mind."

"He's a pleasant fellow and a good customer. He's bought a lot of propane and gas over the years. Once a month, he brings the folks staying there into the station and treats them to ice cream and hot dogs. They're always nice, always cheerful."

"Nice and cheerful in a weird way?"

"Just in a normal way. Like a happy family. They talk and laugh and get a thrill out of eating junk food like the rest of us."

"But Marielle wasn't happy."

"She used to be, but few months ago, something changed. That's when she first approached me."

"What did she say?"

"Nothing, she slipped me a note that said: *Help me leave.* I didn't quite know what to make of it at first. There were always new faces, it was my impression that people came and went whenever they wanted to."

"But Marielle's situation was different."

"My sister Carole was abused and I know the signs. She finally got up the guts to leave the bastard and got killed for her trouble."

"I'm really sorry, Lenny."

"Thanks. Me, too."

"How did you know to pick her up last night?"

"She called the station from a phone at the compound and gave me the details of where she'd be waiting. She'd never called me before, so I'm guessing it was a risk. Marielle wasn't open about anything on the drive down, but it was obvious she was desperate."

"The cops will do everything they can, just like you did."

Lenny scuffed his boot on the asphalt. "Which isn't much, I'm damn sorry to say."

Sam thought about Margaret Nolan first, then remembered the last thing Remy Beaudreau had said to him.

Know you have a friend in the LAPD if you ever need anything.

"I'd like to call somebody, run this by him. Maybe there's something more he could do."

Lenny's eyes lifted back up to the sky. High, thin clouds had moved in, streaking azure with translucent white. "I appreciate that, Sam."

"And I want you to stay at my place tonight."

"Thanks, but I have to get back to the store."

"You trusted Mike to open this morning, can't he close, too?"

"Absolutely. He's not all there, I give you that, but he's more reliable than the sunrise. I just can't leave my own shop hanging."

"What's Mike's story?"

"He's a good kid and a hard worker, just different. His mother told me she figured he had an accident when he was a kid that scrambled him a bit."

"She *figured*?"

"He's adopted and the agency didn't have much information on him."

Sam knew better than most not to make assumptions about somebody without knowing their situation, and he felt badly about being cynical about Mike. "Mike gave me a free bag of beef jerky when he got the impression I was related to Clint Eastwood. I guess I owe you."

Lenny smiled. "No, you don't. I guarantee Mike paid for it out of his own pocket and there will be an envelope with the money and a note waiting for me. Aside from you, there's nobody I trust more."

"Then trust me when I tell you not to go back to Furnace Creek tonight. I don't want you on your boat, either. Sanchez is right about being careful until this gets sorted out."

"You have a bad feeling, too."

"Caution and common sense are highly undervalued. Call Mike and get things squared with him."

He sighed in resignation. "I'll need to get some things from the boat. Overnight bag and my groceries. Got some nice T-bones and I'd like to pay my way."

"I've got the alcohol covered. Hop in."

Chapter Eighteen

NOLAN FOUND IVAN LUKIN INTRIGUING BECAUSE she couldn't get a clear read on him. His home was as opulent as a royal residence, his suit a sartorial triumph that hadn't been purchased off a rack anywhere. The whisper of an accent sounded cultured and generic European; his manner was refined and without conceit. But she sensed a coarseness thrumming a low frequency just beneath his polished presentation that contravened his gilded office and his bespoke suit. He was comfortable in his habitat and clothing, but he didn't quite belong.

He dragged his fingers through thick, dark hair that didn't show a trace of gray and looked perfectly natural, although Nolan was sure it wasn't. In spite of his obvious passion for plastic surgery, it was clear he wasn't a young man—mid-sixties, she figured. Did anybody really believe that face-lifts made you look younger? To her, enthusiasts of the knife just looked like old people with bizarrely tight skin.

"This is such shocking, devastating news," he lamented over a crystal glass crowned with a chunk of lime. "Please tell me what happened to Blake."

She let Crawford give him an abridged, sanitized version and by the end of the short, sad tale, he was engaged in a struggle with emotion.

"My God. How could he have possibly ended up . . . how could this . . . was it an accident?"

"We haven't been able to determine cause of death yet."

He turned his big leather chair to face a wall covered with framed prints of articles from business publications like *Forbes* and *The Economist*. Several featured photos of Ivan Lukin and Blake Lindgren together. "The two of us over the years. I couldn't have built Krasnoport without him. I also can't imagine this world without him." He swiveled back to face them. "How I can help you, Detectives?"

"He has no family left living except for a cousin in memory care. We're hoping you can fill in some blanks. It appears you two were very close."

"We were, professionally."

"But not personally?"

"Our relationship always remained within those boundaries."

"Even after twenty years?"

"Blake was an extremely private person."

Nolan understood the dynamic. She couldn't imagine herself having a personal relationship with any of her bosses, no matter how long she worked for them. "Was he close with any other colleagues?"

He shook his head morosely. "I really don't believe he let anybody in. You may know this already, but Blake's son Michael was kidnapped."

"We do know."

"He withdrew almost completely after that and never recovered. Twenty years may seem like a long time to us, but if you've lost a child and don't even have the closure of knowing what happened . . ." Lukin's gaze drifted back to the vanity wall. "He was so vibrant before the tragedy, so engaged with everyone around him. That was the secondary tragedy. There are so many sorrowful repercussions that emanate from a single evil act."

"We see it all the time," Crawford agreed. "The kidnapping must have affected his work."

"In an unexpected way—he became more dedicated, more driven, more focused. I imagine it was his way of coping with the brutal reality of his loss."

"Was there ever any office friction that you noticed?" Nolan asked.

"Never. He was well-liked and respected. I can print out a list of his coworkers if you'd like to speak with them."

Nolan nodded. "That would be helpful, thank you."

Crawford pulled out his pocket notebook, a rebellion against the fully electronic era. "Was he at work yesterday?"

"No, he took the week off."

"Did he say why?"

Lukin gave him a pained smile. "He always does this time of year. Michael was abducted in August."

"So he didn't have a work engagement that would have brought him to the Bel-Air?"

"Definitely not. Blake always took client meetings in our downtown offices."

"I suppose you wouldn't know of any personal reasons, like a friend outside the office?" Nolan asked.

"No, I really wouldn't."

So far, Lukin was presenting an insular, one-dimensional man. But even the most lackluster people had some dimension. There was more to Lindgren, something that had brought him out of exile and to the Bel-Air to die or be killed. "He divorced a year ago."

"Yes."

"Was it contentious?"

Lukin took a dolorous sip from his glass. "I believe it was extremely painful. After all the years he and Zoe stayed together, sheltering one another, and then to have the marriage finally fragment . . . another heartbreak in his life."

"Did you know his wife?"

"I met Zoe a few times at office functions. Christmas parties, team-building events, things like that. She was a beautiful, vivacious woman. But after the kidnapping, I never saw her again." He looked away briefly and squeezed his temples like a man engaged in mortal combat with a migraine. "Does she know yet?"

"We haven't been able to reach her."

"When you do, will you inform me immediately so I might extend my condolences and support? Blake was the only family she had in the world, and divorce or no, I imagine this will be extremely difficult for her."

"We absolutely will." Crawford turned a page in his notebook. "Have you had any contact with Mr. Lindgren during his time off?"

"Not for a week."

"Did he have any substance abuse issues that you know of?"

The question seemed to startle him. "It wouldn't be possible with the demands of his job. And he certainly never showed any signs of it."

"Did he demonstrate any mood changes recently? Depression, for instance?"

"He's been depressed for twenty years, Detective. But I did notice that it seemed to deepen after the divorce. And I recently overheard him having a rather heated phone conversation. That was a few weeks ago and it was very out of character. He never had a sharp word for anybody, so I assumed it was Zoe. I remember being surprised by that."

"Why?"

"The divorce has been final for some time. With everything settled and no children, there wouldn't be a reason to have contact with her any longer. Or fight with her. Then again, are things ever settled after a divorce?"

Crawford scrawled *loose ends/wife?* in his notebook. "In my experience, lawyers argue and yell a lot."

"It wasn't Blake's style. And if it had been work related, he would have come to me immediately."

"He was private, but you knew about the divorce."

"That is a very difficult thing to conceal."

"Did he confide in you?"

"Not voluntarily. He only informed me when he had to cancel travel to appear in court. I asked if I could do anything to help, but he declined and we never spoke about it again."

"Did you overhear anything he said on this phone call?" Nolan asked.

"His office door was closed. It was only at the end of the conversation when he walked out into the hall that I heard anything. He said something like, 'Zoe, we can't do this over the phone.' I don't remember his exact wording."

Nolan leaned forward slightly in the ornate, gilt chair she'd been offered. "After the phone conversation, did he act any differently? Agitated, perhaps?"

Lukin sipped his drink with a pensive expression. "He seemed distracted; perhaps more melancholy than usual."

"Mr. Lukin, did you ever suspect he was suicidal?"

He rubbed his jaw pensively. "I admit I was vigilant. But no, I never really did. Is that something you're considering?"

"We have to consider everything at this point. Including homicide."

Lukin folded his manicured hands and regarded her curiously. "If it was homicide, then your job should be very easy."

"How so?"

"Because your killer would be more stupid than most, attempting to conceal a body in Swan Lake. Of course, you can really never overestimate the stupidity of criminals, can you?"

"It's dangerous to underestimate them."

"An interesting point, Detective. I never thought of it that way. If you're looking for insight into Blake, Zoe would be the one to speak to. She knew him better than anybody. She might be the only person who really knew him."

"We plan to." Crawford closed his notebook and tucked it in his pocket. "Mr. Lindgren was general counsel for Krasnoport."

"Yes. Not the most glamorous position in the field of law, but international trade is extremely complex and difficult to navigate, especially between Russia and the US, and especially now. Blake was without peer. Over the years, he had generous offers from my competitors, but none I wouldn't match or better to keep him."

"What sorts of things do you import and export?"

"The bulk of our business is agricultural and manufacturing products. As I said, not the most glamorous."

But obviously very lucrative, Nolan thought. She slid a card across his desk. "Please call us anytime if you think of something that might help us."

"I most certainly will. And please be in touch. I would like very much to know what happened to Blake, and also to provide for the memorial service if such a thing would be appropriate."

"Of course."

"Thank you. Let me print that list for you. I hope it helps."

•

"Wife first or Lindgren's house, Al?"

"House. If there's anything more to the guy, and I think there has to be, that's where we'll find it."

It was full-on rush-hour gridlock, which gave them ample time to work the list of colleagues Lukin had given them while staring at taillights on Sunset Boulevard. All of Blake's coworkers confirmed what Lukin had told them: he was a quiet man who was universally liked, devoted to his work and staff, but as distant as Mars.

"Nice, boring guy with sad baggage," Crawford remarked. "Not the type to have a target on his back."

"No. Right now, the alleged fight with his ex is the most interesting thing about him. But what's there to fight about?"

"Hurt feelings, bad blood. People torture themselves over it all the time."

"What's your gut so far?"

"Lindgren was a chronically depressed shut-in stinging from a divorce. He's fighting with his ex. He's been off work for a week thinking about his son and stewing in his misery. I can see a guy like that doing something stupid, like drinking or drugging himself into a stupor and falling into a lake."

"That doesn't sync with what Lukin said."

"Passive suicide. If you're on the edge of a cliff and your feet are stuck, add lubricant. But why would a hermit go to the Bel-Air to kill himself? He was the apotheosis of antisocial, and people go there to be seen."

That greased a seized gear in Nolan's brain and she almost missed her turn. "Remy told me people also go there to disappear in one of the private suites. There's a Swan Lake suite. Maybe it all meant something to him."

"A poetic suicide is a nice thought, love the drama, but we cross-referenced the reservation system with his name and credit cards."

"So maybe the reservation wasn't under his name or card. Let's check out the recent rental history of the suites, see if we can link him to the hotel another way."

"You have a feeling about something?"

"I have a feeling Blake Lindgren might have been a little more complicated than anybody gave him credit for."

The Bel-Air's premium service didn't disappoint—they were as equally accommodating to police as they were to the wealthy—but the results did disappoint. The recent rental history of all the suites included an entourage from Brunei; a flamboyant, well-known Oklahoma oil billionaire and his extended family; and a Florida couple who'd rented the Swan Lake suite for their honeymoon. Nolan was disheartened, but they'd followed her tenuous theory to its terminus. Now it was time to see the environment where this sad and disconnected man lived, and hopefully find some answers.

Chapter Nineteen

WHAT KIND OF AN IDIOT WORE *a leather coat to the desert? Grisha wouldn't need the gun he always kept concealed beneath
it, not out here. But habitual paranoia had kept him alive this long.
He seemed unaware that his deadliest adversary was his own abused
body, breaking down cell by cell.*

*A future here? In the middle of a desert? Fuck your mother, your
brain is on fire from the heat, Pasha.*

*This place is remote, far from anything. Hours from Los Angeles,
twenty-five miles from the nearest town. I think very few people know
it even exists. It would be a good place to conduct business.*

*Away from those bastard Armenians. Yes, I get it, but if we came
here, they would know it exists, and then so would everybody else.
We're better off in the city. No one notices thieves and murderers there.*

Sometimes the best way to hide is in plain sight.

Not in our line of business.

You lack vision, Grisha.

Yes? Then help me see.

*The Russians had God taken from them by the Communists; the
Americans have lost him on their own. Who needs God when life is
good? Struggling to survive has meaning, it defines the soul. If people*

lack that existential motivation, life becomes empty and pointless. They succumb to drugs, diseases of the mind and body, real or imagined; to hopelessness. I would give them a sense of belonging; a larger purpose; a place where they feel important, like they matter in the scheme of things.

But they don't matter. Do you think the universe mourns the death of a human any more than the death of a fly?

The universe doesn't mourn death and neither do I. But some people need to believe it does.

You're talking shit again. What do you care about making a bunch of idiots happy?

I don't, but happy idiots are useful. There is always ripe fruit for the picking if you're creative enough to exploit the desolation of the human soul.

Sometimes, it was important to remember the beginning of the journey in order to continue. Gregory was aggressively stupid, so it had taken a long time to make him understand, but Paul had ultimately accomplished the impossible. And his success had surpassed even his own exalted goals. But reality was interfering with his work now, and that was unacceptable.

He furiously paced the vestry of his lovingly restored chapel, trying to concentrate on the words and tone of his welcome speech. The content was fixed and his command of riveting prolixity flawless, but it took fervent focus to deliver it with the required spiritual theater. And how the fuck was he supposed to focus on spiritual theater, on *anything*, when the whore and his daughter were missing, Gregory was losing his shit and wasn't returning his calls, and Ivan's lurid specter was hovering over him? Jesus Christ.

Jesus Christ is the answer. You are Saul who changed his name to Paul; a disciple in His domain, sharing the good news. Deep breaths, eye of the hurricane.

He threw his speech on the floor of the austere cell and sank into a crudely made wooden chair. Its poor construction and the misery it brought to anyone who sat in it was intentional—all part of the stage set. It reassured every person he counseled here that he eschewed material comforts in order to serve a greater purpose, just as Jesus had.

But Jesus had never had a problem giving speeches. Probably because he'd believed every word he spoke. Paul's inspiration had to come from elsewhere. His eyes slid to the decanter of Château Margaux breathing on his plank desk. Drinking a vintage bottle after the first convocation was a ritual he relished, but today of all days was reason enough to adjust the timeline. He was sure that Jesus, being a big wine drinker himself, would approve.

•

Things were going so well, Paul wondered if he shouldn't drink before all future convocations. The veil of darkness had lifted, his focus was pure and sharp, and his words flowed freely. The depth of conviction with which he spoke actually moved him. Oh, yes, his little chapel was brimming with the Holy Spirit of St. Margaux.

The sun streamed through the stained-glass windows at the perfect angle, casting divine light into the nave, and the audience of three men and seven women seemed captivated by the atmosphere and his inspired presentation. Only Emily Nolan, a meticulously dressed and coiffed middle-aged woman in a field of dilettante hippies and rich degenerates became visibly alarmed when he mentioned the simple shifts they were all required to wear during their stay. If he was reading her right, that news had been harder to take than giving up her phone. There was always one control freak in every group.

He had to remind himself that people like her were plagued by fear and insecurity and required a little extra finesse. It was incumbent on him to win her heart and mind so she didn't corrupt anyone else's. He went off-script and improvised, tailoring his words just for her.

"You are all equal in God's eyes. He is only interested in the interior of his lambs, not the fleece that covers them. Exterior trappings are meaningless, and a distraction from spiritual pursuits. During your time here, I encourage you to liberate yourselves from the petty vanity of the world you left behind and focus on what pain, suffering, or loss has brought you here. Healing can only begin when you redirect focus from yourself and give the root of your trauma undivided attention."

He noticed some guilty nods. That was good. They *should* feel guilty for their selfishness and narcissism.

"This is not a luxury retreat, but a spiritual one; a place where you will prepare your soul to receive your God in whatever incarnation he or she will come to you. Some of you may have never experienced the power of holy, unconditional love, or felt like you had a place or purpose in the greater universe. But the universe is waiting for you. God is waiting for you. All of this is waiting for you.

"Clear your minds and let God's love fill you with hope and healing and a positive path forward in life. If you can achieve that state of grace, anything is possible. Are you all prepared for this journey?"

Paul heard murmurs and watched heads bob in enthusiasm—even Emily Nolan's—and he felt a surge of warmth and energy. And power. He knew them all intimately from the dossiers Sister Carina had compiled. None of them knew the extent of the research that went into every single person who visited here, so they were always stunned by his omniscience when he counseled them. He would take special care with Emily Nolan, a devout Lutheran who'd lost her son in Afghanistan. This serious woman of God would flourish under his counsel and might end up being his greatest success story to date.

"Then let us begin our journey now. Please follow Brother Angelo and Sister Carina to the Fellowship Hall, where they will give you an orientation and outfit you for our trip into the desert today. As we travel together physically and spiritually, be mindful of Jesus and his battle with Satan in a place exactly like this. Let Him inspire you and be your guide to peace and unlimited possibilities. The desert is unforgiving and cruel, but it is also a place of beauty and miracles. This will be our first lesson along the path to becoming Children of the Desert and children of God."

I think I see your vision now, Pasha. You're a real devil, aren't you?
I intend to become a god.

Once the pathetic little lambs had been shepherded away to ponder their spiritual goals, Paul hurried back to the vestry and called Gregory again. God really was bestowing miracles today, because the son of a bitch finally picked up. "Why the fuck haven't you been answering my calls?"

"Because I've been very, very busy on your behalf; you're welcome. I hope you're not using that appalling language in front of your new flock, Pasha, they would be very disillusioned."

"Did you find them?"

"Your lost sheep? No. They're not on the boat."

"Son of a bitch! Keep looking for them."

Paul heard a nasty snort on the other end of the line. "Right. Keep looking for them in Los Angeles, it's just a small fishing village. Perhaps you can point me in another direction."

"How the fuck should I know where they are?"

"How the fuck should *I* know where they are? You should have thought of that before you became so careless. Are you sure she doesn't know anything?"

"Of course she doesn't!" But Paul couldn't be absolutely, positively, 100 percent sure about that. He felt the dark curtain descend again, the force of the hurricane crushing the air from his lungs. He stood abruptly and started pacing furious circles.

"If she doesn't know anything, then why do you care so much about what happens to her?"

"I don't care about her, I care about my daughter! Who knows what she'll do to her? She's not stable."

"Pasha, this is a very bad situation on top of a very bad situation. They are a liability we can't afford."

"Don't touch them! They come back here."

"That's supposing we find them, which isn't very promising."

Paul gave the loathsome wooden chair a brutal kick and sent it skidding across the floor. "You didn't tell Ivan about this, did you?"

"Fuck your mother, do you think I'm an idiot? If Ivan finds out about this debacle on top of everything else, you won't survive. Do you still have your survival instincts, Pasha, or has all your oratorical bombast entirely blown the sense out of you? Let me give you some advice: forget them, clean your house right now, and get rid of anything you don't want Ivan to see."

"Ivan wouldn't come here."

"No, *he* probably wouldn't. But he'll send his *byki*. Maybe they're already on their way. And if Marielle went to the police . . . well, I don't want to think of what might come of that."

"I told you she won't, goddammit."

"Your voice is not as confident as your words. Has the new product arrived?"

Paul felt a stippling of sweat pop on his brow. "Yes."

"Get it out of there."

"But deliveries are tomorrow . . ."

"If you want to see another colorful sunrise in that hideous oven you call home, get it off the property and have it brought to me. I can make safe arrangements for the deliveries. Do you understand what I'm telling you?"

Paul had a strangely serene epiphany and nearly laughed at the absurdity of it. He was sure he understood exactly what he was telling him: Gregory was planning to fuck him over. It was mildly shocking, but not a surprise. "You weren't so worried about Ivan a few hours ago."

"I was very worried about Ivan a few hours ago, but a man can only strategize one crisis at a time."

"I'll handle the arrangements. I have contingency plans for times like these. I'm sure that's a relief to hear." Paul smiled at the following silence as Gregory recalculated his plan. If he didn't control the product, he didn't control the money or the situation. "I'm thinking of your safety, of course. What if Ivan came to visit *you*?"

"Yes, I see. That is a relief. Take care of your arrangements quickly, then, and go back to your guests. Preach and pray like your life depends on it."

"You are very paranoid, Grisha. It's not good for your heart."

"Can you really categorize self-preservation as paranoia?"

Paul didn't believe for a minute that Ivan or his *byki* would show up. This was simply another one of Gregory's inept maneuvers—part scare tactic, part attempted power grab. "Have a little faith, Grisha."

"That's your job," he snapped. "And stop calling me, it isn't safe. I'll get back to you when and if I have news."

Paul had the feeling he wouldn't hear from Gregory anytime soon. His silence might even become permanent with all his health troubles. Glenn the insect might make himself useful after all.

God certainly did work in mysterious ways.

Chapter Twenty

WHEN HE'D BEEN IN PRISON, GLENN had taken every opportunity to lose himself in fantasy, just like every convict did. None of those epic visions had resembled driving through an ugly dustbowl with a tweaked meathead who'd done ten for fifteen on possession with intent to sell. But even though this wasn't the hookers and blow scenario of his dreams, he had to be grateful he wasn't in a halfway house right now, getting piss tests every five minutes.

Duane Showalter was rambling inarticulately about watch schedules and perimeter duty and surveillance feeds. Sweat dripped down his lank face and into his sparse beard, even though the Jeep's air-conditioning seemed just fine to Glenn.

"This place is pretty desolate," he remarked, trying to work up some kind of rapport. "Wouldn't think you'd need much security out here."

"Father Paul is very serious about it, and you need to be, too. The Children of the Desert is the best thing that ever happened to us, and this is the most important job here. We're the Delta Force of God. That's what Father Paul says."

Glenn coughed to cover his laugh. "That's a lot to live up to."

"Damn right it is." He glared sullenly out the windshield. "The new guys always start at the bottom, work the schlep jobs like maintenance and construction. You earn your way to a security position and a lot of them never make it at all. It took me four years."

Because you're a fucking idiot. "Is that how it works?"

"How it's supposed to work. You didn't even go through orientation, so you must be pretty goddamned special."

Apparently taking the Lord's name in vain wasn't on the no-no tablet of commandments here. Neither was covetousness or drug use. Glenn bit his tongue and started carving his way through Duane's deep resentment. "Nothing special about me, it's just I've known Father Paul a long time. I'm lucky he looked deep inside me and decided there was something to save. I owe him a lot."

The ruffled feathers settled a little. "You sure do, we all do. Nobody else on the outside gives guys like us a chance. Father Paul expects loyalty and he deserves it."

"He can count on me."

He grunted. "First-degree murder rap, huh?"

"Total bullshit. I didn't do it."

Duane warmed up to the classic prison lie. "I hear you. I got a bullshit rap, too."

"It's a two-tiered justice system, Duane. For those who have and those who don't. We never had a chance."

He hammered the heel of his palm on the Jeep's steering wheel. "You're goddamned right about that. Goddamned right."

"So, Father Paul was telling me about his flock, but I haven't seen anybody."

"You won't." He gave him a partially toothless grin. "We're not allowed in the general population. Kinda like solitary."

"Ha! That's a good one, Duane."

"But this job has a lot of perks." He sniffed a couple times to give him a hint. "Father Paul wants us alert when we're on shift, and sometimes they run twelve hours if we're short-handed, and we are right now. We're just a skeleton crew: you, me, and a guy named Karl Hetson. Armed robbery. I'll show you the ropes once you get situated."

He ran the windshield wipers to clear the dust and gestured broadly, resuming his guided tour with the enthusiasm of a manic museum docent. "This is the back quadrant, where we keep it real tight. That's why there are watchtowers and a shitload of cameras. They feed right into that phone I gave you and alert you if something ain't right so you can get on top of it. Binoculars are your best friend. After perimeter duty, you head to a watchtower that's been assigned to you, so we'll go there next." He turned and leveled a severe look. "And you never, ever stray from the perimeter and go interior, that's the law here."

Glenn was extremely curious about what Father Paul was so obsessively paranoid about protecting. It had to be something good and he was going to find out what it was. "What are we looking for?"

"People who don't belong. Lookie-loos. Breaks in the fence or any sign somebody's been messing with it."

"Does that happen a lot?"

"Not on my watch."

Of course not. "So what are we supposed to do about it if it happens?"

"If the fence is broke, we fix it and report it. If we run into a trespasser or somebody thinking about it, we send them on their way with a message strong enough to make sure they never come back."

Glenn's grip tightened affectionately on the AR15 in his lap. "I guess that's what these guns are for."

"Yeah. They make a statement."

"I don't have to tell you that if two felons get caught with these honeys, we go down. So does this whole setup."

"Who's gonna catch us?"

Glenn scanned the vast, barren expanse before him. Duane had a point. "If we run into somebody, how strong a message are we supposed to send?"

"Don't shoot them," he said seriously. "Don't shoot anything unless Father Paul tells you to."

"Not even snakes?"

"Not even snakes. You got a problem with snakes?"

Glenn smiled. "Just one particular type."

Chapter Twenty-One

THE ENDLESS, DONKEY TRAIL OF DESERT road was withering Malachai Dubnik as much as it was his car. The BMW's Z-rated tires were being shredded by rocks, the cabin filters and air-conditioning were choking on dust, and the temperature gauge was creeping too close to the red zone. The windshield and hood of his formerly pristine black beauty were coated in a dense layer of ugly, rust-colored sand that was undoubtedly destroying the soft paint. He should have taken the Rover again, but he didn't recall the travel being quite this grueling. A bad sign that he'd made at least one wrong turn somewhere.

When his onboard navigation system and its locator pin had conked out, he'd been fairly confident he could pick the rest of his way to Children of the Desert without it. Now he was fairly confident he was hopelessly lost in a desolate wasteland with no proper roads, no landmarks, and nowhere to stop to ask for directions. He should have gone through Furnace Creek like he had before instead of trying for a shortcut. By his estimation, the shortcut had added an hour to the trip and ten years to his car.

He pulled over and tried to find the compound on Google Earth, but with no physical address, it was impossible to pinpoint five miles of desert in millions of acres. The phone number he'd called for an appointment wasn't answering and the website wasn't responding to his queries. There was something dubious beneath the sacrosanct veneer of Children of the Desert.

It was mystifying that anybody would come to this hellish wilderness for anything, let alone healing. Maybe self-flagellation was part of the program. It certainly wasn't part of his, and he was beginning to regret this trip as much as he regretted shorting triple volatility using leveraged ETFs a few months ago.

On the upside, he had a particularly strong cell signal—better than he got in Beverly Hills sometimes—which was curious. But there were military installations in this part of the desert, so towers were probably sprouting like cacti all over the place. His tax dollars at work. It was peace of mind in case his beleaguered car followed in the unfortunate footsteps of his GPS. BMW Roadside Assistance would just love rescuing some dumb fuck lost in Death Valley.

After fifteen more minutes of hard driving, he realized he only had one sensible option if he didn't want to die out here: backtrack to Furnace Creek and get directions at the gas station again. The odd clerk hadn't led him astray the last time.

As he wheeled the car around, he thought he caught a flash of something glinting in the distance. He knew the desert played tricks on the eye, so he found his binoculars and scanned the apocalyptic landscape in front of him. It certainly looked like a genuine steel mesh fence and not a mirage. Any sign of civilization was worth investigating more closely.

It was farther away than he thought—it was impossible to judge distance out here—but it was definitely a real fence, and it stretched as far as the eye could see. He picked out two cameras mounted on the posts of a chained and padlocked gate. There was a small structure that looked like a guard tower, but no other buildings in sight.

A few minutes later, a cloud of dust boiled up from behind the fence and a Jeep emerged from the haze. His presence here hadn't gone unnoticed for long. It stopped at the gate and a man in desert camo jumped out and walked through a man-sized door punched into the fence. He was carrying an assault rifle, but there wasn't a name patch on his uniform, and he wore a scraggly beard and long hair. Definitely not military, which made Dubnik nervous. There were plenty of meth labs in the desert, and if this was one of them, the security setup meant it was probably a large operation and cartel-affiliated.

With the sheepish smile of a tourist gone badly off-course, he opened his window. Grit flooded into the car along with an oppressive wall of scorching air that seemed to shrink-wrap him. "I guess you probably already figured, but I'm lost as hell."

The man was rangy and rough-looking, his eyes obscured behind the mirrored sunglasses of a seventies TV cop. He didn't smile back and was squirrelly as hell. Not the disposition you wanted to see in a man who was carrying an assault rifle. "Where are you trying to get to?"

"Children of the Desert, do you know it?"

He lifted his sunglasses and eyed the BMW. "Some kind of spa for rich folks like you. Do they know you're coming?"

"Is it a problem if they don't?"

"It might be. I heard they don't allow private vehicles in."

"Good thing I have an appointment. Can you steer me in the right direction?"

He gestured north with his gun. "The main entrance is about four miles that way. There's no road that goes there from this side of the property, so your only option is to backtrack to Furnace Creek and come in from that direction. Unless you have four-wheel drive in this fancy sedan." He smirked. "I guess you're going to be late for your appointment."

Dubnik's patience was already frayed to the limit, and now this yahoo was pissing him off. This yahoo was also flying on something, which reinforced his suspicion about a drug operation. But he was somehow a part of COD and knew something about it, so he marshaled his restraint and kept playing his role. "So this is all part of Children of the Desert?"

"I didn't say that."

He had said exactly that, but he wasn't going to argue semantics with an idiot. "Pretty tight security for a spa."

He was clearly confused about how to respond. This one was drowning in a shallow gene pool. "This ain't part of the spa," he finally said.

Dubnik looked out the windshield and noticed that Yahoo's companion had decided to leave the air-conditioned comfort of the Jeep and join the party. He was a slab of a man, much bigger and broader than his partner, and he engaged in better grooming practices. Yahoo and Slab. Dubnik slid his gun out of the holster and tucked it between his seat and the console.

"Trouble here?"

Yahoo shot his friend a laconic smile. "Nope. Just a lost soul looking for salvation."

They both thought that was hilarious and Dubnik decided to leave before he shot them both, he was in that kind of a mood. "Well, thanks for the directions. I guess I'll head back to Furnace Creek."

Slab smiled. "Hope you make it. Don't forget to turn left at the tumbleweed."

More infuriating jocularity, but the mood had become ominous. This was one of those rare times when Dubnik still wished he carried his shield and the full force of the law behind it. "Fuck you, too, assholes."

He peeled away and drove as fast as he could without rattling his car into a heap of scrap, and put a half-hour between himself and the troglodyte twins. He stopped at the junction that would lead him to Furnace Creek and decided things felt too weird to pursue anything further today. He was on COD surveillance camera footage twice now, and a totally hairless man intent on breaching the castle fortress was bound to raise some red flags. At least if anybody with half a brain was paying attention. That was definitely up for debate from what he'd seen today, but like in *The Wizard of Oz,* it was the man behind the curtain you had to worry about.

He put in a call to Remy, and when he didn't answer, he left a brief message. "Hey, I just left the backside of Children of the Desert property. Pinhead armed guards playing soldier with assault rifles, big chain-link fence, cameras, a watchtower. Time to assess a new strategy, so I'm going to skip the appointment and head back. Thought I'd call in case I disappear."

Dubnik signed off. He'd meant that last comment to be flip, but the longer he thought about the encounter, the more menacing it seemed. He goosed the accelerator and felt the BMW fishtail in the rocky sand.

•

Duane gave his new recruit a jab in the arm as they watched the BMW disappear in a cloud of red dust. "That asshole was here a couple weeks ago. I couldn't get a plate number, could you?"

"No, the fucking thing was covered in dirt. Do we let Father Paul know?"

"He'll see it for himself on the footage, he looks at it every day. Remember that. These cameras are his eyes. We'll put it in the daily report, though." He chuckled. "Turn right at the tumbleweed. That was priceless, Glenn. You're gonna fit in just fine here."

Chapter Twenty-Two

BLAKE LINDGREN'S HOUSE WAS A CONTEMPORARY, architectural jewel box with a panoramic view spectacular enough to turn even the most strident atheist into a true believer. It appeared to be constructed almost entirely of glass, all the better to take in the scenery. Nolan imagined it was breathtaking at night with all the city lights scattered below.

The front walk was slate and paralleled by a rectangular gazing pool that reflected chic, minimalist clumps of agaves. Pebbled concrete lozenges appeared to float in the still water. Nolan looked for the obligatory koi, but didn't see any.

Crawford gestured to it. "Just in case you want to make your grand entrance walking on water."

"I'm tempted. Do you think it's filled with holy water?"

"Anything is possible up here, closer to God." He looked around appreciatively. "This is exactly the kind of place I'd get if I won the lottery."

"I thought you said you wanted a big Texas ranch."

"If I won the lottery, I could have both. You called the alarm company and had them disable the system, right?"

"Of course I did."

"Just double checking. I don't like surprises." He rang the bell and waited, then knocked and announced himself before sliding the key on the Mercedes fob into the lock. The door opened easily onto a vast, three-story space, sparsely furnished in industrial-contemporary. "I hate being in dead people's houses."

"Me, too, but it's way worse when there's a body. I don't smell one."

"It's a big place."

It was a big place. There were no real rooms, only areas designated by the types of furnishings. They wandered through the foyer, kitchen, dining room, living room, all spotless and ordered; obsessively so, Nolan thought. The palette of materials varied little: steel, granite, leather, fur, brushed aluminum, glass. She glanced at a collection of Mongolian lamb pillows arranged on a massive leather sofa and wondered if Lindgren had been the type to notice a single ovine hair out of place. The house seemed to radiate that vibe.

They found the interior door to the garage, along with his missing Mercedes, which simplified things a little—he'd definitely gotten a ride to the Bel-Air. She made a mental note to cancel the BOLO on the car.

At the back of the house, there was a broad deck with an infinity pool perched at the edge of a steep drop-off. Chaise longues with rolled towels on the seats were arranged perfectly equidistant from each other. There were several other seating areas near an outdoor kitchen, a long bar, and a wood-burning oven. This was an entertainer's fantasy—an odd choice for a couple who had shut themselves off from the rest of the world twenty years ago.

Crawford echoed her thoughts. "Pretty damn depressing to own a place like this and not be able to take advantage of it. Unless they had a secret party life."

"Doesn't seem likely." Nolan walked to the polished concrete fireplace that dominated one side of the main living area. An enormous metal triptych with bas-relief waves consumed the vaulting space above it. "Everything is so cold and impersonal."

"It's my experience that women are the ones who add the personal touches and the wife's been out of here a year."

"Let's go find a place where someone actually lived. There's got to be one."

The bedrooms were equally chilly and sterile, but they finally found a study that seemed to be the sole repository of all things sentimental and human. Most of the room was as sleek and anonymous as the rest of the house, but a long zebrawood credenza crowded with framed photographs of family life stood out in sharp contrast.

There was an engagement shot and a wedding shot, and a half-dozen more featuring the happy couple with a beautiful blond boy. The chronological record ended abruptly with a photo of all three Lindgrens on a beach somewhere, cerulean surf frozen in time behind them.

Crawford pointed to the picture. "Their life stopped here. This is a shrine."

"Drives home the reason why there's no life or joy in this house. You don't have to have kids to feel the pain."

"No kidding." He took a slow tour of the display. "Blake Lindgren was handsome, but Zoe Lindgren was drop-dead gorgeous. Until you go down the line. Frame by frame she loses weight. She's damn near emaciated by the end."

Nolan thought about Sophie again, and how she'd shriveled to a dry, gray husk during her futile treatment. She was no expert on the ravages of chemotherapy, but Zoe Lindgren's weight loss didn't look like cancer to her. "An eating disorder, maybe."

"I never got that. A stunner like her, she doesn't think she's good enough?"

"It's a mental illness. They're complicated."

Crawford walked over to a wall of floor-to-ceiling bookshelves and took a brief inventory. "Ponderous tomes on the law that look like they weigh a hundred pounds each. Hope he didn't have to carry these around campus. Some Russian-English dictionaries. That's it, Mags. Did you see books anywhere else, like for pleasure reading?"

Nolan frowned. "No. Not even a Taschen vanity book on a coffee table."

"I guess Lindgren didn't have any hobbies or interests, and he didn't read for pleasure. That's weird. Even I have a Taschen vanity book on my coffee table." He rubbed his jaw thoughtfully. "Does anybody really serve coffee on their coffee table?"

"The only beverage I serve on mine is wine."

"Beer for me. So, Lindgren lost interest in everything but his job. That fits the profile Lukin gave us." He walked to the desk and poked at the unresponsive black screen of a tablet computer. "It's off. We'll bag it and bring it to Ike." He pulled open the top drawer. It was lined with green baize and empty except for some pens, a magnifying glass, and a leather journal. "Nobody has a desk this clean."

Nolan stretched out her hand. "Give me the journal." She leafed through page by page while Al started riffling through drawers of files. She'd been hoping Lindgren was old-school and kept a datebook or diary, but so far, it contained lots of notes in dry legalese and one entry that looked like a doctor's appointment.

"From what I'm seeing so far, these files are all work stuff, Mags. But there are lots of drawers to go."

"Same with the journal, except an entry from a month ago: MD— 11 a.m."

"A visit to the doc might be a great place to start, what with the shit they're passing off as medication these days. He pops one too many pills and ends up in Swan Lake. I'll keep an eye out for medical records."

Nolan continued to shuffle through the journal and found an anomaly near the end. "Look at this, Al."

He peered over her shoulder at a page that was solidly filled with the notation *UPUHA,* each one underlined so hard, the pen had gone through the paper. "An acronym."

"Maybe a company he was dealing with?"

"One that really pissed him off. At least he was passionate about something. I'll look it up." He started searching his phone.

Nolan slogged through another few journal pages regarding weighty topics like Russia's violations of Ukraine's sovereignty, the annexation of Crimea, and partial suspension of bilateral economic engagement between the US and Russia. Significant issues for a lawyer whose job it was to facilitate trade between the two countries. The remaining pages were blank. "UPUHA was one of the last things he wrote in here. Find anything on it?"

"So far I've got a Lithuanian metal band, one Twitter account that's never tweeted, and a Russian teahouse in Tarzana. He could have been a regular there. I'll give them a call."

"Find out why they're called UPUHA."

He nodded and stepped out of the study.

Nolan browsed through the journal again. Sometimes things looked different at a second glance. As she neared the end, a business card slipped to the desk top: glossy black with a name and phone number, nothing else. Malachai Dubnik. "Al, come here."

He reappeared with a bemused expression and pocketed his phone. "I talked to the owner of the teahouse, a very nice lady who laughed her ass off at me. UPUHA isn't an acronym, it's a name written in the Cyrillic alphabet. Irina."

"Is Irina a real person?"

"Was. She named the place after her grandmother."

"Did she know Lindgren?"

"The name wasn't familiar to her. I texted her his license photo, but she didn't recognize that, either."

Nolan handed him Dubnik's card and he grunted in surprise. "It slipped out of the journal."

"I'll be damned. MD wasn't a doc's appointment after all."

"A PI's bread and butter is spying on spouses, but this appointment was last month. I suppose he could still be trying to nail his ex on something. It could explain the fight."

"Or he was looking for his lost son. Parents never give up on finding a child no matter how much time has passed."

Nolan looked at the journal page again; at the angry scrawl. "Whoever Irina is, he had strong feelings about her. An affair?"

"Possibly. It's a place to start looking. But why would he write it in Cyrillic?"

"I'm sure he had fluency in Russian, maybe it's knee-jerk to write Russian words and names in the language instead of transliterating them to English. You worked with Dubnik back when he was on the job, right?"

"Yeah, I'll call him while you keep poking around. Lindgren just got a little more interesting."

Nolan flipped through another drawer of files, but the photo display kept intruding on her thoughts, so she went back to the credenza for a closer, more thoughtful look. The heart was the most honest part of the human anatomy and whatever had been left of Lindgren's was there, not in his paperwork.

Pretty family, lots of smiles, an increasingly thin wife. She studied the engagement photo, where their life together had started. Zoe Lindgren was indeed a beauty, with wavy gold hair and large, cornflower-blue eyes. A beaches and sunshine face, a real California girl. She and Blake were cheek to cheek, smiling like maniacs. Her left hand was raised to the camera, proudly displaying a diamond solitaire far too large for her slender, delicate hand.

The location was hard to discern—the photo was faded and the background slightly blurred. On the frail premise that location might provide some sort of insight, she helped herself to the magnifying glass. After her eyes had adjusted, she was able to make out the feathery heads of pampas grass. A gazebo. A lake with swans.

Location, location, location.

Chapter Twenty-Three

MARIELLE ROSE FROM MURKINESS WITH A sense of levitation. She was floating like a magician's assistant, suspended by the nothingness that enveloped her mind and body. As the blackness receded, pain skewered her temples and fragmented thoughts began to reassemble. The transcription was poor, but eventually she started to remember the men on the boat and then panic and terror took root.

She simultaneously opened her eyes and vaulted up off a fleece-covered cot; jagged light flashed in her eyes and her vision wobbled. After a few dizzy, staggering steps, she listed to the right and tumbled onto a concrete floor that was rancid with odors of grease and pine cleaner that triggered her gag reflex. She was familiar enough with drugs to know she'd been dosed.

"Serena!" The effort behind the weak scream ignited an explosion in her head and her field of vision began to narrow. Fighting hard, breathing hard, she dragged herself up onto the cot and tried to bring her surroundings into focus. She was in a small windowless room with concrete block walls painted bile green. A bare bulb dangled from the ceiling, casting raw light on a single ladder-back chair. Two doors, the cot, the chair, nothing more. "Serena?" she whimpered.

She had no idea who or what to expect when one of the doors

creaked open, so she curled into a defensive ball. It wouldn't save her if Paul had somehow found them, but the posture was instinctive.

"Ah, Marielle, you're awake at last."

She pressed herself into the corner as a fat man in a leather jacket entered the room. His bloated face was greasy and pink and ravaged with pockmarks; his voice raspy and accented. The stench of cigarette smoke and alcohol wafted across the room. He knew her, but she didn't know him, although he looked vaguely familiar. She'd seen him before, at the compound, she was sure of that now.

"Where is my daughter?"

"Nearby."

The curt, dismissive tone of his voice stoked an outrage that annihilated her fear and pain. "I want to see her NOW, goddammit!"

His eyes were empty, his smile insincere. "You're very spirited. I think it's a good quality. Unfortunately, my friend guarding the door doesn't agree. You did some damage to his face with your fingernails and he's not happy with you. If you can't behave, I'll have to send him in to calm you down. I'm not sure how that would go, he has an unpredictable temper."

Marielle put her face in her hands. She felt her chest hitch, but no tears came. So much for heroics. "I just want to see my daughter. Please."

"Oh, you'll be reunited with her."

"When?"

"When I'm satisfied with your answers."

"What answers? Who are you?"

"I might be the only friend you have right now. Enough with the questions. My turn." He sank heavily into the chair and withdrew a silver flask from his jacket. "Water? Tea? Something stronger? It's horseradish vodka, I make it myself."

She noticed a bulge in his jacket. A gun. She turned away and stared at the wall, trying to gather memories of what had happened on the boat. As if the answers were printed on this stupid, fucking, puke-green wall. "What do you want?"

"I just need some information about Father Paul, and then you can see Serena."

"You're . . . not with him?"

"He's very upset that you left, you know. He wants you back."

She felt something inside shatter so completely, she wondered if it would ever mend. "He'll kill me. He'll kill us."

"He wouldn't kill Serena, I hope that makes you feel a little better. But he might kill you. I guess you could say that your fate is in my hands."

Who *was* he? Obviously not a nice man; a criminal, she had no doubt. But what did he have to do with Paul? What, what, *what?* "You might kill me, too."

He shrugged. "I hope I won't have to. No child should be without a mother. To avoid such a tragic outcome, I would recommend your full cooperation."

"And then I'll see my daughter?"

"Yes. I would very much like a happy ending."

"What information do you want?"

"Tell me about life in your little desert ghost town."

"It's not a town, it's a prison."

"So you aren't allowed to leave the town?"

"What would be the point? There's nothing but desert for miles around."

"You didn't answer my question. *Were you allowed to leave the town?*"

"No. Not alone."

"How do you know there's nothing but desert for miles around?"

"If you have eyes, it's obvious. When Father Paul takes us to Furnace Creek, we drive forever. There's nothing in sight."

"Why do you go to Furnace Creek?"

"To get sodas and ice cream and hot dogs at the gas station." A distant memory flared briefly in her muddled brain. "I've seen you there, haven't I?"

"I'm asking the questions, Marielle. So this gas station is where you met Lenny."

Her throat tightened. God, poor Lenny. "Is he alright?"

He stared at her impassively. "Have you explored other parts of the property?"

"I told you, there's nothing there, why would I?"

He took a sip from his flask. "I can tell when people are holding back information. It's a special skill I have."

"I'm not holding anything back."

"Really? It seems odd to me that you wouldn't have explored the property in your effort to find an escape. Maybe you saw something you'd like to tell me about."

Her face grew hot. "There's an abandoned mine. It didn't seem important."

"Everything is important. What else did you find?"

Whatever alliance he had with Paul, it seemed to be tenuous. He suspected him of something and she saw opportunity in reinforcing his suspicion. But she had to be careful, because he was too interested in what she'd seen and what she knew. Which was nothing, but he wouldn't believe her. "There were bodies in the mine."

That drew his undivided attention. "Tell me about them."

"They were old and dried up. Like mummies. I think they've been there a while."

"Or maybe not so long. You would be surprised by what happens to bodies in the desert." He reached into his jacket and withdrew the rock she'd picked up. "I found this in your duffel bag. Is this from the mine?"

"Yes."

"Why did you take it?"

"Because I knew Serena would love it. I'm going to give it to her for her birthday."

"All children should be so pleased with a rock as a gift. Parents these days are doing a horrible disservice to their offspring by spoiling them. Tell me about other things you found."

She shook her head. "An abandoned mine, mummies, and a stupid rock only an eight-year-old would find enchanting. There's nothing else there, we're lucky to see a lizard. It's the end of the world. If you haven't been there, you should go and get a preview of Hell."

He tipped his head, considering. "What about other buildings besides the ones in the town?"

"I've never seen any."

"Do you see other people you don't know?"

"Security guards sometimes. A few of us are allowed to help with the retreats. Do you know about the retreats?"

His face contorted like he'd just tasted something repulsive. "I know about the retreats. Why did you leave?"

"I told you, it's a prison."

He shook his head with a mournful expression. "You're not being cooperative like you promised. I'll give you one more chance."

"I . . ."

He pulled his chair closer and leaned forward. "Why did you leave, Marielle? Did you see something?"

She lowered her head. "If you know Father Paul, you know why I left."

"Tell me."

"He's . . . he's a monster."

"Father Paul, a monster? Maybe we're not talking about the same person."

"I can't go back. I won't go back."

"Tell me how Father Paul is a monster."

Tears finally sprang from her eyes and spilled down her cheeks. "He wants to take Serena."

"Where?"

"No, he wants to *take* her. As a bride."

His hooded lids dropped like a stage curtain and his voice was low, ugly. "You're lying."

"He told me he was taking her. He said it was God's will. He's insane."

Livid red crept up his neck to his face, then he lurched out of the chair and slapped her across the face. "His own eight-year-old daughter? That's a disgusting thing to say! I don't believe you!

"I don't care what you believe, you bastard."

He muttered in a foreign language. "Did he ever show you other parts of the compound? Tell you about the work he does there?"

Marielle scowled at him. "His only work is lying and hurting people."

"I think you have more to tell me."

"I don't."

"I'll leave you alone for a while, maybe your memory will improve." He walked to the door, then paused and looked over his shoulder. "Why did you hide in a boat instead of going to the police? Or hadn't you gotten that far?"

The crux of everything, she realized. Something illegal was going on at the compound, this asshole was a part of it, and he wanted to make sure the law wasn't brought in. "I can never go to the police. I'm a criminal. Let us go and you'll never hear from us again."

He chuckled, the sound of glass being crushed. "Everybody in your position says the same thing, but promises made in desperation are worthless. Incidentally, there is no way out of this room, so don't even try. There are also cameras." He pointed to the second door. "There is a bathroom for your convenience. There may or may not be cameras in there, I couldn't tell you." Another broken glass chuckle, along with a leering, haughty smile. "If you somehow managed to make it out of this room, your disfigured friend will be waiting for you and I can't take responsibility for his actions."

As much as she hated this man, she was panicked to see him leave—he was her sole tether to Serena. "Maybe I can help you. I've been with Paul from the beginning. I'm his wife. At least his first wife."

"Possibly. We'll see about that."

"My daughter. I want to see her."

"When I'm finished speaking with her. Enjoy your privacy, Marielle."

The thought of this pig talking to her daughter launched her off the cot and into a senseless charge directed at his inflated gut. He swatted her down easily and she sank to her knees on the cold floor.

"I like you, Marielle. You care about your daughter. But don't ever do that again."

She wouldn't do that again. The next time, she'd kill him.

Chapter Twenty-Four

PAUL WAS LACING UP HIS DESERT boots in preparation for the evening's journey while he tried to ignore the incessant reflux of acid corroding his esophagus. A man could only take so much stress, so much bullshit, before something gave way. But he couldn't let that happen, not now—there was business to take care of and lambs to lead.

He jumped when his phone jittered on the desktop, something he hadn't been expecting. So Gregory had something more to say after all: a new angle, a new persuasion, a new ruse. But he wasn't going to let that traitor fuck him over. He would be the one doing the fucking.

He snatched the phone off his desk without looking at the caller ID and answered sharply. "This better be good news."

"Uh . . . Father Paul? This is Sheriff Brandeis."

Paul flipped a switch in his mind, the setting on his voice box. All unctuous, holy goodness, all apologies. Brandeis was a parasite, but a useful one, no doubt calling to remind him of the department fundraiser. It was that time of year when corrupt politicians started wheedling for contributions. "Sheriff, I'm so sorry, I didn't realize it was you. I've been dealing with a very dishonest person, and my patience . . . well, I'm flawed and not above frustration. God is perfect, but I'm sorry to say that I'm not even close."

"No worries, Father Paul, none of us are."

"What can I do for you?"

"I hate to bother you with a minor annoyance, Father, but we received a request from LAPD/Marina del Rey to follow up on a missing person's report. A young woman and her eight-year-old daughter disappeared from a boat down there."

It took a long moment for the shock to subside. That lying cocksucker. Gregory *had* taken them and he was trying to lay some kind of a trap, just like he was with Irina and the product. Setting him up for Ivan. Setting him up to vanish, and Marielle and Serena would vanish with him . . .

"Father Paul?"

"That's terrible news. I just said a prayer for them and I ask you to keep them in yours."

"I will."

"Sheriff, I'm confused. Why did Marina del Rey call you and why are you calling me?"

"They believe she might be in our area. Possibly even on your property."

"*My* property?"

"I don't have any photos, but the mother was described as slim and fit, with long, dark hair and a fleur-de-lis tattoo on her left shoulder. The daughter is blond. First names are Marielle and Serena. No last names. Have you seen them?"

"There's nobody here by those descriptions or names, Sheriff." Which wasn't a lie, Paul thought manically as he wiped the sudden, rapid runnels of sweat from his face with the sleeve of his cassock. "I can't imagine what led the police here, but they're obviously not well-informed."

"The man who reported it said they left your compound last night and he's concerned about an abusive situation. Any troubles of that sort up there?"

Lenny. *Judas.* And what lies had that bitch told him? "Absolutely not, Sheriff. That would never be tolerated and I would report it to you immediately. This is a sanctuary, a place of peace. I'm very sorry

for whoever Marielle and Serena are, but they never left the compound because they were never here. This person who reported it
must be confused. Or perhaps the other party is confused. Either
way, there's some mistake."

"I agree. With what little information LAPD had, I figured they
were dealing with a troubled runaway. You understand, I had to
check."

"Of course you did."

"I'll let LAPD know they're on the wrong track, then." He let that
final comment hang for a moment before he spoke again. "How are
things with you, Father Paul?"

"Very good. I'm about to take a new group out to the desert. And
you?"

"Busy getting ready for the department fundraiser next month. I
hope you're planning to join us."

"You know I wouldn't miss it, Sheriff. It's been a particularly fruit-
ful year for us, so I can safely say we will be exceeding last year's
donation by quite a bit."

"We're always grateful for your generosity, Father Paul. Take care
and let me know if there's anything you need."

"I will, thank you. May God bless and keep you and your family."

"Looking forward to seeing you soon."

Paul slammed his phone down over and over until the screen
cracked. He'd pissed up a rope this time and the irony wasn't lost on
him. In trying to save himself and Children of the Desert he'd done
the opposite, and now unintended consequences were cascading out
of control. If he'd just let Marielle go, she probably wouldn't have
gone to the police. If he hadn't taken Gregory into his confidence, the
police wouldn't have gotten involved. He should have *never* trusted
that bastard in the first place, but he would pay for his sins.

No, no. That wasn't right at all—none of this was his fault. *He*
hadn't screwed himself—Marielle had first; then Gregory; and finally
Lenny, who also had to die now because he was the only outsider who
could connect them to the compound.

He fumbled in his desk for his pill box and selected the pharmaceutical-grade MDMA. Ecstasy was exactly what he needed, it's what everybody needed. Humankind could benefit from the alchemy and the clarity of thought it offered.

He stared at the crucifix on the wall across from his desk. He could blame Jesus for all of this, too, but he didn't believe Jesus had been anything more than a charismatic mortal like himself. It hardly seemed fair to blame a visionary opportunist two thousand years dead for his problems.

As time passed and the X started to manipulate the gray folds of brain tissue, the teeming chaos in his skull dissipated and transformed into a crystalline vision. Gregory wanted to get rid of him; Ivan wanted to get rid of him, too, but he didn't know about any of the current subterfuge. Neither of them knew about the arrangement with Sheriff Brandeis, who would shoot himself in the head before he interfered with Children of the Desert or the generous Father Paul. Gregory also didn't know Lenny's call to the police had exposed his treachery.

Paul smiled as he recognized his great strategic advantages. He knew exactly where that son of a bitch would be holding Marielle and Serena, and he wouldn't be expecting him. After he cut this evening's jolly jaunt into the desert short, he would head to LA to bury that vodka-sodden waste of rotting flesh and reclaim his property. Things would be thorny with Ivan when Gregory went missing, but he'd explain that he'd run off with money and product and had been undercutting them all along. A dead man couldn't defend himself.

His identity would also protect him. Father Paul was a man beyond reproach, a man of God who did wonderful things and had the endorsement of the governor through his prison reform program. Ivan was nothing more than a well-dressed thug, and with meticulous planning, he could bury him, too, without risking his desert kingdom.

As serotonin suffused his body with rapturous warmth, his thoughts turned to humanitarian matters, specifically poor Emily

Nolan. She was the most damaged of all his new sheep, and her travails weren't egotistical and self-inflicted, unlike the rest of the whiners and addicts. Her personal demons were real. And he felt a connection with her, because he'd just lost a child, too. He could help her. They could help each other.

There was a soft knock on his door and Sister Carina entered without permission. Normally, the impertinence would have infuriated him, but he was feeling deeply magnanimous. "What is it, Sister?"

She looked at him with big, brown eyes, round and soft, like her young body. "I hope Sister Marielle is feeling better."

His sweet, caring, irredeemably stupid Carina. "It's a terrible flu, but she and Serena are resting comfortably."

"That's good news. I definitely missed her help with the retreat today. I felt awkward without her."

"You did a wonderful job, Sister Carina. I'm very pleased."

"Thank you."

He watched a flush creep from her neck up to her cheeks. Some people blushed from the bottom up. It was fascinating.

"Is there something I can do to help, Father Paul? Check on them for you, bring them some broth or tea?"

"No. She insisted they remain in strict quarantine for a few days so they don't pass it on to anyone else, and I believe that's the wisest course. Is there anything else?"

"We've finished orientation and the group is getting settled in their quarters. They're looking forward to their trip into the desert. I told them to gather in the Fellowship Hall in half an hour."

In his escalating euphoria, time was stretching like taffy and thirty minutes seemed like an eternity. "We should take advantage of that time, don't you think?"

Her plump, pink lips lifted in a smile and she started wriggling out of her androgynous shift. He preferred it when she came to his private quarters dressed like a slut, with all her piercings in, but in the end, all of God's creatures were the same inside.

Chapter Twenty-Five

SAM PULLED THE MUSTANG INTO THE garage, helped Lenny unload his truck, then gave him the nickel tour of the house. It was funny, the things you never noticed until somebody else was seeing your domicile for the first time—cobwebs, lint on the rug, a basket of folded clothes not yet put away. He wasn't a slob—his mother had trained him well—but he wouldn't win any housekeeping awards, either.

Lenny spent a long time in front of the bookcase where Sam kept a modest display of photographs that he considered mileposts in his life. He hadn't realized it until now, but they all represented significant loss: his favorite wedding portrait; a group shot of his number two–seeded USC baseball team before they'd whiffed it in the first round of the Lake Elsinore Regionals; a candid of him with Shaggy, Wilson, Rondo, and Kev in Afghanistan. It was a disturbing subliminal expression of where his mind had been the past couple of years.

Lenny undoubtedly recognized this, but he was a kind and considerate man and focused on the most benign. "Didn't know you were a ballplayer, Sam. Division I is a big deal."

"I wasn't that great, but I loved the game."

"Did you ever dream of the Majors?"

"Absolutely. But I never told anybody and I was never delusional about it. I just played my heart out and knew I was lucky for the opportunity." It felt good to have another body in the house, and he imagined Lenny was glad for the company, too. Worry was easier to take with a friend. And a few cocktails.

"Nice place you've got here, Sam."

"Thanks. I wish I had a spare bed for you, but I use the guest room for my weights."

"The sofa looks fine to me." Lenny shrugged off his overnight bag while Sam put the steaks in the fridge.

"Can I interest you in a beer? A bourbon? A margarita?"

"Whatever you're having."

"I'm in the mood for margaritas. I haven't gotten around to installing a patio yet, but I have a couple chaise longues in the back-yard."

"Sounds perfect. It'll be nice to rest my eyes on some greenery for a change." He looked out the kitchen window at the palms waving frantically in the stiff, hot wind. "Santa Anas are coming in early this year. I guess the desert is following me."

"I know the feeling."

"That you do."

"I always liked them. It's the only time West LA is hot at night."

"Is that a persimmon tree?"

"Yuki's pride and joy. I'm trying to take good care of it for her. How did you know?"

"Growing up, we had one. Hate the fruit, but they're good-looking trees. Can I give you a hand?"

"I'm good, Lenny, make yourself comfortable outside. I'll be right out with the drinks."

While Sam mixed a pitcher of margaritas, heavy on the tequila, he checked his phone again. No word from Remy yet. If he was working a case, he might not hear from him for days, and he had a dismal feeling Marielle and Serena didn't have days. There probably wasn't much more he could do anyhow, but it didn't hurt to ask.

•

Remy hated the swimming pool because it roused a disturbing montage of recollections from Charlotte's time here, but he found himself out here often in spite of it. Or maybe because of it.

In her manic phases, she swilled vodka straight from the bottle and pranced around the stone deck to the warped soundtrack in her mind. In her depressive phases, she sulked away to the pool house and didn't emerge for days.

It was out here that she'd kissed him on the cheek and told him it was *so* ridiculous to be a homicide cop; she'd screamed at him and pounded on his chest in blind fury, demanding more money; she'd giggled about going to Disneyland to become a different, better person. Maybe she had gone to Disneyland that day, but not to become a better person, because at one point she'd stopped at a bank and cleaned out his accounts. He hadn't seen her since.

He sipped a Dr Pepper and stared at the turquoise water, ruffled by the emergent Santa Anas. By tomorrow morning, the pool, the yard, and the streets would be littered with palm fronds too weak to withstand the furious gusts. The burgeoning wildfires already burning in the Malibu Hills would spread, and the west side would be acrid with the smell of smoke and coated with ash.

The Santa Ana winds were sometimes histrionically referred to as the hot breath of Satan. In Remy's opinion, LA was always plagued by the hot breath of Satan, but it was almost entirely man-made, and Charlotte had been swept away by it.

Coming off his early-afternoon martini buzz, he hadn't checked his phone for hours. Fully sober now, he picked it up and listened to an ominous message from Mal. He wasn't answering, so he left his own message and followed up with a text.

The only other call was from Sam Easton, which surprised him. He didn't think he'd ever hear from him again. His message was vague and sounded apologetic, asking for a favor. Remy definitely owed him a big one.

He answered on the first ring, like he'd been sitting on his phone. "Mr. Easton, I just got your message."

"Thanks for the call back, Detective. Listen, I really hate to bother you . . ."

"No bother. I'm on vacation. What can I do for you?"

"Truthfully, maybe nothing. It has to do with a mother and daughter who went missing from a friend's boat today . . ."

"Did you report it?"

"With Marina del Rey, but the circumstances are . . . well, it's kind of convoluted. Hard to explain over the phone. It is possible for us to meet up?"

"Where are you?"

"Home. Mar Vista. I'd like you to speak with my friend."

"I'm intrigued. Give me your address, I'll come over."

•

Sam answered the door and was again startled by Remy Beaudreau's intensity. The energy was omnipresent in the way a stalking predator's was. It burned in his black eyes and emanated from his lean frame as he moved in a room. It was a more significant presence than the flesh and bone of the man himself, and Sam remembered the first time he'd met him. He'd sensed at once that Remy Beaudreau had some very persistent demons clamoring just below the surface that required effort to restrain.

Perhaps more startling was the detective's generous gift of one of Sam's favorite bourbons—Jefferson's Ocean, aged at sea. It supposedly crossed the equator four times before it went to market. Whatever mileage it had on it, it was like drinking velvet.

They exchanged a genial handshake. "I asked you for a favor, and you bring me one of my favorite bourbons. Hardly seems fair."

"The gesture is overdue, Mr. Easton. It's ninety proof, so be careful with it."

"I think our past association puts us on a first-name basis, don't you?"

He smiled and some of his intensity diffused. "Hell, yes."

Sam lifted the bottle. "Thanks for this. Will you have some?"

"If you're opening it, absolutely."

Sam introduced Lenny and went to the kitchen to pour lowballs while his guests engaged in obligatory small talk. They'd obviously hit it off: by the time he returned to the living room with the drinks and the bottle, Remy was sharing an amusing anecdote about his only trip to the desert—in July—the worst possible month to visit unless you enjoyed frying eggs on the hood of your car. His warmth with Lenny disabused Sam's gloom and doom impression while reinforcing his belief that this was a complicated man; and someone he'd enjoy getting to know better.

They savored bourbon together and continued the pleasantries for a few minutes, but the issue at hand was sucking the oxygen out of the room. Remy drained his glass and got to the point.

"Tell me about the missing women."

"It's your story, Lenny, go ahead."

"I don't have much to tell, but I'll do my best." He began recounting his tale, and when he mentioned Children of the Desert at the onset, Sam watched the detective's expression darken.

"Do you know it?" Sam interrupted.

"It's come up recently. More than once. Go ahead, Mr. Jesperson."

Lenny continued metronomically and in great detail, and hearing it for the second time, Sam realized he was a great witness. He wouldn't be the guy who misremembered the color of an assailant's shirt or the presence of facial hair.

Remy remained staunchly detached and unreadable through the rest of the telling, and Sam had the feeling that he was keeping everything locked down tight after he'd called him out on his perceptible reaction to Children of the Desert. In his limited experience dealing with cops, he'd developed the impression that showing emotion was not only a rookie move, but a cardinal sin.

Lenny finally concluded and brought out the necklace. "I told her I'd buy her a phone and pay for tickets to wherever she wanted to go. She gave this to me as collateral, which was nonsense, but she didn't take no for an answer. A woman bent on running wouldn't have given it to me. It's the one thing she had of value that she could have pawned for a fresh start. Detective, I know right here," he tapped his chest, "that Marielle and Serena are in trouble. I think Marina del Rey is doing everything they can, but Sam thought it might be worth a shot, asking you in. I appreciate your time more than you can imagine."

"It's no trouble. I'll see what I can do to help." Remy stood abruptly. "I'll be in touch."

Sam was perplexed by the hasty dismissal, so he dogged him to the door, then outside as he strode toward his Porsche. "What was that about, Remy?"

He turned and gave him his dark, unreadable eyes. "I was rude. I apologize. Just bad form on my part."

"I'm not talking about etiquette. This means something to you. We have a few secrets between us, so tell me about this one. No bull-shit."

He sighed in resignation. "Marielle has been missing for eight years."

"A cold case?"

"Something like that."

"Are you sure it's the same woman?"

"The fleur-de-lis tattoo and the necklace confirmed it."

"Who is she?"

"Her real name is Charlotte. She's my sister."

Chapter Twenty-Six

"I LEFT A MESSAGE FOR DUBNIK . . . what is it, Mags?"

"Take a close look." Nolan handed Crawford the engagement photo and the magnifying glass. He examined it carefully, then returned it to its proper place in the procession of the Lindgren family's brief history of happiness.

"This is what got Blake to the Bel-Air, what do you bet? Whatever they were still fighting about, they called a cease-fire and met up at the long-ago happy place to honor their son on the anniversary of his disappearance. Remember what Lukin overheard: 'Zoe, we can't do this over the phone.'"

"That works. Things obviously didn't go very well."

"Suicide, crime of passion, they both fit, take your pick."

"If he was murdered, it was slick. Premeditated."

"A crime of passion doesn't preclude premeditation."

"It's hard to conjure a scenario where there's that kind of passion after twenty-some years of marriage and social isolation together."

"Sounds like the perfect recipe for murder to me. Who knows what was going on between them? Zoe Lindgren is what we have right now. At the very least, she has some answers we need. This is a secondary crime scene, so let's seal this place up, get some unis to keep eyes on it, and go talk to her before we dig in here any further."

The uniforms arrived quickly and started securing the scene, which predictably drew a lot of attention from passersby, and would ultimately draw the media vultures. Lindgren's name hadn't been released, but they would look at property records. They would find out the same pair of detectives who'd worked the Bel-Air were also at Tanager Way and put two and two together. Then they'd speculate and disseminate misinformation. There was a special place in hell for them.

While Al squared a patrol schedule with the sergeant, Nolan walked toward the street to intercept a shirtless jogger standing at the end of the drive with his panting German shepherd. It was evident from the man's physique that he spent more time in the gym than he did pounding the pavement with his dog. And like all well-conditioned people you encountered in Los Angeles, they were eager to get as naked as legally possible to display the bounty of their labors.

He was gaping at the fluttering yellow tape despoiling the property, probably wondering what possible crime would dare intrude on such a tony neighborhood. Rubberneckers irritated the hell out of her, but she couldn't blame them—curiosity and self-preservation were human nature.

She smiled down at the shepherd sitting patiently at its master's feet, pink tongue lolling. "Beautiful dog."

"Thanks. This is Bridget. You can pet her, she loves people."

Nolan let the dog smell her hand as a courtesy, then scratched behind her ears. The dog smiled and groaned happily.

"What's going on?" he asked. "Is Blake okay?"

Two questions she wouldn't answer. "So you know Mr. Lindgren?"

He gestured toward a red tile roof, the only thing visible above a foliage-covered wall adjacent to the Lindgrens'. "No, but he's my neighbor. Was he robbed or something?"

"No crime occurred here." He seemed relieved that his property value was still intact, but not entirely satisfied by her evasion.

"So why are the cops here stringing crime scene tape if there wasn't a crime?"

Just a follow-up on a little homicide, nothing to worry your pretty little head about. "What's your name, sir?"

Curiosity instantly forgotten, he slipped off his sunglasses with a raffish smile, apparently believing it would render an introduction superfluous. The vanity and insecurity in this town was beyond comprehension, but Nolan actually did recognize him as the lead in a hot new Netflix series, ironically about a Los Angeles homicide detective. She'd never seen it, but she had seen his handsome face plenty of times in the media. They were obsessed with his off-screen antics, multiple rehab stints, and cynical, much re-tweeted observation that there were only two types of people in the entertainment industry: those in rehab and those who would be there soon.

"I'm Roan Donnelly." He seemed disappointed and maybe a little pissy that she wasn't throwing her underwear at him. Witness cooperation was always paramount, so she played to his neediness.

"I recognize you. Love your show. I'm Detective Margaret Nolan."

Roan bloomed with effervescent joy and nearly shook her hand off her arm. "Great to meet a *real* detective!"

"I think you do an excellent job portraying one." She was enjoying lying a little too much. More aftereffects of the martini?

"Thanks!"

"Can you tell me anything about Mr. Lindgren?"

"Not really, just that he's private and quiet. And he loves Bridget like a guy who really misses having a dog. He definitely talks to her more than me. We probably haven't exchanged a hundred words since I moved here four years ago. Just a 'hi' and a neighborly wave when we see each other. SOP in LA, and much appreciated from my POV."

Nolan dug deep to keep her eyes from rolling. The English language was being insidiously dismantled one acronym at a time. WTF?

His eyes darted to the crime scene tape. "He didn't do anything, did he? I mean, he doesn't seem like the kind of guy who would do something crazy enough to bring cops around."

"No, he didn't do anything. Did you know his ex-wife, Zoe?"

"Yeah. We hit it off, actually. She was lonely."

"Can you be more specific about 'hit it off'?" Or was that HIO?

He shook his head vehemently. "Not an affair, if that's what you're thinking. She was like a mom to me and I really miss her and Marshmallow."

Nolan raised a brow in question.

"Her cat. Beautiful white Persian. I hit it off with Marshmallow, too, and believe it or not, so did Bridget. It was like that show *Unlikely Animal Friends*."

Nolan would never admit to anyone that she watched *Unlikely Animal Friends* with a box of Kleenex on her lap. "Are you still in contact with Mrs. Lindgren?"

"No. She promised to keep in touch after the divorce, but she didn't. I get that and didn't take it personally. She has issues; I understand."

"Like?"

"Like she's a raging alcoholic. Zoe could drink me under the table, and that's saying something. But I'm clean now," he added hastily.

For the fifth time, according to the tabloids. "So you partied together?"

"We drank together but we didn't party together. She didn't do drugs."

Note to self: partying included drugs. "Tell me about your relationship."

"Classic enabling. I heard her crying one night by their pool and asked if I could help. We were both drunk, so I invited her over, and we drank some more. She said Blake hated her and their marriage was over."

"Did she say why?"

"Maybe, but I wouldn't remember. I probably didn't ask. We just got wasted together. That's the only thing that matters when you're in that toxic headspace. But I'm sure it had to do with her drinking, she was pretty out of control."

"Did you spend much time with her?"

"Whenever Blake was out of town on business, which was a lot. We had addiction in common and if you've never been there, it's better than sex."

"What happened to the relationship when you got clean?" She watched his face transform into a frowny face emoji. Pictograms were the second phase of the evil plan to annihilate verbal communication.

"At first, Zoe was really supportive and even stopped drinking. But it didn't last. If anything, she got worse. I told her about my miracle in the desert and said I'd take her there, but she wouldn't go. I couldn't be around that anymore, so we stopped hanging. Then she moved out."

Against her better judgment, Nolan asked, "Miracle?"

"Yeah. I've been everywhere for rehab and it never stuck, so I wanted to try something new. Alternative, you know? I'd been hearing from friends about this place called Children of the Desert, and thought, what the hell? If it worked for them, it might work for me, and it did. I've been sober for over a year."

Children of the Desert was becoming an annoying presence in Nolan's life, like a cheesy pop song on heavy rotation. It also reminded her that she really needed to reset her relationship with her mother. Pride goeth before the fall. "Tell me about the place."

"Well, like the name says, it's in the desert. Things are stripped down to just the basics. You learn how to love yourself and God, stop making excuses, and ask others for forgiveness so you can forgive yourself. It's not specifically for addiction, it's more of a broad holistic approach to being the best person you can be. The program really helped me understand how important it is to break free from selfishness, which is where all your problems start."

Nolan wasn't certain he was entirely embracing that aspect, but she reserved judgment, and wondered if the approach would actually be something positive for her mother. "I'm glad it worked for you."

"Thanks. I am, too. It saved my life." He shook his head sullenly. "I hope Zoe's doing okay. I should probably reach out."

Nolan gave him her card. "Thank you for speaking with me. I may want to be in touch again to follow up . . ."

Roan snapped out of his morose reverie like he'd just gotten a director's cue and reached into the pocket of his abbreviated jogging shorts and traded cards. "My private number." He winked. "Don't go sharing that with all your girlfriends."

OMG. "Your privacy is safe with me."

"So is Blake okay?"

"As I mentioned, no crime has been committed on the property."

He smiled knowingly. "You can't discuss an active investigation. Now I'm really curious."

"Thank you so much for your time, Mr. Donnelly."

"Roan. No problem. Really nice to meet you. Be sure to check out my next episode. You won't believe what happens next."

"You might be surprised."

"Yeah, I suppose you've really seen it all. Hey, maybe I could talk to you sometime about the job. Authenticity is extremely important to me."

He didn't wait for an answer, assuming he'd made an offer no sane person would refuse. He blinded her with a white smile and waved over his shoulder as he and Bridget jogged up to his gate and entered the hallowed ground of Roan's World. If there had been anything substantive between his ears before his love affair with drugs and alcohol and fame, it had been vaporized and replaced by the thin air of success and validation.

Roan Donnelly was charming in a superficial way, at least if you didn't mind egomaniacs. She hoped he was being smart with his money. Life and fame had a long track record of vanishing faster than an alcoholic could polish off a pint of booze, something he would know about. Insert drunk emoji.

Chapter Twenty-Seven

IN SAM'S OPINION, FINDING A SIBLING who'd been missing for eight years was a monumental occurrence that should have elicited joy, but Remy was dour and preoccupied. Of course he was. His sister hadn't reached out to him during a very serious time of need, which had to cut to the bone. There was obviously painful baggage between the two of them, but it was none of his business, so Sam modulated his reaction. "I'm really glad for you, Remy. This is good news." *Isn't it?*

He leaned against his car and sighed tiredly. "It's good news for me, but maybe not such good news for Charlotte. She was mentally ill when she disappeared. Easy to exploit, and the PI I hired to find her was looking into Children of the Desert as a possible. It's buttoned up, you can't get in unless they want you in, and you obviously can't get out, either, unless you're a guest. He went back today to try again and ran into a paramilitary presence on the backside of the property. I think Lenny is right—she's in trouble. And so is the niece I didn't know I had."

At the mention of heavy weaponry, Sam's thoughts veered sharply. It would be easy to hide criminal activity in the middle of Death Valley, especially if you fronted it with a legitimate operation in the unimpeachable business of saving souls. "There wouldn't happen to be a Russian connection to any of this, would there?"

"That's a very strange question."

"Yeah, I know. Probably a stupid one, too, but I was up in Death Valley running this morning and heard about Children of the Desert from Lenny's employee at the gas station. It was an offhand comment, but weird enough that it hit me the wrong way."

"What did he say?"

"Sometimes when they visited, he heard *yob tvoyu mat*—'fuck your mother' in Russian—obviously used as an insult, sometimes as a rude exclamatory. Like, 'Fuck your mother, I just got another parking ticket.' The parlance of people you don't want to meet in a dark alley."

Remy's flat expression morphed into incredulity. "Are you talking about Russian organized crime?"

"When you say it out loud, it sounds pretty idiotic."

"Actually, it doesn't. LA has plenty of *bratva* and they're well diversified. And they're always fighting with the Armenians. The desert would be a good place to form a new position of strength. Some of the best criminal enterprises in the world rise out of the sand."

"I was thinking the same thing. I take it COD isn't on law enforcement's radar."

"No. Not ours, not the feds, but maybe they should be. Thank you for telling me."

"Charlotte isn't on law enforcement's radar, either, is she? That's why you hired a PI."

"She was an adult who left on her own. I had to work it on my downtime. Clearly, I didn't get anywhere."

"I suppose there's no chance of getting a warrant."

"Not based on Lenny's gut feeling. Sanchez is right, there's no evidence of a crime. It's just speculation based on a few hours he spent with a stranger who has a history of erratic behavior. Kidnapping is a very serious charge. Even if we could pull paper, legally we need a specific location to search, and the property can be measured in square miles. Five to be more precise."

"An aerial map of the area would show structures."

"And what if they weren't holding them in a structure? The Inyo sheriff would have checked it out by now, so our hand is blown. And you know better than anybody how easy it is to hide people in that kind of terrain."

Sam did, all too well. "So your hands are tied but you want to find your sister, who might be tangled up with the Russian Mob. What are you going to do?"

"I have to think about it."

Sam knew exactly where he was. They'd both been here before, probably many times in life, but more recently, they'd both been here together. History had a wicked way of repeating itself. "Forgive me for being a presumptuous asshole, but you don't have to think about it, you've already made up your mind."

"She was there, Sam. Maybe she's been there for the past eight years and I believe she's back there now, being held against her will. Lenny is right, she wouldn't have given him her necklace if she was planning to rabbit. I have to try. I know you can appreciate the value of Machiavellian theory under certain circumstances."

Sam had never been a fan of Machiavelli, but it wasn't his sibling and niece in potentially grave danger. "You can't just run up there and badge guys with automatic weapons and expect something good to come out of it. We need a better plan."

"We? This isn't your fight, Sam."

"I'm making it mine, because this is personal for you, and personal can lead to stupid."

Lenny walked out onto the front porch, waving his phone. "Detective Sanchez just called. The Inyo County sheriff talked to Father Paul and he said there's never been anybody named Marielle or Serena at the compound. That's bullshit, I've seen them together dozens of times at the station."

Remy met his eyes. "She could have given you a different name. Or used another one there."

"I heard him call her Marielle. 'Sister' Marielle. More than once. He's lying. What are we going to do about this?"

Sam put his hand on Remy's shoulder. "Come back inside, let's put everything on the table. I'm not going to let you walk into a potential shitstorm alone, if that's really the direction you're going."

"Whatever shitstorm you're talking about, I won't, either," Lenny said gruffly. "Get inside and tell me what I don't know."

They resumed their places in the living room and Sam refilled glasses. It was Lenny's turn to listen, and his expression was hard as he processed things.

"Father Paul had me fooled," he finally said, looking at Remy. "If there's nothing the police can do . . . well, then you couldn't dream up two better desert guides than Sam and I. If you do decide to go off the reservation, you'll need us."

Remy shook his head vehemently. "I won't put either of you in danger, period."

"Think of us as consultants."

"No, Sam."

"So what's your plan?" Judging by Remy's sour expression, he'd obviously taken the query as a taunt, and Sam wasn't positive he hadn't meant it as one. Remy was a good detective, maybe even a great one, but he needed a reality check.

"I'm working on that."

Sam watched a plastic bag sail across his front yard and tangle in an oleander. The winds always dislodged garbage and deposited it in plain view. Maybe they were trying to shame human civilization into better behavior. If that was the case, the effort was wasted. "Did I ever tell you part of my job in the Middle East was helping Special Forces coordinate and execute extractions of high value assets in enemy territory?"

Remy shook his head. "No, you never did. Your point is?"

"His point is that whatever you decide to do, it's going to take planning," Lenny interjected a little churlishly. "It's your decision, but we're here if you want our help."

"You need our help, Remy. Don't be a stubborn ass," Sam said.

"That's second nature, I'm afraid." He lowered his head and rubbed his eyes. "I have to call Maggie."

"Detective Nolan?"

"Her mother is there now for a retreat."

Sam rocked back on his heels as the Santa Anas churned around the house. It was during a hot wind like this with a different name that he'd almost been obliterated by a roadside bomb. Bad things came in on bad winds. "I have issues with paranoia sometimes, Remy. It goes with PTSD."

"I understand."

"Maybe this is going to sound paranoid, but I think she should get her mother out of there."

"I'm sure she'll agree. It's better to be paranoid than sorry."

"I told that to my shrink a few times and regretted it."

Remy's perennially dark expression eased with a faint smile. "Don't ever be completely honest with a mental health professional."

Sam switched into tactical mode so easily, it scared him. Re-assimilating into civilian life hadn't been nearly as smooth. He still wasn't there. "That could be the way in without causing an incident. If I can get past whatever security there is in Detective Nolan's car when she gets her mother, I can slip out and search five miles of desert in my sleep. No one will know I'm there."

He considered for a long moment. "That's risky as hell."

"In my biz, success is all about forward reconnaissance. Do you know anybody who has a drone?"

His brows lifted. "I have several. A hobby of mine."

"Then you're going to be my forward observer. Make your call, then let's figure this thing out."

Chapter Twenty-Eight

EMILY WAS SHOCKED—BY THE BARREN, DEPRESSING room and its flimsy twin mattress; the single, scratchy towel in the bathroom; the rickety wooden chair in the corner that looked like the handiwork of a child. As an Army wife, she certainly wasn't accustomed to anything remotely resembling opulence, but this was like a monk's cell—and outrageous considering the price tag. What would the meals be like? Bread and water? At least there was air-conditioning and indoor plumbing. According to Father Paul, God had blessed the property with natural springs. Something to be grateful for.

She wasn't happy about wearing a dreadful sackcloth uniform or turning over her phone, either. She understood the point of eliminating external distractions in order to focus on internal healing and growth. The materials they'd been given at orientation were comprehensive on the topic. But it was one thing to sacrifice creature comforts in the interests of self-improvement, another entirely to forfeit your identity.

She sat down on the bed and felt her fingers itch for her phone as if it was a phantom limb. It was not her intention to shop online or stream movies at night, but Margaret worried her. She hadn't responded to her earlier calls, which meant she was working a case.

Two months ago, she'd almost lost her life to the job. What if something terrible had happened and Margaret needed her? It didn't seem unreasonable to ask for an exception to the rule under the circumstances.

And then, with absolutely no warning, she began to weep. The outburst terrified her, because she was afraid she would never be able to stop.

•

Father Paul sat patiently in the wooden chair while he waited for her to compose herself. He was a handsome man, with sandy hair, kind blue eyes, and an open, sympathetic expression. It was a face that engendered trust, and he seemed infinitely patient, which helped calm her. She finished the cup of tea he'd brought her, then blotted her eyes and straightened, envisioning as she always did during trials that her spine was unbending steel. "I'm so sorry about this, Father Paul. I'm keeping the others waiting. Maybe you should go without me."

His voice was gentle and reassuring. "Please don't apologize, Emily. Everyone who comes here cries. It surprises and distresses most of them, but it is a catharsis, a natural part of the cleansing process. When the soul is suffering, it must find release. No one here will judge you and they're happy to wait. You're among friends who are experiencing their own suffering. Like you, some are just beginning to realize it."

She glanced at him through tear-fogged eyes and nodded.

"People are afraid to confront the wounds they've come here to heal, even though that is their intention. We are all very adept at constructing neuroses and fears to divert our attention from what's truly troubling us. They are obstacles to our happiness and must be broken down so we can face our true reality and learn to accept it. Once we accept it, we can improve upon it. That is our work here. Now tell me what's troubling *you*."

She wound a tissue around her index finger nervously. "It's my daughter, Margaret. She's a homicide detective and I wasn't able to reach her before I came here. I'm afraid something may have happened. I need to speak with her."

"Emily, there is a phone line here that is answered twenty-four hours a day in case of emergencies. We gave this number to your husband, so you don't have to worry."

"But . . . what if he lost it? Or if he had to rush to the hospital, he could have forgotten to bring it with him. He never remembers to put important numbers in his phone. I can't be out of touch with my family."

"We'll call him and make sure everything is okay."

Panic fluttered in her heart and it took all her strength to keep her voice steady and unyielding. "I really must insist on my phone, Father Paul."

He folded his hands together on his lap and she focused on them to avoid meeting his eyes. His right hand was brown from the sun, but a blanched, shiny web of scarred flesh wrapped up and around from his left palm.

"The reason we take away phones and computers is not for punishment, Emily. It's to prevent regression into negative behaviors in the face of challenge and pave the way to successful healing. We have found in this program that resistance, avoidance, and deflection are very common. Allowing outside interference that might enable our guests to backslide is contrary to our purpose here."

"I'm not sure I understand how that applies to my request."

"Loss of control is something we all fear. Ironically, people come here because they have already lost control of some aspect of their life, but they haven't been able to truly confront or accept it. Relinquishing denial of fear is the first step in conquering it. Giving up communication with the outside world is a part of that."

Emily bristled. "I don't want to communicate with the outside world, I want to communicate with my daughter because I fear for her safety."

"And you don't trust us to make that call for you?"

"A parent needs to hear their child's *voice*."

His eyes narrowed slightly; shrewdly, she thought, and something about that frightened her.

"I do understand that, Emily. I've recently lost a child and I would give anything to hear her voice again."

Her indignation ebbed and she felt the familiar, unrelenting sorrow return. "Oh, no. I'm very sorry, Father Paul."

"Thank you." He leaned forward and turned his left hand palm-up, exposing an angry white expanse of scar tissue. "I noticed you looking, so I'll answer the question you were too polite to ask. I had a cruel father who held my hand down on a hot griddle to teach me a lesson. He had many lessons to teach. You see, we all have our reasons for being here and we must be honest about them. Tell me about Max."

The blood drained from her face, leaving it stiff and cold. Oddly, the rest of her body was suddenly warming and softening, and she felt the angry knots life had tied in her unwind. It was such an alien feeling of peace, she was deeply mistrustful of it.

"It's alright to talk about anything here, Emily. God knows what's in your heart and he's here for you. Can you feel his love?"

Emily felt something, but she wasn't sure it was God's love. "I've been praying so hard, but he hasn't come to me before."

"God comes when we're ready for him." He stood and extended his hand. "Let's go to the desert."

Emily stood and took his hand, felt the hard, smooth flesh melt into her own, reminding her of his tragic story. "I'm sorry about your father."

"In a way, it was a gift. I wouldn't be here otherwise."

"What will I find in the desert?"

"Salvation." He led her out of her room. "Tonight, as we walk the path of our savior, I want you to look up at the stars and see them as the souls of the departed. Max's star is up there, and I want you to find it tonight. I want you to find each other. Your lost child is crying for you, Emily. You have to let him back into your life. If you don't, you'll never know peace."

•

Mike swept the flashlight in a tight arc as he walked toward the tomb in the mine, watchful for aliens. He knew for sure they were here now because they'd taken the woman and the little girl and he had to be careful. He couldn't save them if he got himself killed.

He felt for the screwdriver in his pocket and gripped the handle tightly. If you couldn't burn them to death, screwdrivers were the next best way to kill them because you had to take out their eyes. That's where their souls were and if you didn't get rid of the soul, they could come back, and they'd be mad. Most people didn't realize that and he wished movies about aliens were more realistic. It would probably save lives.

When he reached the fence, he clicked off his flashlight and climbed through. It was safe to navigate by starlight now because there was no more danger—aliens couldn't stand to be around the dead. That was another weakness that people didn't know about.

The musty smell of the tomb was comforting as he settled into the soft darkness and lit several small candles. He momentarily lost himself in the hypnotizing beauty of the flames. They were so tiny, but so powerful. A single spark could ignite a fire that would burn for miles and destroy millions of acres, killing all the aliens in its path. Aliens feared fire more than screwdrivers. He thought about Sam Eastwood and his brush with death and realized he should write a survival manual about these things he knew to help people like him.

His mummy friends were in the same place they'd always been. It really was surprising what happened to bodies in the desert. The fat man who smelled had been right about that.

Mike sat down in the sand and ran his hands along the dry, wizened remains, absorbing their power. It was more important than ever to build up his protective shield with the aliens so close. But what you took had to be replaced or it wouldn't work anymore. He knew they liked beef jerky because it was always gone when he came back, so he dumped a packet all around them and arranged it carefully.

When Sam Eastwood came to the gas station again, he would give him the biggest bag Lenny kept in stock and tell him the truth about how to use it. He was nice and if anybody needed a protective shield, he did. When they didn't get you the first time, they always came back. Sam Eastwood would need a good screwdriver, too, and he had plenty to share.

Chapter Twenty-Nine

NOLAN WAS NAVIGATING THE IDYLLIC, OCEANSIDE enclave of Santa Monica for the second time in twelve hours, but the endemic serenity had changed with the full-on arrival of the Santa Anas, which always seemed to blow with more fury once it was dark. They buffeted the car, abused the statuesque palms lining the streets, and sent random debris sailing through the night air. It was chaotic compared to her sunny, peaceful morning bike ride along the Pacific.

She trolled Seventh Street slowly, postponing the inevitable. Every cop dreaded notifications, even if it was a potentially hostile ex-spouse who was about to get the news. Learning a former loved one had been murdered hurt no matter what animosity plagued the relationship. Unless, of course, you were the murderer. She hadn't liked Zoe Lindgren for a murder scenario before she'd learned she was an inveterate drunk, and it seemed even less likely now. But she was keeping an open mind.

Crawford had been silent for most of the drive after she'd filled him in about Roan Donnelly, Zoe's prodigious alcoholism, and her mother's flirtation with celebrity, New Age enlightenment. That was bound to come up at some point, and she had to keep him in the loop. Especially since Remy already knew, thanks to the evil combination of vodka and hormones that had entirely obliterated her discretion.

She'd anticipated a question eventually, but the topic surprised her. "Your mom isn't at Children of the Desert for rehab, is she, Mags?"

"God no. I wish she would drink, it might be helpful. It's all about Max."

"Maybe it will be good for her."

"That's what my father says."

"You hate the idea of her being there."

"I didn't say that."

"You didn't have to. But I get it. Remember when I told you about Corinne listening to Reverend Bandy podcasts?"

"Yes."

"That's her thing. She gets something out of it that I can't give her. Maybe I'm the reason she listens. I don't understand, but it makes her happy, and that's good enough for me."

"Don't judge, that's what you're saying?"

"I'm saying that there's no harm in letting a person you love look for something they need. It's not an insult. We're not everything to everybody. Ever."

"I always wondered why they call you Obi-Wan."

"If you haven't figured that out by now, you're a shit detective."

She turned off Seventh onto Alta and parked in front of a well-lit, showpiece Craftsman home where the former Mrs. Lindgren lived. An array of carefully placed landscaping lamps illuminated the flower gardens and the façade of the house. She imagined her Woodland Hills rental with landscape lights trained on her single clump of moribund bird-of-paradise and almost laughed.

Culturally and topographically, Santa Monica and the Hollywood Hills were as different as Helsinki and Helena, and she wondered if the adjustment had been difficult for Zoe. Even if your only world was contained in a bottle, it would be hard not to notice.

"Nice hedge roses," Crawford remarked.

This was the commencement of ritualistic, banal small talk meant to postpone the inevitable. "You can't even identify grass, Al."

"It's a hedge with roses on it, it's self-explanatory. Corinne tried them out a few years ago, but they never took. Hey, did you ever get your bird-of-paradise to bloom?"

"It's thinking about it."

"Did you fertilize it or what?"

"I put a bag of composted manure around it." The conversation was entering absurd territory, but neither of them made a move to get out of the car.

"My uncle Bernie was a raging alcoholic, too. For a lawyer, he was a great guy, with a nice place by the ocean just like this one. When he was in his cups, anything that came out of his mouth should have stayed between him and his God. We knew never to visit or call after three o'clock."

"At this hour, she might not be in great shape."

"Which could work to our advantage. She might confess to murdering her husband straight out of the gate, then we can go home."

"Since you're familiar with the minds of drunks, you take the lead."

He unclipped his seat belt with a sigh and heaved himself out of the car.

As they mounted the steps onto a spacious porch, the front door creaked open and a huge ball of white fur burst out and almost put them both on their asses.

"Jesus," Crawford muttered. "It's going to be Thanksgiving before my heart slows down."

"Just think of how the poor cat feels. Marshmallow! Come here, kitty!"

"Marshmallow?"

"Donnelly told me about her cat. Kitty, it's okay!"

"Like it's going to come to you now." He rapped on the doorjamb. "Mrs. Lindgren? Zoe Lindgren?" The door was already ajar, so he pushed it open farther and took a step over the threshold.

"Mrs. Lindgren?" He jerked backward, covering his mouth and nose, and looked at Nolan. "Call it in."

•

They were both mouth-breathing against the stench of decay as they entered the living room, but the swarm of flies snapped their jaws shut. They knew where they'd been, and it was better to inhale death than to swallow it.

Zoe Lindgren was on her back on the floor, mottled and bloated. She'd been here a while. The fabric of her dress had a blotchy, abstract gray-and-purple print that blended disturbingly with her exposed flesh. For all the flies that had stirred at their entrance, most weren't deterred from their gruesome feast, which was concentrated on her ruined, empty eye sockets.

"Sweet Jesus," Crawford mumbled. "I was on the way to seriously considering she'd murdered Blake, but now I'm thinking it's the other way around. An ex is always a good bet for a rage killing and Zoe told Donnelly Blake hated her."

"But did he hate her enough to put her eyes out? This is pure nut job, and so far, Blake presents as pretty stable."

"In his work life. But he was plenty bottled up in his personal life and people like that can snap. They were arguing recently. That could have been the catalyst."

"Why would he go to the Bel-Air to meet a woman he'd already killed?"

"To kill himself. A full circle kind of thing. Your vision of a poetic suicide may have been right on."

"Or somebody wanted them both dead."

Crawford sucked his cheeks, an annoying habit he had when he was thinking. She wondered if he did it at home, too.

Corinne: Do you want bacon and eggs or bagels and lox for break-fast?

Al (sucking his cheeks): Let's go to Malibu for fish tacos.

"The MOs are light years apart, Mags. Murder-suicide fits better.

There's no sign of struggle, no sign the house was tossed. The door was open with no sign of tampering. Rage killings aren't stranger killings—she knew him."

Nolan looked at the coffee table—a half-empty bottle of gin, a totally empty glass, a bag of cat treats. It was a sorry tableau that confirmed what Donnelly had told her. "Or she was too drunk to lock her door and some psychopath walked in; or came through a window and let himself out."

"Zoe?"

They both jerked their heads toward the high voice, powerful enough to be heard through the closed front windows. A gracefully aging Westside doyenne—an actress or singer, Nolan figured from the strength of her vocal projection—was passing by Zoe's hedge roses, cradling Marshmallow against her ample bosom as she walked up to the porch. "Zoe, I've got Marshmallow, she was in my agapanthus again. Pretty, naughty girl always seems to get out at night."

"I'll get this." Nolan stepped out and closed the door on the horror behind her. The woman gave her an uncertain smile, but it faltered when she noticed the stranger she was confronting was wearing latex gloves and a grim expression. She was putting things together and she hugged the squirming cat like a child seeking solace from a stuffed animal. "I was just bringing Marshmallow back, she gets out sometimes. I live next door . . ." Her voice drifted away in the wind.

"Can you keep Marshmallow at your house for a while?"

The woman's face turned as white as the cat's fur. "Oh . . . oh God. Zoe?"

"I'm sorry, ma'am."

Tears trickled down her cheeks and she worried Marshmallow's pelt with shaking hands. "I'll take care of her. Oh God," she repeated. "I knew she'd kill herself drinking."

"May I ask you a few questions, Ms. . . . ?"

"Cohen. Sylvia Cohen. Yes, but I have to put Marshmallow inside first, she's so scared and she can't be out at night. The coyotes have been a terror lately."

Nolan waited while she deposited the cat into the safety of her home—another well-lit showpiece, this one of a more Spanish revival bent. Ms. Cohen returned with a fistful of tissues stained with mascara.

"This is so horrible. What can I tell you?"

"Were you friends with Mrs. Lindgren?"

"No. I tried to introduce myself when she moved in a year ago, but she never answered the door. The only time I ever saw her was when Marshmallow got out. The poor dear, she was so tragic, always very impaired. Something terrible must have happened in her life and I felt just awful for her."

"Have you seen any unusual activity or visitors here recently?"

"No, just the gardeners and her housekeeper. Delivery people. Occasionally, I see a silver Mercedes. Not very often, though."

Blake Lindgren's? "What type of Mercedes?"

"I wouldn't know the model, but it was a large sedan."

"Do you remember the last time you saw it?"

Ms. Cohen frowned. "Not specifically. Earlier this week, I think."

"Do you remember hearing anything out of the ordinary, maybe a fight?"

"No." Her eyes expanded into large brown saucers. "You don't think she was murdered, do you?"

"Zoe *was* murdered."

She clamped a hand over her mouth.

"Please think hard about this week, Ms. Cohen. Even the smallest thing you might remember could help us. I'll come to speak with you in a little bit."

She nodded and hurried back to her house, then turned before she mounted her porch steps. "Should I be worried?"

"I don't believe there's a threat to the general public, but it's always wise to keep your doors locked and your security system armed."

Ms. Cohen's expression was pure, resigned sorrow. "I always do. Such a world we live in."

Nolan clicked on her flashlight and did a circuit around the house, paying close attention to the windows, doors, and the surrounding foliage. There were no disturbances in the shrubbery and the window casings showed no signs of tampering. The back door was locked. Everything seemed intact and undisturbed.

Crawford was swiping his phone when she reentered the house. "Looks clean outside."

"Inside, too, so far. No murder weapon in the general vicinity of the body. Who was the lady?"

"Ms. Cohen, the neighbor. She's taking care of Marshmallow."

"Our only witness. If cats could talk. What did Ms. Cohen have to say?"

"'I knew she'd kill herself drinking.'"

"That's better than the truth. Did she know her?"

"No. Zoe would never answer her door. She only saw her when Marshmallow got out, and she was always impaired, as Ms. Cohen put it. She hasn't noticed or heard anything unusual, but she's seen a silver Mercedes sedan here occasionally, specifically earlier this week."

"We know who that belonged to. Setting up a date for the Bel-Air, maybe. It really bugs me that we don't know how Blake got there. That's a key."

"There are a couple private car services I haven't been able to reach yet."

"Or his killer picked him up. If he was killed."

If, if, or, or. Homicide investigations were lousy with conditional conjunctions. "What are you doing on your phone?"

"Hers, not mine. I found it by the body." He passed it to her. "Factory setting screen saver, the only photos are of her cat, and she has four contacts: Blake, Roan Donnelly, Ivan Lukin, and get this—Irina. Whoever she is, her phone is out of service. I put in a call to the provider."

"Lukin said he didn't really know Zoe and never saw her after the kidnapping."

"But he never said he didn't talk to her. He's Blake's boss, it makes sense she'd have his number. Check out her phone log, Mags."

"Huh. She called Lukin multiple times in the past few months."

"Right. But no texts between them and no calls from him."

Nolan's brows ticked up. "Drunk dialing?"

"That's my guess. She's feeling melancholy, maybe she wants some insider info on Blake or wants the boss to mediate their argument, who knows? We'll ask him about it when we call to give him the bad news. Which we should do right now."

Nolan continued scrolling through the sparse call log. "She made a call to Blake on Monday. No calls to or from Irina. Who the hell is she?"

"I'm hoping there are some answers here. We'll gut the place once CSI is finished processing. She was killed here, there could be some dandy evidence. That's one thing we've got going for us."

"Neither one of us is going home tonight." She looked around and felt an overwhelming sense of emptiness, even though the house was abundantly furnished in country French—a choice that would send any aficionado of Craftsman architecture or period-appropriate décor into apoplexy. Maybe after dwelling at Tanager Way for a couple decades, she'd had it with simple and masculine. The only commonality between the two houses was the lack of personal items, and she wondered if they would find a private shrine out of sight here, too. "I'll call Lukin."

"Put it on speaker."

He answered promptly, his voice anxious. "Detectives?"

"Yes. We're sorry to bother you so late . . ."

"It's not late at all. Do you have news? Were you able to reach Zoe?"

"We're at her house now. We found her deceased. I'm sorry, Mr. Lukin."

There was a long silence. "I . . . I can't believe it. Was she murdered? Was Blake murdered? If they both were, there's obviously a connection between the two."

Thanks for the tip, we never would have thought of that. "We haven't confirmed that yet," Nolan sidestepped. "We did discover that she made several calls to you in the past few months. You never mentioned that."

"I didn't think it was worth mentioning."

"Why?"

He sighed. "Zoe began calling me occasionally after the divorce was final. It was very inappropriate, but I don't think she even realized who she was calling. Her messages were always incoherent. She had obviously developed a serious problem, but Blake never said anything to me about it. Of course, he wouldn't."

"Did you tell him about her calls?"

"There was no point. It would have only embarrassed and upset him."

"Did you ever speak to her?"

"I answered the first few calls, wondering if there wasn't some sort of an emergency with Blake, but never after that."

"You didn't think to block her calls?"

"I considered it. But I had a great deal of sympathy for her and given her condition, I worried that one message might be an actual emergency. Blake was out of town so often and I had doubts that she would have the presence of mind to call 911 if she really needed to."

"Did you save any of these messages?"

"I reviewed, then deleted them as they came in. They were very sad. Disturbing." He sighed anxiously. "After you left my house, I was reminded of something. It's probably meaningless . . ."

"Go ahead."

"Before the kidnapping, when Blake was sociable, I remember him mentioning that he proposed to Zoe at the Bel-Air. I wouldn't know, but I suppose it's possible they might have planned some sort of reconciliation there. That's the only thing I imagine might have brought Blake out of his hermitage."

Nolan and Crawford shared a glance. "We became aware of that. But thank you for telling us."

"Certainly."

"Is there anything else?"

"No."

"Thank you for your time, Mr. Lukin. We'll be in touch when we know more." As she signed off, the first of the squads pulled up with lights, no sirens. Circus Number Two was about to begin.

Chapter Thirty

MARIELLE SEARCHED FOR CAMERAS ONCE THE fat man had left. At first, she camouflaged her intent by pacing the room and covering her eyes in a gesture of despair while she peered through her fingers. She grew bolder when she found no immediate evidence of surveillance and conducted a more exhaustive search with no repercussions. All she found were cobwebs and mouse droppings. The cameras had been a bluff.

Next, she listened at the door. After what had seemed like an interminable wait in silence, she tried the knob. When nobody burst through the door to swat her down again, she jiggled it more aggressively. Nothing. The guard at the door had been another bluff. Two deceptions were enough to give her hope. Now it was time to find a weapon.

Marielle considered the chair, but it was fairly solid, and breaking it apart against the wall would make too much noise. But the cot had a metal frame. She sank to her knees and began examining it. The screws were too tight to budge without a tool, but the metal itself was flimsy, so she braced her foot against one of the legs and tried to bend it. It didn't yield much at first, but after working it back and forth, over and over, the metal began to weaken at the stress point.

With aching arms, she worked faster, her eyes stinging from sweat mixed with tears.

When it finally snapped in half, a surge of adrenaline rushed her body and her hope transformed to cautious optimism. The broken edge was jagged and sharp; deadly, if she aimed right. All she had to do was wait.

•

Serena burrowed into the corner of a corduroy sofa and pulled a tattered red blanket over her head. It smelled like mildew, but it was better than the harsh, smoky stink of the man who kept coming in and asking her questions she couldn't answer. And he wouldn't let her see Momma. He was awful. She wished Lenny was here, he would save them.

She'd never really stopped crying the whole time she'd been locked in this room, but the tears came faster and harder when she heard his footsteps outside the door again. She pulled the blanket tighter over her head, wishing herself invisible as the door creaked open.

"There's no need to cry or hide, Serena. I've been nice to you, haven't I? Didn't I bring you juice and some snacks to make you feel better?"

She shivered at the rough voice. "My head still hurts. I want to see Momma."

"And she wants to see you, very much. Shall we go to her?"

She tentatively peeked out from beneath her concealment. "I can see her?"

"Yes. She needs a little encouragement and I think you're perfect for the job."

"What kind of encouragement?"

"I'd like her to tell me some things. I don't think she's been honest with me."

"Momma is always honest, she never lies about anything!"

"Keeping things to yourself is the same as lying, isn't it?"

"I . . . I don't know. If I encourage her, can we go back to Lenny's boat?"

"Of course."

"Why did you take us?"

"You ask too many questions, little girl."

She recoiled at the sudden, sharp tone of his voice, and his ugly face softened.

"Ah, but you've been through so much, and you're scared and confused, aren't you?"

Serena swallowed a sob and nodded.

"I brought you here to keep you safe."

"From what?"

"From Father Paul. He is a very bad man."

Serena pondered this confirmation of her own suspicions by a grown-up. "Then you saved us?"

"I did."

"But won't he keep coming after us because we left?"

His thick lips curled into a smile that didn't look very happy to Serena.

"I wouldn't worry about Father Paul."

Chapter Thirty-One

A CSI UNIT ARRIVED AT ZOE Lindgren's house shortly after the patrols, nudging up to the curb between two of them. Nolan and Crawford went out to speak with the second and hopefully last crew of the day. Roscoe Miles was in charge, but he was the only one Nolan recognized. The rest of them looked very young. If there was another murder tonight, they might have to call up kindergartners.

Neighbors were staring out their windows or standing in yards in tight clusters, indulging their schadenfreude. Alta was a short street and the barricades on the east and west ends were keeping out vehicles, but Nolan heard helicopters and knew they belonged to TV stations and not LAPD. Homicide detectives Margaret Nolan and Alan Crawford at their third scene of the day—media gold.

A very small, very evil part of her brain envisioned a fierce Santa Ana gust upending one of those helicopters. Of course everybody on board would survive the crash. She wasn't *that* evil.

Roscoe smiled at them sympathetically as he unloaded gear, his face bi-colored in the flashing bar lights of the squads. "You two are keeping us and the media busy today. What's the connection here?"

"Ex-wife of the Bel-Air vic. This is bad, Ross. A mutilation."

"Damn. I hope none of my kiddos ate a big dinner."

"They do look young," Crawford commented.

"Everybody looks young to us. Actually, most of them are seasoned and they're all good. You have nothing to worry about."

Crawford brightened when he checked the ID on his ringing phone. "Department of the Coroner, praise the Lord. Be right with you, Ross." He and Nolan ducked into the privacy of their sedan, away from telephoto lenses and directional mics.

"Crawford," he answered.

"Hello, Detective. Otto Weil here."

"Thanks for the call, Doc. Maggie is with me. Sad to say, but we're at a new scene and sending another one your way. Lindgren's ex-wife, Zoe."

"I'm sorry to hear that. Similar circumstances or MO?"

"Not even close. This was a very brutal murder."

"How so?"

"Her eyes were gouged out. Do you have time to look at her?"

"I'll make time. Let whoever shows up know I'll be taking the autopsy."

"Thanks. Are you finished with Blake Lindgren already?"

"Yes. Very interesting case. He died a sick man, but his body and organs were in excellent condition."

"Sick how?"

"Antemortem vomiting and diarrhea, convulsions, myocardial infarction."

"Drugs?"

"There was no alcohol in his system and no indication of drug use or abuse. Of course the comprehensive tox screen will take some time to confirm."

"So he died of a heart attack?" Nolan asked.

"That was secondary. Primary cause of death is asphyxiation due to pulmonary edema, which means his lungs suddenly filled with fluid."

"He drowned, then."

"No. He was dead when he went in the water."

Even though they hadn't dismissed murder as a possible cause of death, the news still jolted Nolan. "Do you know what caused the edema?"

"They're very common in people with congestive heart failure, except as I mentioned, Lindgren's organs were all quite healthy." He sighed heavily into the phone. "My findings are consistent with organophosphate poisoning. That will also take some time to confirm. We're working on it now."

"You mean, like pesticides?"

"Yes, exactly."

"The company he works for deals in agricultural products. Any chance the killer took a long-term approach?"

"None. The pathology indicates a singular, significant incident of toxin exposure, most certainly on-site."

Nolan's skin crawled with imaginary poison. "Why do you say that?"

"No significant decomposition, even factoring in the preservative effect of submersion. I'd say he hasn't been dead longer than fourteen hours. And more practically, if you'd poisoned someone in a different location, why would you bring them to the Bel-Air for disposal?" He sighed dolefully. "It's a shame the water washed away trace evidence, it might have been helpful."

The cold, imperturbable pragmatism of scientists always amazed her—so different from the cold pragmatism of homicide cops. She was undeniably jaded, as her father had pointed out; but still, she always saw a victim as a person first, and invested in their life before death. Whereas Weil was blandly lamenting that water had been an inconvenient bulwark to his postmortem examination, as if Lindgren had been a disappointing experiment.

Crawford was frowning so hard, his brows obscured half his eyes. "Have you seen something like this before?"

"Never. Not in this country."

"What do you mean?"

"I was having some difficulty believing what I was seeing, so I consulted a colleague in Germany. She helped treat Alexei Navalny after he was poisoned with Novichok. It's an agent many times more deadly than VX gas, developed in the Soviet era . . ."

"Nerve gas?"

"I suspect a nerve agent of some kind. They're all organophosphates and many are volatile and soluble in water. Non-persistent, it's called. That may explain why he was put in Swan Lake."

"Jesus!" Crawford barked in panic. "Why didn't you tell us this right away? We have to shut that place down!"

"Not to worry, Detectives," he cajoled in that smooth, unflappable voice. "I've reported my preliminary findings to the FBI, as per protocol. I'm sure they're already at the Bel-Air by now, but they won't find anything. The dosage required to kill is in micrograms. Literally a single drop in a beverage, for instance, which is what I think happened here."

Crawford had regained control, but Nolan could hear the lingering tightness in his voice. "Why?"

"Because it's too dangerous to deliver it externally—for instance, leaving it on the surface of a drinking glass or doorknob where it could be spread. First of all, that method potentially endangers the killer. Secondly, if it sickens others, the poisoning is no longer a secret. That's where the Salisbury killers made a grave error. I think your killer learned from that."

"Just how sure are you this isn't going to spread? Or that it hasn't already?"

"I've checked with all Los Angeles County hospitals and there have been no patients admitted with symptoms of this type of poisoning. And we all had contact with the body—I have spent the better part of three hours inside it—and we're not dead. Neither are the swans. I consider that to be convincing evidence."

Nolan waited to speak until the wave of nausea had passed. "Salisbury?"

"In 2018, a Russian double agent for the UK and his daughter were poisoned in Salisbury. The highest concentration of the agent—Novichok, in this case—was found on their front door. They both survived, but barely, and many others were sickened. A few months later, a British national found a perfume bottle seven miles south in Amesbury and gave it to a woman named Dawn Sturgess. She sprayed it on her wrist and died a week later. Authorities believe the man had found the discarded delivery system of the Salisbury poisonings. Very sloppy." A phone rang in the background. "I have to excuse myself, Detectives, but I'll be in touch with new information as it comes in. Good day."

Nolan was having difficulty finding intellectual accommodation for what Weil had just told them. Al was sucking his cheeks again.

"Nerve gas," he finally mumbled. "Holy shit. If Blake was killed by the stuff that Putin's thugs use to off political opponents, then he pissed a Russian off. We need to find out if he was working on something else besides the boring stuff in his journal and files."

"Lukin would know."

"What if the Russian he pissed off is Lukin?"

"Assassinate his most valuable employee with nerve gas? That would be kind of leading, wouldn't it? He also pointed out that only a stupid killer would dump a body in Swan Lake, and he didn't strike me as stupid."

"No. But you can't just pick this shit up on the street. Not here, not in Moscow. This is high-level stuff."

"Krasnoport might have some high-level enemies. Call Ike and see if he got anything from Lindgren's computer yet."

Crawford nodded. "I'll have him start looking at Krasnoport, too. Maybe there's some international brouhaha going on."

While he called Ike from the car, Nolan went back into the house, where the techs were diligently dusting for prints, bagging evidence, and placing numbered markers. A photographer and videographer were building the visual documentation—a twisted parody of paparazzi.

Roscoe was kneeling next to the body, speaking into a tiny recorder. Two of his youngsters were keenly watching and listening. On-the-job training. "Ross, can you ballpark a time of death?"

He sat back on his haunches and looked up at her. "Not with the accuracy of a coroner."

"You've been at more crime scenes than any coroner. Give me your best guess."

"Around forty-eight hours."

"That was my thought, too. Thanks."

She returned her gaze to Zoe's body. Blake had been dead for fourteen hours, Zoe for forty-eight. Different killer than her husband's or the same killer trying to make the two murders look unconnected? Conventional wisdom said the same perp, but mutilation was pretty far to go to throw investigators off course. Without the kind of rage that came from a personal connection to the victim, it would be hard to gouge somebody's eyes out. That made Blake Lindgren an excellent choice for his ex-wife's murder and Ross's timeline supported that. Or maybe that was part of the killer's plan.

Crawford was back in the house, beside her at Zoe Lindgren's final, ignominious resting place on the floor by a half-empty, sexy blue bottle of gin. "Ike's into the computer. The only thing that's jumped out at him so far is that Blake had a lot of bank accounts. Five have IBANs: international bank account numbers. God, I'm still freaked out. This is creepier than hell."

That was one thing she and Al could agree on. "IBANs aren't unusual for a guy who was obviously pretty wealthy and dealt in international trade."

"Offshore accounts are always red flags. Ike's looking into the locations of the banks now."

"So Blake may have been dirty."

"It would explain an assassination. Ike's also printing his current case files for us in case we missed something. I also told him to search the drive for 'Irina.'"

"And he'll dig into Krasnoport?"

"With all his heart and soul. Between the bank accounts and nerve gas, he's all over it. He's a spy novel freak."

Nolan suddenly realized Ike hadn't been the only one distracted by the perverse, outrageous news of a possible poisoning by nerve gas. It had overshadowed the more pedestrian, procedural aspects of the case. "Weil said Lindgren was poisoned on-site. That could only happen somewhere private, so the body had to be moved. Lindgren was six-feet and over two hundred pounds. You'd need a couple men to move that kind of dead weight."

"So we have to dance around the feds and check all the Bel-Air room registrations again, dig a little deeper."

"Not all the rooms. It has to be one of the suites, they have private entrances. The Swan Lake suite was the only one that wasn't occupied this morning. The rest of them are still full of Oklahoma and Dubai oil money and I'm guessing they're not assassins."

"The honeymooners from Florida."

Nolan gestured to the body. "I'm not sold on Blake doing this to his wife."

"I'm not, either, even though it sounds good."

"I was thinking about a setup. The killer had to get rid of them both, so he frames a dead guy for his ex-wife's murder. Ross's speculative time of death works with that."

"I can go there. Hell, at this point, I can go almost anywhere. She was with him for over twenty years. If Blake was in the deep somehow, Zoe was right there. Drunk or not, clueless or not, she would be a loose end."

"Right. Keep digging around, I'll call HazMat response and tell them to focus on the Swan Lake suite."

Chapter Thirty-Two

MARIELLE STOOD BY THE DOOR WITH her back pressed against the wall, her heart pounding a frenetic cadence in the cage of her chest as she heard footsteps drawing nearer. Fat Man had a gun, so surprise was her only advantage—she had to move fast when he entered. One chance. His life or theirs. And then she heard Serena's voice, and her grip on the jagged metal bar she'd harvested from the cot loosened. How could she attack and possibly kill a man in front of her?

You don't have a choice. He's either going to turn us over to Father Paul, which is a death sentence, or kill us himself because he thinks I know something. Please forgive me, Serena.

Time slowed and warped and the turning of the doorknob seemed to happen in a different dimension far removed from reality. This wasn't reality, it couldn't be reality. Just a movie, a video game, a caprice of an overactive imagination . . .

"I have a surprise for you, Marielle," he said as he entered the room.

And I have a surprise for you, she thought hysterically as she plunged her improvisational weapon into his neck.

Nothing registered in Marielle's brain for a moment except the warm blood on her hands and face and the fat man gurgling on the floor as he clutched his neck. Then the nausea came in a great, odious wave, along with a trembling that would shatter her into pieces if she couldn't get it under control.

When Serena's scream jolted her back to the present, maternal instinct obliterated everything else. She scooped her up in her arms, whispered soothing nonsense into her ear, then bolted out of the room and started running down a hallway—running away from bad things and running toward the unknown which had to be better because it couldn't get much worse. These walls were concrete block, too, with cages on the bare lightbulbs lining the walls. Not a house, something industrial. A warehouse? It was important to pay attention, to notice every detail, because it might matter. It might save their lives.

In the faint light, she saw that the long hallway dead-ended in a windowless double metal door with push bars to open them. She didn't pause to think about what she would do if those doors were locked, or what was down the hall in the opposite direction if she had to backtrack. Doors meant escape and that's where she would go.

•

Paul stared in disbelief at the metal bar embedded in Grisha's neck; at the lake of blood pooled around his head and shoulders; at the ghastly gray face and blown pupils. His breathing was ragged and sweat slicked his face. The entire drive down, he'd envisioned the various ways he would kill Grisha, but finding the job already done was a shock.

Marielle had surprised him once again, that fucking sow of Satan. This was *his* job to finish. She was taking things from him one by one. And as much as Gregory deserved to die, this was inhumane and barbaric. Now he took solace in envisioning the ways he would kill *her*.

"We both underestimated her, Grisha, and now you're a mess. You shouldn't have sent your men home, but I suppose you had plans you didn't want to share with them. Killing women and children is offensive even to the *podonky* you keep around."

"Find . . . h-her."

"Oh, I will. She won't get far. And she'll pay. Now, what to do about you?"

"H-help m-m-me."

His voice was faint, the stuttering syllables dissolving in his gasps for air. It was amazing he could speak at all. Paul knelt down and put a hand on his clammy brow. "I would call an ambulance, but that would bring up some difficult questions. Besides, I'm afraid you're not going to make it, so there's really no point."

"P-p-lease."

"Why should I help you? You were going to fuck me. That's no way to treat an old friend."

"N-no. Protect. F-from . . . Ivan."

"Don't lie on your deathbed, Grisha, it's beneath even you. God hates liars."

"Not . . . lying."

"Your judgment is out of my hands now. Shall I leave you like this or put you out of your misery? It doesn't matter to me either way."

He blinked frantically. "Butyrka . . ."

Of course Grisha would bring up Butyrka in his final, desperate moments as a last chance at salvation. Emotional blackmail was one of his few talents. "Yes, you kept me from rotting in a Russian prison, but I think I've repaid that debt. I got us to America and made us rich, didn't I? That's something Ivan never would have done, he's a greedy pig. I even did time here so he wouldn't get suspicious. And what did I get from you?" He thrust his hands palm-up in front of his dimming eyes. "Do you remember? Do you remember any of the lessons you taught me in that shithole apartment in Golyanovo? *I* remember."

"I saved you, Pasha," he said softly, but clearly—a miraculous moment of cogency. The death knell, Paul knew; he'd seen it many times. Then he uttered a strange, wet sound and tears leaked down his cheeks, dropping to the floor to mingle with the blood.

Paul felt a strange combination of revulsion and what he imagined was sympathy, or at least some semblance of it. There was no love between them, there never had been, but they shared a history. A Russian history. It was like a polluted, underground river, but it ran deep.

Paul reached into Grisha's leather jacket and found the ubiquitous silver flask, then cradled his head and put it to his lips. "Drink your disgusting horseradish vodka, Grisha, it will make you happy."

Most of it dribbled down his chin, but Paul was certain the quiver of his lips was meant to be a smile as he closed his eyes. This seemed like the right time for mercy. He would have done it for an animal, and Grisha deserved that much.

•

Almost to the door. Marielle pushed her legs harder while Serena's frightened whimpers shredded her heart. "Shh, Serena, please be quiet. We're going to get out of here and everything is going to be okay . . ."

The gunshot that split the air made a liar out of her. She dropped to the hard, concrete floor inches away from the door and covered Serena's shuddering body with hers. Dear Jesus, they had to get out of here, but where had the shot come from? She didn't know which way to run, but she did know that right now, they were trapped in the hallway without a place to hide.

She held her breath and listened. If there was anybody else here, the gunshot would have sent them scrambling, but she didn't hear anything. No alarmed shouts, no frantic footfalls. The door right in front of her seemed like the only option, it had always been the only option. It led somewhere, and please, God, let it lead outside.

She looked down at Serena for the first time since she'd jammed a piece of metal into another human's neck with the intent to kill. Her eyes were huge and wet and filled with terror as she stared at her mother's gore-covered face.

For the first time in too long, Marielle thought of her own mother, her father, and poor, dear little Louis, with the angels now. Remy broke through her mental fortress again, too, his presence stronger this time.

She should have gone to him. None of the mess she'd made of her life had been his fault, she knew that now. If she and Serena survived this, she didn't know how she would be able to piece all the broken hearts and lives back together again.

"Honey, I'm sorry I had to hurt that man, but it was the only way to make us safe, do you understand?"

Serena swallowed. "But he saved us from Father Paul."

"He's a liar. He's *with* Father Paul and they're both bad men. But we're going to be alright, baby, just hang on tight. Really tight." When she felt Serena's arms clutch her neck, she got to her feet and pressed softly on the door. It opened slowly onto a dim, cavernous room. Now or never, all or nothing.

She took a hesitant step inside and let the door close quietly behind her. The room was rank with a miasma of smells she couldn't immediately categorize, but the prevailing top note was petroleum. In the feeble light of more caged bulbs, she could make out large crates stacked four and five high on pallets, a metal staircase rising to a dark second level, and a table with an overflowing ashtray and empty beer cans. A dirty white van hooked to an enclosed trailer was parked along a wall. The van had gotten in here through a garage door, and that was how they would get out.

Marielle was so focused on an escape route, her peripheral vision hadn't caught the tall shadow approaching until it delivered a fierce blow to her right shoulder that sent her and Serena tumbling onto the greasy concrete floor. Starbursts of agony flared in her vision as she groped for her daughter, then she froze and quailed at the voice above her.

"It's so good to see you, Marielle. Especially Serena. I was so worried I'd lost you both."

Chapter Thirty-Three

NOLAN AND CRAWFORD WERE DRAFTING IN the techs' wake when a low-fidelity version of the Tannhäuser Overture erupted from her suit, reminding her of unplayed messages.

"Wagner, Mags? Really?"

"I'm impressed you know that."

"Don't be. My knowledge comes from a Bugs Bunny cartoon."

"I want this played at my funeral. Remember that if you outlive me." She hoped one of the messages was from her mother, but none of them were. "Remy. He called three times."

"I doubt he's trying to reschedule a social engagement, so you'd better call him back."

Nolan stepped out into the turbulent, hot night and gulped the air greedily, hoping it would scour the cloying film of decay from her throat and mouth and nose. Most of the rubberneckers had retreated, but the media were still clamoring behind the barricades. She started pacing while she listened to Remy's phone ring.

"Maggie. How's the case?"

"Cases. We're at Zoe Lindgren's place in Santa Monica right now. Somebody put out her eyes."

"Jesus. Are you thinking murder-suicide?"

"It was in the running until things started getting really weird.

Blake Lindgren was murdered and Doc Weil thinks he was poisoned with nerve gas."

"*What?*"

"Yeah. The feds are probably there now. Check your computer, I'm sure it's trending."

"Have they taken over the case yet?"

"Part of me hopes they will, but we haven't heard from the Special Agent in Charge yet."

"You will. God, this is insane. Who poisons somebody with nerve gas?"

Nolan noticed that Sylvia Cohen had closed her curtains and turned off her outdoor lights. "The way things are rolling out, it might make sense."

"How so?"

"There's a Russian component to this through the company he worked for, and nerve gas seems to be popular with the KGB set. Or whatever they're calling themselves nowadays."

Remy was quiet for a very long time, which unsettled her. He wasn't a cheek-sucker and usually never took more than a second to respond to anything. "You're thinking too hard. What's wrong?"

"SVR is the current name of their foreign intelligence service. KGB had too many negative connotations for the new Russia. Bad PR."

"You're not thinking about the historical nomenclature of Russian intelligence, are you, Remy?"

"No. I'm wondering if there are any connections between the two murders aside from the obvious. In particular, with Children of the Desert."

Nolan felt a faint warning tingle travel down her arms. "Blake Lindgren's neighbor went there on a rehab retreat. It's a popular place."

"Can you reach your mother?"

"I've been trying but she's not answering her phone. Why?"

"I may have your excuse to get her out of there."

Nolan's stomach started squirming. "What the hell is going on, Remy?"

"Do you remember the missing person's case I told you about?"

"The one your PI friend is looking into."

"Right. He was there today and saw a paramilitary presence. There's a Russian component there, too."

"Criminal activity?"

"There's no other reason for men with big guns. Marielle, my . . . my missing person escaped from COD last night with the help of a man named Lenny. She was kidnapped today from his boat in Marina del Rey where she and her daughter were sheltering."

"And your friend thinks they took her back there?"

"He doesn't know I found her yet. I haven't been able to reach him."

"So where did you get this information?"

"Sam Easton. He's friends with Lenny and contacted me."

"*Sam Easton?*"

"I'm at his house now."

Nolan braced her arm on the porch railing as her mind churned through surreal, impossible bits of information; scattered pieces of a puzzle that may or may not fit together. "Is your PI Malachai Dubnik?"

"Yes, why?"

"We found his business card in Blake Lindgren's personal belongings. We think he was looking for a Russian woman named Irina."

"Have you spoken with him?"

"We haven't been able to reach him, either." She lifted her eyes to the street and saw the coroner's wagon pull up. "I've got to go, the coroner just got here. Can you come over?"

"Text me the address."

"Is my mother in danger, Remy?"

"I don't think any of the guests are. The retreats are aboveboard. But I wanted you to know. As I told Sam, it's better to be paranoid than sorry."

"I don't care how aboveboard the retreats are, I want her out of there."

"I thought you might. From what Mal told me, it's virtually impossible to contact COD, but there's probably an emergency number for family of guests."

"I'll ask my father."

"See you soon."

Crawford walked out onto the porch. "What did Remy want?" He froze when he saw her expression.

"Things just got more bizarre, Al."

Chapter Thirty-Four

SAM HADN'T OPENED THE TRUNK WHERE he kept his Army things since he'd locked it over two years ago. He wasn't sure what to expect from his emotions, but he figured they would be a collection of negative and positive. Hopefully the opposite poles would neutralize without prompting a nasty flashback.

He took a deep breath, lifted the lid to Pandora's box, and was hit by the repugnant smell of the mothballs Yuki had insisted on using. Her rationale was that his uniforms were an important part of his past and must be preserved. One day he would need access to the memories they held and it wouldn't do to have them defiled by insects. Not in the spirit to argue at the time, he'd sat mutely on the bed and watched her wrap them carefully in tissue, then place them on top of his medal cases and all the other bits and pieces of a former military life.

He lifted the tissue from his Army combat uniform, pristine and unworn in battle. Thankfully, they hadn't returned the bloody shreds of the one he'd almost died in, if there had even been that much left. He doubted it.

When the ACU didn't sink fangs into his flesh, he ran tentative fingers across the fabric. The familiar feel of it was a direct a portal to Afghanistan, but it didn't initiate a flashback—the memories that hadn't been taken by the roadside bomb seeped in more than flooded.

There were plenty of bad ones in the stew, but they seemed hazy and distant. What he felt and remembered most was the warmth of camaraderie and good times with his men. Shaggy, Kev, Wilson, even Rondo—their ghosts had never left him. But this mental journey back to Afghanistan imbued them with life for the first time since they'd actually drawn breath. It felt good; right.

Sam would never understand why they'd died and he hadn't; and he would never fully vanquish his survivor's guilt. The dead knew why they died but the living never had answers, which gave them a distinct advantage that pleased him.

He spent a long time reacquainting himself with his past, then removed the desert camo and closed the lid. This time, he didn't lock it.

Lenny was at the kitchen table with a mug of coffee, making notes on a printout of an aerial map of Children of the Desert Remy had found with the property ID number. He looked up with a weary, concerned expression. "I'm writing down everything I know about this place, including where I picked up Marielle and Serena. It's not much."

"But it's something. Thank you."

"Are you sure this is a good idea, Sam?"

"Not at all. It's probably a huge mistake."

Lenny grunted his assent. "You and Detective Beaudreau must have quite a history for you to stick your neck out like this."

"A short one, but an important one."

"If those men with guns see you, Sam, they just might shoot you dead."

"I won't let them see me. And I won't be going in blind. Remy's going to solve that problem with his drones. We can identify buildings and where guards are stationed." Sam poured himself coffee, wondering if he was totally insane or if it just felt that way. Dr. Frolich would have a ready answer, but he wasn't going to call her to find out. He sat down next to Lenny and looked at the map. It was a lot of real estate to cover.

Lenny rolled his tongue along the chew lodged between his cheek and gums. "Say you find Marielle and Serena, and I pray you do. Then what?"

"I get them out."

"I know you can run a marathon without breathing hard, but getting out won't be so easy with three of you, especially with a little girl and possibly some bad guys on your tail." He winced. "They might be injured."

"I can do it."

Lenny pointed to a red X he'd drawn on the south side of the map. "This is where I picked them up. Marielle scouted this area for a month and never saw any patrols. The fence is lower here, too. Maybe you ought to go in that way instead of trying to sneak in through the main entrance with Detective Nolan."

"After Marielle and Serena's escape, they'll be tight and watching everything. And if she's back there, they'll be even more vigilant. Now they know the police are involved with her disappearance and they're smack in the bull's-eye. All it would take is a perimeter patrol with night vision goggles to spot me climbing over a fence and game over. It's better to get inside the fence without risking exposure. The Trojan horse plan is always a good one."

Lenny tapped his pen on the map. "Detective Beaudreau said there was paramilitary presence on the backside, which is the north side. That means there's something there to protect." He circled a cluster of buildings. "Whatever it is, it's in there, so you'll want to steer clear. Hopefully they're not keeping them there."

Sam turned the map. "The buildings here on the south side?"

"It's the town, if you could call it that. It used to be a silver mine back in the 1800s, with some cabins for the miners, a hotel and saloon. A chapel, too. It used to be open to tourists. The retreat center went up after COD bought it. I've never seen guards or patrols on the south side when I've driven by the main entrance or gone inside the gate for a delivery. They might not even go near the retreat center. It would look pretty bad to the paying guests."

"That's good news."

"You can use my station as a staging area. You'll need one."

"Did you ever think your shop would be an operations command center?"

Lenny chuckled. "Honestly, I think I've seen stranger things in my life. How are you doing, Sam? I mean, this has got to bring back the past."

"It does. But it's not all bad. I can remember some good things now, too." Sam pushed himself up from the table. "Let's grill those steaks. It's late and I'm starving."

Chapter Thirty-Five

DUBNIK PULLED INTO HIS GARAGE, CHECKED his rear and side mirrors, then his gun. He decided not to holster it before he got out of the car. Paranoia wasn't his customary frame of mind these days, and he didn't like the feeling. In fact, it pissed him off, because it was irrational. Whatever was going on at COD wasn't going to follow him to Brentwood; neither were Yahoo and Slab. But cop instinct was something imprinted on you from the academy to your time on the force, and it kept getting stronger the longer you served. It was stupid not to listen to it. It had saved his life before.

He closed the garage door and let himself into the house, disarming and rearming the alarm. Aside from the wail of the Santa Anas and the incessant smacks of embattled palm fronds against the house, all was peaceful.

He poured himself a nightcap of scotch and retreated to his office to pick up email and listen to his messages. On the way home from his disturbing trip to Children of the Desert, he'd detoured to his globe-trotting, sometimes gal pal's house. While he'd been enjoying her excellent cooking and the solace of her other charms, his phone had been equally busy. Remy had called and texted multiple times and so had Al Crawford, which meant there was something official going on. He tried Remy first, and he answered immediately.

"Mal, where the hell are you? I've been trying to reach you."

"I'm at home now, just got here."

"Your last message was a little grim, I was getting concerned."

"I'm sorry about that. I had my phone turned off for a while. Greta is in town."

"She's a good reason to turn off your phone."

"The message I left was meant to be in jest, but the more I think about the whole situation up there, the more wrong it feels. Crawford called me, too, do you know anything about that?"

"Yes. I'm on my way to meet up with Al and Maggie in Santa Monica."

"You're supposed to be on vacation."

"I am. Blake Lindgren was your client, right?"

"Yes. *Was?*"

"He was murdered and they found your card in his personal belongings."

"I'm very sorry to hear that. He was a nice man."

"Were you looking for a Russian woman named Irina?"

"I was. Do they think she's connected to his murder?"

"It's a possibility. Whatever you know, you need to tell Maggie and Al."

"I don't know much, but I'm happy to share what I do know. What's the story with Lindgren?"

"He was poisoned and dumped in Swan Lake, submerged a few hundred yards away from where we were enjoying martinis today."

Dubnik's jaw slid open in disbelief. "That's crazy."

"His wife was murdered, too, in her home. Eyes were gouged out. That's where I'm headed now."

"God, that's horrible. But why are you involved?"

"Russia and Children of the Desert are pinging the radar from all angles. I know for a fact Charlotte was there, Mal. And I think she's there now. She escaped last night and was kidnapped today from the boat where she was hiding."

Dubnik squeezed his temples. "You could have led with this, Remy. Tell me."

"No point wasting our breath on the phone, there are too many moving parts. Can I pick you up? We can go over there together and I'll tell you what I know on the way. Crime Scene should be wrapping things up by the time we get there."

"Sure. I'll bring my files."

Chapter Thirty-Six

AS NOLAN PROBED ZOE LINDGREN'S DEN, she fought hard to still her frantic heart and push secondary distractions to the back of her mind.

Distractions like the possibility your mother might be embedded in some criminal enterprise. No big deal. Happens all the time.

But Roan Donnelly and a lot of other people had come out of COD not only alive and well, but better for it, so there was no point dwelling on the issue until Remy arrived with more details that would either salve her apprehension or completely freak her out. Right now, she owed a tragically sad woman her complete attention.

Her gloves were smudged with fingerprint powder—it was hard to avoid once Crime Scene had finished their work. It wasn't surprising that most of the prints belonged to Zoe Lindgren, being an alcoholic shut-in. Another set that turned up frequently had been left by a small person—presumably a woman, presumably the housekeeper—who was already in the process of being printed for exclusionary purposes. They'd matched Blake's prints on a few common surfaces that any casual guest might touch.

They already knew he visited occasionally; maybe trying to normalize post-marital relations, or maybe for welfare checks. By the quantity of half-empty liquor bottles stashed everywhere, she had been in desperate need of a guardian. It was something of a miracle that a killer had gotten to her before the gin.

That was it for prints, and the amount of trace collected would take time to sort and compare to what had been gathered at the Bel-Air and on Tanager Way. There might be fibers or soil or other random detritus that would link the two murders, but it wouldn't necessarily lead to a killer. Or killers.

Like her husband, Zoe was no sentimental packrat, but unlike her husband, she kept no private display of family photos. Nolan was beginning to think she kept no photos at all, until she found a scant few in a plastic bag. They were unframed and buried beneath old, unopened bills in a desk drawer. It seemed odd to her that a mother and wife of twenty-plus years would shun a photographic chronology of her family—at least the good parts of it.

She began to pile them on the desk one by one. It was a trifling collection that didn't even scratch the surface of the life of a fifty-year-old woman. Where had they all gone? Had she intentionally disposed of her past or had somebody else? It was something to think about.

It was also something that suffused Maggie with deep sorrow. Two people totally erased with so little to remember them by. The only things they'd left behind were big, expensive houses that had been vacated in all the ways that mattered long before their deaths.

In the limited omnibus spread before her, there was the same engagement photo from the Bel-Air that Blake had on his zebra-wood credenza and some wedding shots. None of their son, Michael, which seemed odd. But the last photo in the grid made her spine crawl. It was of a smiling, stunningly beautiful young Zoe wearing a crown and the sash of Miss California Teen USA. The edges were burned and there was some blistering on the surface. Al had mentioned a fire the night Michael had been kidnapped, but that didn't explain the two perfect burn holes where her eyes should have been.

Crawford walked into the den. "Find a computer or anything else useful?"

"No computer, but look at these photos. From what I can tell, they're the only ones in the house, and they were buried in a drawer."

He stared at Zoe's ruined beauty shot for a long moment. "Creepy foreshadowing, wouldn't you say?"

"Very. But she could have done this to the photo herself as an indirect form of self-mutilation. That would sync with an eating disorder, which is essentially a form of self-mutilation."

"But she didn't gouge out her own eyes. And why would she keep this?" He puffed out a sigh and shook his head. "From beauty queen to alcoholic to homicide victim. Makes you realize how unstable life really is. No pictures of the kid?"

"No. Anything on your end?"

"SAC Daley called. He wants our coverage soonest, as he put it. Like we've had time to write a report. I needled him about the Bel-Air, but he wouldn't say boo, just that they were concluding their operation. He's kind of an arrogant prick."

Nolan actually found a smile. So Daley's rep wasn't just nasty gossip. "What else?"

"Blake's phone records came in. Nothing unusual. Calls and texts to and from the office, and the call from Zoe on Monday. The manager of the Bel-Air is losing his mind, but he's pulling the file on the honeymooners and sending it our way. Aside from the bank accounts, Lindgren's hard drive was a bust. No private journals in a lock box, no mention of Irina. I did a search on Krasnoport. There's no history of litigation here or abroad and the company is in good standing with the IRS. Ike's digging a little deeper right now, looking at the companies they do business with."

"Is Remy here yet?"

"Just arrived. Dubnik is with him, too. Christ, this is turning into one big hairball. What are you going to do about your mother?"

"I'm going to call my father and see if there's an emergency number where I can reach her."

"Meet us outside when you're finished. Good luck."

She put the photos back in their plastic sheath and made the call. Daddy would probably panic in his quiet way, but she couldn't white-wash this. He had every right to know; maybe more than she did.

"Hello, Margaret. What can I do for you?"

Such an odd greeting from a parent. As if he was a sales associate at a call center. "Hi, Daddy. I'm trying to reach Mom. Did she give you a contact number at Children of the Desert?"

"It's here somewhere. But she has her phone."

"She's not answering. Has she been in touch with you?"

"No. I imagine they're keeping her busy."

"I suppose they are. But I really need to speak with her."

"What's wrong?" he asked warily.

"I've been thinking about what you said today. I'd like to reach out."

"That's very thoughtful, Margaret. She'll appreciate that."

Nolan took a deep breath. "There's something else."

"What?"

"Al and I are on a case and some things have come up about Children of the Desert. Possible criminal activity. I want to get her out of there."

"My God. Is she in danger?"

"I don't think so. Just a precaution."

"I'll leave now . . ."

"Let me talk to her, Daddy. If she thinks there's something strange going on there, I need to know about it. The police need to know about it."

"Yes. Okay." She heard papers rustling. "Found it." He rattled off a phone number. "You call me right after you've spoken to her. I'll be ready to go. And I hope you'll eventually tell me what the hell is going on."

Daddy never swore or even said *hell*, and it startled her. "I don't know myself what's going on yet. But I'll call you once I get through to her."

Reaching Children of the Desert via the emergency number wasn't a problem. A woman with a soft voice answered brightly after a few rings.

"This is Los Angeles Police detective Margaret Nolan. My mother, Emily Nolan, is staying with you and I need to speak with her."

The woman hesitated. "It's awfully late . . ."

"This is an emergency number, right?"

"Yes."

"This is an emergency. Get her now."

Nolan counted her heartbeats while she waited. And waited. There wasn't even a crappy canned soundtrack to listen to. After five minutes, she was beginning to wonder if the chipper woman with the soft voice had dropped the phone and gone to bed.

Finally, her mother's sleepy voice came on the line. "Margaret, what's wrong? Is York alright? Are you?"

"We're fine. Are you okay, Mom? I've been trying to reach you. And you sound a little . . ." she wanted to say spacey, but decided that was impolitic. Besides, she'd just been dragged out of bed.

"I have a terrible migraine. And they took my phone away. They took all of our phones. I wanted to call you earlier."

"They can't do that." But of course, they could. They could do whatever they wanted to.

"I'm upset about it."

"So am I. Daddy is coming to pick you up."

"Oh my God, something *is* wrong. Tell me."

"We're okay. But I'm working a case and Children of the Desert has come up several times. I don't have time to explain, but we want to bring you home."

"This sounds serious. Should I be concerned?"

"You're fine, and Daddy will be there as soon as he can. Mom, have you seen anything unusual? Suspicious maybe?"

"Not really."

"You don't sound certain about that."

"No, nothing. But I'm glad to be out of here, Margaret. Aside from confiscating our phones, the lodging is atrocious, not at all what I expected. And Father Paul—he's the deacon—seems very nice and caring, but I think his methods are a bit Draconian. I'm not at all pleased. I hope I'll get a partial refund."

Nolan didn't think she should count on that. "Is there somebody with you now?"

"Sister Carina is waiting for me outside the door. She's the one who got me out of bed."

"Put her back on the line."

After Nolan explained to a flummoxed and resistant Sister Carina exactly what was going to happen, she shoved her phone in her pocket.

"You look upset, Maggie."

She started at Remy's voice. She hadn't even noticed him enter the den. "I just got off the phone with my mother. She's fine, but she wants to leave, and the COD woman I spoke to is a pain in the ass. My father's going to go pick her up."

"He hasn't left yet, has he?"

"No, I have to call him back first."

"Before you do, I need to tell you about some plans Sam Easton and I are thinking about."

Chapter Thirty-Seven

SISTER CARINA WAS WEAVING HER FINGERS together in distress. In the stark light of the overhead fluorescents in the media center, she looked alarmingly young to Emily. Not a spot or line or even a pucker marred her smooth face. Of course, most people under thirty looked like infants to her.

"I'm so sorry to see you leave, Sister Emily. Father Paul told me you're special and the most promising student he's ever had. I've never heard him say anything like that before."

Emily didn't like being called sister or student or special, at least in the current context, but she kept those thoughts to herself. "I'm sure there will be others."

"Can I help you pack?"

"No, but thank you."

She tipped her head with a look of concern. "Are you feeling alright? You look pale."

"It's just a headache. I get migraines sometimes."

"Would you like some herbal tea? Lime tree tea works wonders for migraines."

Emily thought of the soporific brew Father Paul had given her when she'd been crying; the trip into the desert she barely remembered. There was something terribly wrong about that, and she thanked God she was getting out of here. Whatever had happened, she'd sort it out later. "I've had quite enough herbal tea. I would appreciate something caffeinated if you have it. That always helps my headaches."

"We have a nice black Russian tea, I'll get you some."

"I appreciate that, but before you do, I'd like my phone. My husband will be here in a few hours and I need to be in touch with him."

"I'll have Father Paul return it to you."

"I'm dealing with a family emergency. I need my phone now."

She shrank apologetically. "Of course. I don't know where he keeps them, but I'll page him immediately."

Emily suddenly felt ashamed for taking out her angst on this poor young girl who was so eager to please. None of this was her fault. "Thank you. And I'm so sorry if I seem sharp, I'm just very worried."

Her brows peaked in empathy. "I understand, Sister Emily. This is a difficult time for you. I'll get in touch with Father Paul, then make you some tea."

"You're very kind."

•

Paul was in his bedroom in the gloriously refurbished old hotel. The restoration had turned out even better than the chapel's. Sometimes he imagined himself as Rufus Cadogan, the original owner of the silver mine: a monarch of a bygone era, watching riches comes out of the ground while he indulged his desires from the comforts of his beautifully appointed quarters.

In researching the history, he'd discovered that the original owner had kept a suite of rooms here. But Paul kept the entire place all to himself. Every square inch: the guest rooms, the dining room, the gaming and whoring parlors, the bar and restaurant and lobby. It was a grand mansion; it was the American dream. And Marielle and Serena were back where they belonged. After a disastrous start, the day had ended well.

He was changing out of his bloody cassock when he received a page from Sister Carina, which ruined his jocular mood. Whatever the stupid slut wanted, it would have to wait. He put on a track suit, popped an upper, and snorted a few lines of coke. Sleep wasn't an option tonight.

He walked down the hotel hallway to the room where he was holding Marielle and Serena. He'd put them in the room Gregory used on his visits, which seemed appropriate. Hopefully, his ghost was there now, haunting her.

Glenn had bound and gagged Satan's sow and tied her to the four-poster bed for good measure; Serena was spared the indignity because she would never leave her mother's side. Not that it mattered—they were both still sedated, and would remain that way until he was ready to pass judgment.

Glenn was standing near the bed with his gun slung over his shoulder. An unlit cigarette hung from his mouth.

"I told you no smoking in the buildings."

"I know, that's why it's not lit. Helps with the cravings."

He seemed alert and vigilant; serious about his duty, if not overly enthusiastic. "You don't need an AR15 to guard two drugged women, Glenn."

"You said to watch them. That's what I'm doing. The gun is in case we get unexpected company. You said to watch for that, too."

Sister Carina paged him again, then texted.

Come to the retreat center NOW.

Stupid slut. She was prone to melodrama—an infuriating trait—and if she was paging him because she'd broken a fingernail or crashed a computer, he was going to have to teach her a lesson she wouldn't forget. He brushed away the pellets of sweat that had burst on his brow.

"Something wrong, Father Paul?"

"I need to take care of something at the retreat center." He withdrew a leather pouch from his jacket and unzipped it to reveal a row of tiny syringes with caps instead of needles. "If either of them wakes up before I get back, squeeze one of these under the tongue. Marielle might need two to keep her sleeping, but don't give the girl more than one. If she starts making noise after one dose, tape her mouth. But don't hurt her."

"I won't."

"And if I'm not back in twenty minutes, call me to check in."

"I will."

"How do you like the job so far?"

"I like it just fine."

"I thought you might. Duane said you were going to fit in here."

"I believe I will."

"Good, because I have a bigger job for you later. A very important one."

"What's that?"

"I'm going to show you where to go to make deliveries. It's not far from here."

"What are we delivering?"

Paul clenched his fists behind his back. In his mind, Glenn's head was being crushed between his palms. "That is none of your business."

He smiled. "I suppose it's not. But I can guess."

"Don't get ahead of yourself, Glenn. Arrogance is a sin. I'm trusting you with some important duties. I also trusted the two men you're replacing, but they failed. I think you know what happened to them."

"I won't let you down."

"You'd better hope not."

•

Glenn walked to the window and watched the Jeep drive away. Did Snake really think he was so stupid, he couldn't figure out that drugs and guns were on the delivery menu? Once he got into a routine, he'd just disappear with a load one day and get set up on his own. He had a place to go where Snake would never find him.

He turned and examined his prisoners. What was so important about a woman and a little girl? But who the hell knew what was going through Snake's mind. He didn't seem very stable tonight, not at all like the cool customer who'd visited him in prison.

He poked the woman with the muzzle of his gun, but she didn't respond. The girl didn't, either. Dead to the world; there was no way they were waking up anytime soon. He'd just go down for a quick smoke, five minutes max. He had plenty of time before Snake got back.

Chapter Thirty-Eight

AS PAUL GOT INTO HIS JEEP, he considered Glenn. He was a long-term liability because he knew that Father Paul was really Snake Jackson; he was also a treacherous, selfish bastard, so he might try to leverage that knowledge at some point. He would have to watch him carefully. And eliminate him when all this uncertainty was resolved.

He approached the retreat center where his lambs were undoubtedly sound asleep. Emily Nolan would be for sure. He was making great progress with her. Maybe he could convince her to stay a few extra days.

He found Sister Carina fretting in the media center. He dug deep for forbearance so he didn't hit her. "Is there a problem, Sister?"

"I'm sorry to bother you, Father Paul, but it's Emily Nolan. She's leaving us."

"What do you mean?"

"Her daughter called. She's a Los Angeles police detective and they're coming to pick her up. She said it was a family emergency, but I have the recording right here. Listen to it."

Paul did, and his mood went black.

I'm working a case and Children of the Desert has come up several times. I don't have time to explain, but we want to bring you home.

"What does she mean, Father Paul?"

Good question. What the *fuck* did she mean? Paul kept his voice calm and low. "Sister Emily told me her daughter is frustrated because she hasn't been able to help her with her struggles. It was my impression that she finds it difficult to accept the possibility of others succeeding where she has failed."

She looked at him incredulously. "That's so selfish. She obviously doesn't care about her mother's soul."

"We'll pray for her."

"Do you really think Sister Emily is disappointed?"

"No, she was just telling her daughter what she wanted to hear. It's a destructive pattern of codependency. This is such a shame. Sister Emily has stepped onto the path of healing, but she needs our guidance."

"Maybe you can convince her to stay?"

"I'll go speak with her."

He was shaking with fury when he left. The fucking cops. He wanted to believe his own story about the daughter being a selfish, manipulative bitch, but the longer he thought about this development, the deeper a cold, unyielding dread sank into his bones. What if they knew something and sending her mother here had been a setup from the beginning? A "family emergency" was a perfect way to give the bitch cop daughter legal access. Her daddy would drive right through the gates with her in the car and she would pretend to see something, make shit up, then call her other fucking cop friends.

He started to hyperventilate and ducked into the Fellowship Hall to calm himself and come up with an emergency plan. There was no damage to control yet, but a good tactician came up with a plan before he needed it.

He took the coke vial out of his warm-up jacket and did a couple bumps, knowing the numbing powder would focus him. And it did. In the brief time it took the drug to enter his system through the tissue in his sinus cavity, he clearly understood what he had to do:

take care of Marielle and Serena, then get Irina and the product off the property.

•

Mike hid behind a clump of thorny plants and watched the glowing ember of a cigarette wobble in the dark. Anybody else would have seen a man smoking, but Mike knew what it really was. He knew this for sure because he'd seen it bring the missing woman and the little girl into the building. It was a clever disguise that had even fooled Father Paul, but it didn't fool him.

In all the time he'd been watching, he hadn't seen any other aliens, and felt confident that he'd absorbed enough protective power to easily take care of just one. Even if there were others in the building, they would be weakened by his death.

"Go ahead, make my day," he whispered as he emerged from his cover and crawled toward the building.

Chapter Thirty-Nine

NOLAN HAD JUST STEPPED INTO AN alternate universe, she was certain of that. Remy had lost his mind and had somehow talked Sam Easton into losing his. Or maybe it was the other way around. "You can't be serious about this, Remy."

"There's no other way. I believe these women are in imminent danger, Maggie, and we can't justify a warrant. Not in time."

From what he'd told her, there wasn't even enough to justify the surveillance to get a warrant at some point in the future. "No kidding. The Inyo sheriff interviewed Father Paul, who's lying, according to this Lenny person who didn't actually witness a kidnapping. Do you have *any* proof that they were taken from the boat and didn't just leave on their own?"

Remy shook his head. "That's the problem."

"And they only went missing today?"

"Yes, so the law isn't on our side. That's why we need to do it this way."

Don't let the silly laws get in your way, she thought gloomily. Remy had always crossed lines, but this was something entirely different. "So you're going to send Sam Easton to trespass into a privately owned compound guarded by armed soldiers who might be Russian Mafia to find a needle in a haystack that might not even be there?"

"It was actually his idea."

"Sam Easton would be the first to admit his judgment might be questionable. I think it's suicide, and I'm afraid that's what he has in mind. You're willing to let Sam take that risk for an eight-year-old cold case and a kidnapping you don't even know really happened?"

"I know it happened."

She sighed impatiently. "If there's a child involved, it doesn't have to be an interstate incident to get the feds involved."

"We don't have time."

Nolan clenched her fists in frustration. "What the fuck is wrong with you, Remy?"

He looked at her so intensely, she felt it in her stomach. "The woman is my sister, Maggie. The girl is my niece."

Nolan's thoughts slammed to an abrupt halt. Nothing made sense until it did. She would have done anything, stupid or not, to save Max. "Jesus."

"I hope he's paying attention."

"You want my father to sneak Sam in."

"That was also Sam's idea. I'm leaving soon with my drones to scout the area. Then we're planning to meet in Furnace Creek and make a decision based on whatever information I'm able to glean from the birds."

"Oh my God. This is nuts. It's not remotely safe."

"I know. But you understand."

She nodded reluctantly. "Did you tell Dubnik about this plan?"

"Yes."

"Does he think you're crazy?"

"He always has."

"My father thinks the world of Sam Easton, so he might not be on board with this."

"But he's an old warrior, so he might be."

She shook her head. "This is outrageous. Come on. We need to pull all our stories together before you leave."

•

Nolan had never met Malachai Dubnik before, but she found him suave and charming. He had presence and savoir faire and he was one of those rare men who made bald sexy. His eyes were kind and his manner gentle.

Some detectives called him a traitor and grumbled derisively about him going private, even though personality conflicts and politics had pushed him out. In her opinion, he'd made the right decision. If you got shit-canned from Robbery-Homicide, there was nowhere to go but down. Staying on the job with a humiliating downgrade wasn't an option if you had any self-respect. The grumblers were just jealous as hell because he was a roaring success on the outside with a bank account to match while they were still running down the clock to pension, living in rentals like she was because they couldn't afford a house in LA.

After curbside introductions and a brief chat, they'd agreed to meet at a Starbucks on Montana Avenue, away from the crime scene and the scrutiny of lingering eyes and ears. Everybody badly needed the caffeine, but Nolan was craving something stronger, like another Bel-Air martini. They probably all were.

After a half-hour information share, Dubnik leaned back in his chair and sipped his grande Americano thoughtfully. "So you've got a dead husband and wife, kidnappings past and present, a Russian import-export company, and maybe the Russian Mob up in Death Valley hiding behind a cult. Oh, and nerve gas, we can't forget about that. I certainly don't envy you."

Crawford tore into a second blueberry muffin. "Tell us what you know about Irina, Mal. She's a wild card right now."

He slid a folder across the table. "Copies for you. Her name is Irina Walters and she's a Russian national, naturalized as a U.S. citizen in the early nineties. She ran an adoption agency in Calabasas called Loving Hearts, and the Lindgrens adopted Michael through them in '97."

"We didn't know he was adopted."

"From an orphanage in Siberia. The country was a mess back then and there were a lot of parentless children waiting for stable homes. Maybe there still are, but Russia banned American adoptions in 2012. That's another story."

"But Blake just hired you to find her recently?"

"About six months ago. He said he'd been looking for her through his Russian channels for a while, but he couldn't track her down."

"That's odd he was looking for her after all this time," Nolan remarked.

"It struck me as odd, too."

"Did he tell you why?"

"He said he wanted more history about his boy. He'd finally accepted that Michael's remains would probably never be found—he'd been chasing that for years—but he needed some kind of closure."

Nolan frowned. "They surely had all the history they could get out of the orphanage before they adopted him. That's part of the process."

"Russian orphanages aren't very judicious with record keeping, and they're certainly not forthright with prospective parents. He believed Irina had additional information. I'm really sorry I wasn't able to give him what he was looking for."

"You never got a handle on her?" Crawford asked.

"I'm no closer today than I was six months ago. The agency folded in 2011 and she went back to Russia, which is like getting swallowed up by a black hole. Good luck with that. Social media has made finding people a lot easier, but not so with her."

"We found an out-of-service number for her on the wife's phone."

"Local?"

"Yeah."

"The numbers I tracked down are out of service, too. But they're all out of Russia. Moscow. Probably all throwaways."

Crawford thumbed through Dubnik's file. "You found several complaints and pending lawsuits filed against the agency, right around the time it shut the doors. That would explain the vanishing act."

"Exactly."

"What kind of complaints?" Nolan asked.

"Negligent misrepresentation of children's health and history, which explains where Blake was coming from. I talked to some of the plaintiffs and it's pretty tragic. Some of these kids coming from war-torn or chaotic countries are badly damaged from lifelong institutionalization, abuse, prenatal exposure to drugs and alcohol and so forth. If adoptive parents don't know the history and aren't educated and equipped to deal with these special needs, it's impossible to provide adequate care. Not fair to the new parents or the kid, and dangerous, too."

Nolan had heard horror stories of international adoptions gone wrong. It was rare, but heartbreaking all the way around and nobody came out a winner. Except maybe the adoption agency that charged an arm and a leg for their services.

"One of the families who sued told me their family still fears for their lives," Dubnik continued. "Their adoptive daughter ran away at sixteen and disappeared. This was years ago, but they still regularly receive death threats from her and nobody can track her down."

"Did the Lindgrens ever lodge a complaint or file a suit?"

"No, but maybe they would have eventually. Behaviorally, Michael was on the extreme end of the spectrum. Fire-starting, rage, violence, according to Blake. He killed the neighbor's dog with a carving knife when he was ten."

Nolan looked at Crawford. "That explains who defaced Zoe's beauty queen photo."

Crawford nodded and stuffed his empty muffin wrapper in his empty coffee cup. "A budding young sociopath."

Dubnik's expression was grim. "His diagnoses were reactive detachment disorder and callous-unemotional, but yeah, basically. And then he was kidnapped. Poor kid's life was hell from beginning to end."

"A lot of arrows pointing at Russia right now," Remy said.

"Yeah, so be careful. Lindgren may have poked the bear somehow. And it's not that cute mascot they use at the Olympics." He slid another folder across the table. "The file on COD. If they're bad news like they seem to be, then you'll find it incredibly ironic that the state is financing a felon rehabilitation program at Children of the Desert. It's been very successful, and now I know why. Nothing like turning criminals over to smarter criminals."

Crawford shook his head in disgust. "Half the state government is comprised of criminals in my opinion."

Dubnik leaned forward and looked at Remy gravely. "From what I saw there and what you've all told me, you need to be very careful if you go up there looking for Charlotte and Serena. I have no doubt Sam Easton is beyond competent, but he's one man. I'd stake my life that those dirtbags I ran into with AR15s are part of the prison program. And one of them was higher than a giraffe's ass."

Chapter Forty

EMILY WAS ENJOYING THE BLACK TEA that Sister Carina had brought along with a plate of dark, buttered bread. Her headache had vanished entirely, and all the stress of the day was fading into the background of her awareness. If she hadn't been waiting for York, she would have easily fallen asleep, which was strange, since the tea was caffeinated.

She heard a soft knock on her door—certainly considerate Sister Carina, inquiring if she needed anything else. When she answered, she was nonplussed to see Father Paul himself, and dressed in a track suit. Of course nobody would wear their clerical garb twenty-four hours a day, but it was odd to see him out of context. "Father Paul. I wasn't expecting you personally. I'm sorry if I got you out of bed."

"Sister Emily, I just heard the news. I'm saddened to hear you're leaving us, but it's understandable. I hope the emergency isn't very grave. We'll all pray for you."

His eyes were glittering strangely. Sister Carina must have gotten him out of bed. "Thank you."

He turned over her phone with a gentle smile. "You've made such incredible progress here in a short amount of time. I hope when things are resolved, you'll come back to resume your work."

She had no intention of coming back, but she didn't want to be mean-spirited. "I will."

"If it was anything other than a family emergency, I would plead a convincing case for you to stay. Will your daughter be picking you up?"

"No, my husband."

"Travel at night to Children of the Desert is difficult if you're not familiar with our roads. Or lack thereof. We would be more than happy to bring you to Furnace Creek to make it more convenient for your husband."

"That's considerate of you to offer, but he'll pick me up here."

"Let Sister Carina know when he's close so she can open the gate for him." He gestured to her phone. "And if he changes his mind about meeting you in Furnace Creek, let her know that, too."

"I will."

He took both her hands and smiled beneficently. "I will pray for you, Sister Emily. May God bless and keep you and your family during this time of crisis and always."

"I appreciate that. And thank you. Good night, Father Paul."

"Good night, Sister Emily. I'll see you soon. I hope."

Paul walked calmly into the media center, where Sister Carina was dusting and tidying desks. She was annoying, but very industrious and generous with her time and body. He should be more charitable with her. She was still just a child, after all, barely fourteen.

She looked up with bright, eager eyes. "Will she stay?"

"Unfortunately, Sister Emily must be on her way to attend to worldly troubles, but she will contact you when her husband is due to arrive so you can open the gate."

"I'll be waiting."

"Thank you. Direct him to the portico. And if there is anyone else in the car with him, let me know immediately. Page me, text me, call me."

"But I wouldn't want to wake you, tomorrow is such a big day . . ."

"*Immediately*, Sister Carina."

"Of course, Father Paul."

"And don't answer the phone."

"We have to keep the emergency line open . . ."

"Do *not* answer the phone. The only call you will answer is from me, do you understand?"

She gulped and nodded.

"You gave her some black tea?"

"Yes."

"Excellent." He wasn't anticipating that things would go sideways, but it was always wise to keep wayward lambs tranquilized. They had a better memory of their experience that way.

Back in the Jeep, he took deep breaths while he stared up at the infinite array of stars above him. He felt a little better knowing that bitch cop daughter wasn't coming along for the ride. Emily had no reason to lie about that. Maybe there was no grand conspiracy, and bitch cop daughter had meant something else when she'd told her mother some things had come up in a case she was working. He'd hosted plenty of useless Hollywood losers here on their futile quest for salvation—maybe God had done the world a favor and killed one of them.

When his phone rang, he knew it was Glenn checking in, right on schedule. He was certainly being a good soldier, at least for the time being. But he'd always been slick that way, so he couldn't read too much into his model behavior.

"Father Paul. I haven't wakened you, I hope?"

His gut writhed at the sound of the hateful voice. "Ivan. No, you didn't wake me. How are you?"

"Not so well, I'm sorry to say."

Paul felt vomit creeping up his esophagus and he swallowed hard. "There's something wrong?"

"Gregory is dead."

He didn't have to feign disbelief. How the hell had Ivan found out about it so soon? Goddammit, he wasn't prepared for this. "No. No, that's impossible. I spoke with him earlier, he was coming here tonight."

"I'm sorry to be the one to share the unfortunate news."

Ivan's tone was dark and malevolent. That only happened when he was furious. And when Ivan was furious, people died. "How?"

"Someone drove a piece of metal into his neck. He bled quite profusely. A horrible way to die."

"It's those fucking Armenians. They're fucking animals."

"They are, I agree. But then he was shot in the head, which doesn't sound like the Armenians. They would let him die like a pig. That may have been an act of mercy, what do you think?"

This was the role of a lifetime, and Paul embraced it with extraordinary passion. "It wasn't an act of mercy, it was amusement for some fucking *ubiytsy* thugs. They get impatient when people take too long to die. Find them for me, Ivan."

"We're doing our best."

"How could this have happened? Where were his *byki*, or are they dead too?"

"His *byki* said they were dismissed after they were asked to take a woman and a little girl from a boat in Marina del Rey and secure them. You wouldn't happen to know anything about that, would you?"

Paul wiped clammy hands on his thighs. "What would I know? I live hundreds of miles away. I take care of things here. I never knew what Gregory did in LA."

"Yes, I thought so. I know you have always had a difficult relationship with Grisha, so I wish you some peace tonight. I've made arrangements for a proper burial."

Which meant a hole in the desert. Paul's mind raced, stumbling over what a remorseful person who'd been blindsided by the news would say. "I need to be there. I need to see him." Yes. That was good.

Ivan made a thoughtful purring sound. "But I thought you already had. Maybe you didn't say a proper good-bye. Rest well, Pasha. Don't let the scorpions bite."

Chapter Forty-One

BY OUTWARD APPEARANCES, THE BEL-AIR HAD settled back into an untroubled sanctuary of privilege, as if the earlier disturbances had never occurred. A groundskeeper was laconically sweeping pieces of wind-pruned foliage off the drive—an exercise in futility with the Santa Anas still roaring—but that was the only visible action from the street. The Bel-Air had gotten the all-clear, and hopefully the ruffled guests had been pacified back into customary ennui. And what a great story to tell at dinner parties.

Nolan parked behind Crawford's Buick and draped her arms over the steering wheel. Her bones and muscles and brain ached and her teeth felt fuzzy. She had a toothbrush in her purse, but it was probably fuzzy, too. "What did Corinne say?"

"Good luck and don't forget to eat. That last comment was meant for you, not for me. The woman's got a wicked sense of humor."

"We'll order a pizza when we get back to the station."

He glanced at her. "Mags, if you want to go get your mother, I have no problem with flying solo for a while."

"I'm not leaving you to hold the bag. I couldn't stop my father from going and there's no point in the both of us making the trip. He's going to have company anyhow."

"So he's okay with the whole batshit crazy idea?"

"To tell you the truth, he sounded a little jazzed about it."

"I've met your father and he doesn't strike me as a man who gets jazzed."

"He does in his own, very quiet way. He's got two missions up there now. York Nolan doesn't do retirement well. Even though he's wearing Tommy Bahama shirts and drinking chardonnay at brunch these days."

Crawford chuckled. "No way."

"I couldn't believe it myself."

"A lot of people lose their sense of purpose when they retire from a job they love. And apparently their good taste."

"He definitely loved his job."

"I love mine, too, but I never had any taste to begin with, and I don't think I'll lose my sense of purpose when I retire. Plus, I won't have to worry about staying alive."

"We should always worry about that."

"Yeah, but it would be nice to get rid of the service weapon during family gatherings. I can take out Corinne's jackass brother in hand-to-hand combat." He rolled down his window and stuck his face into the hot wind of a climatically raucous LA night. "That's wild about Remy's sister. I feel like I don't even know the guy after all these years."

"I'm not sure anybody does."

"I wonder what the backstory is."

Nolan thought about Remy's brother and wondered if that was a piece of the puzzle. "We might never know."

"I hope they can find her without things getting ugly."

"That's what I'm worried about."

He rolled up his window, silencing the wind. "So this Irina person. The Lindgrens end up dead six months after Blake started looking for her. That can't be a coincidence."

"Agreed. So let's go unpack this mess."

•

Homicide was never empty, whatever the hour, but tonight it was relatively quiet. The majority of the on-duty detectives were out in the field; the on-calls were at home, hoping their phones wouldn't ring. Nolan could almost hear herself think, which was nice but strange.

While Al went to brew a pot of coffee, she ordered a large pepperoni pizza and printed out the Bel-Air file on the Florida honeymooners: William and Rochelle Dugard of Coconut Grove, a posh Miami neighborhood. Two nights in the Swan Lake suite. The scan of his driver's license showed an attractive man, thirty-one in November according to his DOB; five-eleven, one-ninety, an organ donor. A few charges from the mini-bar and room service. They'd paid with an American Express under William's name.

Nolan did a quick search and found a photo of the couple at a 2012 fundraiser for Miami's Lowe Art Museum. She dug a little deeper, called the Bel-Air and spoke to housekeeping, then went to find Al.

He was in front of the coffee maker, half-asleep and hypnotized by the slow drip of a machine that had probably never been cleaned. "Pizza?"

"On the way." She placed a printout on the counter. "Here are our honeymooners in 2012."

He reanimated from his zombie state. "They're about a thousand years old. And this was ten years ago."

"Right. They're both long-dead from natural causes and the honeymooner thing is bullshit. I rattled a Bel-Air housekeeper out of bed and had an interesting conversation. She was in charge of the staff that tried to take care of the Swan Lake suite during this guy's stay."

"Tried?"

"She got a lot of complaints from the maids. Anytime somebody tried to service it, they were shooed away by a 'very big, unfriendly man' posted outside the door."

Crawford grunted unpleasantly. "I'm guessing he wasn't Secret Service. What was the room like when he finally checked out?"

"Spotless. Like nobody had ever been there."

Crawford rubbed his unshaven jaw. "Blake didn't arrive at the Bel-Air in a suitcase, we know that from Doc Weil. So he had a compelling reason to go there. Zoe has always been the obvious one, but maybe that's where we're wrong. When you consider Blake's offshore accounts, maybe it was a clandestine business meeting with the competition. Things crater, they poison him, and toss him in the drink."

"Or he was double-timing Lukin and he found out about it. He made a point of telling us about the Lindgren marriage proposal at the Bel-Air the second time we spoke to him, and even suggested Blake and Zoe may have met there to reconcile."

"Which never happened."

"For a while, we were thinking murder-suicide. Maybe that was the setup."

Crawford poured himself a cup of the sludge he'd just brewed. "You called that early on, the possibility of the killer framing a dead guy for his ex-wife's murder. Problem is, why kill her? She dropped out of the picture after the divorce."

"You said that if Blake was in the deep, Zoe would be a loose end whether she knew anything or not. So possible motive for both killings, but her mutilation still gets me."

"We're speculating about sociopathic criminals, Mags. I wouldn't worry too much about the MO."

"We're missing something, Al. Let's go see if Ike has anything for us."

Chapter Forty-Two

REMY WAS SITTING AT THE FURNACE Creek station's snack bar, eating a stale bismark while he reviewed drone footage on his tablet. Stale or not, the sugar-dusted donut shell wasn't bad and the jelly inside was still gooey; the coffee was fresh; and he'd nailed it with the video. So far, so good.

Nobody on the ground had had a clue about the eye in the sky—a big mistake in the Children of the Desert security protocol—and between the night vision zoom and thermal imaging, he had a footprint of the entire compound that might even please the Pentagon.

Lenny was an intent observer, uttering sounds of approval every few frames. "This is solid, Detective, and it's exactly like you said: all the security is on the north end."

"And exactly like you said: the south end is clear."

"Thanks to you, Sam's not going in blind. You just gave him a real chance."

"Assuming Marielle and Serena are being kept in one of the south buildings. But he still has to get in, find them, then get out."

Lenny chewed his lip, suddenly troubled. "There are a lot of moving parts to this. A lot of opportunities for things to go wrong. This phone tracker thing. You sure we'll always know Sam's location?"

"As long as his phone is on, we'll know exactly where he is at all times."

Lenny seemed slightly less apprehensive. "That's good. Have you been piloting drones for long?"

"Ever since they were available to the public."

"Not to be rude, but how much does a rig like yours cost?"

"Too much for a hobby, but worth the price, as it turns out."

Lenny scraped crumbs off the counter and refilled their cardboard coffee cups. "Sam will find your sister and your niece, Detective. Don't doubt it."

Remy looked at the kind, sun-wizened face of the man who had given Charlotte and her daughter a real chance, too, although he didn't seem to realize it. If he did, he wasn't taking credit for it. "We wouldn't be here without you, Lenny. Don't doubt *that*."

"I guess we all came together for a reason. Sam texted while you were busy with your video. They'll be here soon."

Remy considered Sam Easton and York Nolan—two strangers, thrown together under bizarre circumstances, taking a long road trip together. "I wonder how the ride's going."

"Those two men have more in common than not, so I suspect it's going just fine."

•

Sam looked out the passenger window of the Nolan family Escalade, watching the empty, moonlit desert pass in a blur. The colonel was comfortable driving at high speed and seemed to be enjoying himself on the empty freeway. Three months ago, when his daughter had been trying to hang a double murder on Sam, even the most overactive imagination couldn't have conjured a scenario where they would be driving to Death Valley together in the middle of the night.

And yet here he was, near the end of their journey, talking desert warfare with an old soldier as if they'd shared a battlefield and had been friends for years. Brothers in arms shared common experiences and an unbreakable bond, but the two of them shared more than even that through Max's death and what could have been his own.

At the halfway point of the trip, after strenuous queries from the colonel that seemed more fatherly than military, Sam had acquiesced and talked about his own odyssey to Hell and back. It had never felt good talking about it with Dr. Frolich, even though their conversations had established a positive path forward. But sharing it with York Nolan was easier; even a little cathartic. He understood—not in an academic way, but in a real way. Sam's own Army father had been betrayed by a weak heart and hadn't lived to see him almost die, so he wasn't there to help with the aftermath, but he imagined they would have had a similar conversation.

When Sam had finished his story about Afghanistan, he'd reciprocated and asked about Max. The colonel spoke candidly about his son in a crisp, reserved manner, but there was emotion in his measured words. It brought the survivor's guilt to the surface once again. It was the same old question without an answer, on an endless playback loop. Why him and not me?

"I wish I'd known your son, Colonel. I think we would have been friends."

"I do, too. I can't get you to call me York, can I?"

"Properly addressing a superior officer is a hard habit to break. It wouldn't be right."

He nodded absently. "It was good to talk about Max. Thank you for listening."

"It was an honor to hear about him."

He tapped the navigation display. "We're almost to Furnace Creek. Another twenty miles."

"At the speed you're driving, we should be there in five minutes."

That elicited a chuckle from the stern, formal man. "This is a tank of a vehicle, but it's got an engine to match. I made sure of that before I bought it."

Sam stole a glance at him. He was still a handsome man, and he saw a lot of Margaret Nolan in the planes of his face, and especially in the gray eyes. "I read a review once that described a car as a hairy-chested brute."

He smiled and patted the steering wheel. "That's this sweetheart. Margaret tells me you've got a hairy-chested brute of your own. A real classic."

"A Shelby Mustang. It was my grandfather's."

"Tell me about it."

Sam did, and by the time he'd finished, they were off the freeway and driving toward the scant lights of Furnace Creek. The colonel pulled into Lenny's lot, parked next to his truck, and leveled a hard look at Sam. "I'm damn glad you made it back, son. I believe God spared you for a reason and I'm not sure this is it. Are you positive about this thing?"

"No, I'm not. But I am sure this is something I want to do. Maybe need to do."

"You had a long journey back."

"I'm not sure I'm entirely back yet."

"No, I imagine you aren't. And being out in a desert at night, dressed and equipped for a military mission . . . you've made a lot of progress, Sam. Don't let this be a step back. And don't get yourself killed here at home, soldier. That's an order."

Chapter Forty-Three

IKE BONDI, INSUFFERABLE ROGUE OF THE LAPD, didn't care that he had a bottle of Jack Daniel's in full sight on his desk. He had his detective's shield, but his cyber skills were a far more valuable attribute, so people looked the other way or didn't look at all. Don't ask, don't tell. He'd been pulled off the active roster three years ago and cosseted in a private office where he dwelled in various shades of gray. He knew how to produce results while covering his ass, and there was no reason to let a little alcohol problem interfere with good clearance numbers.

He looked up from his screen and smiled. "You guys look like you could use a drink."

Crawford stripped off his suit coat and sank into a metal folding chair. "At this point, one drink would be too many and a thousand wouldn't be enough. What do you know?"

"I know that three of Lindgren's five international bank accounts are in Russia. What do you call a Russian banker who isn't corrupt?"

"What?"

"A used-car salesman." He chuckled at his joke and took a pull from the bottle of Jack. "There are no passwords for the accounts on his hard drive, so I don't know what kind of money we're talking about or where it came from. I can't dip into that kind of action or it's lights out. The captain's watching me." He made a slashing gesture across his throat.

"Glad you're keeping your nose clean," Nolan needled fondly. "Where are the other two banks based?"

"The Caymans."

"Money laundering?"

"Money laundering, reverse money laundering, whatever. I don't think Lindgren was poisoned because he wanted to diversify his portfolio."

"What's reverse money laundering?"

"The opposite of cleaning dirty money."

"I figured that out. You want to be a little more specific, Ike?"

He gave her a lopsided grin. "God, I love it when you get annoyed, Maggie. Is that wrong?"

"On so many levels. Talk or I'll shoot you."

"God, that would be a dream."

"Ike . . ."

"Yeah, yeah, sorry. Reverse money laundering is just what it sounds like, taking clean money and putting it into a dirty entity that does bad things with it. Like a nonprofit that takes donations and funnels it to overseas terror organizations or other shitbags."

She looked at Crawford. "Children of the Desert is a nonprofit."

Ike leaned forward, intrigued. "What's Children of the Desert?"

"A New Age retreat in Death Valley that is starting to look like a front for the Russian Mafia. Everything we have you looking at is connected somehow. Pure speculation, of course."

He rubbed his hands together gleefully. "I'm on it."

"Malachai Dubnik already dug into it for somebody else and it's clean on paper. He gave us his file."

"Copy me on it and I'll still look into it. No offense to Mal, but I have special skills."

"What about Krasnoport?" Crawford asked.

He shrugged. "Like you said, Al, no litigation, good-standing with the IRS, gold-star corporation that gives to charities, etcetera ad infinitum. But get a little deeper and it's got a dark side. I'm not the SEC, but I'm sure if you got some forensic accountants into his stuff, their heads would blow up. You know what a matryoshka doll is?"

"No."

"Those Russian nesting dolls. You open one and there's a smaller doll inside it, and that one has another inside it, and so on."

Crawford gave him a thumbs-up. "Way to keep up the Russki theme, Ike."

He scratched the dark haze of whiskers shadowing his jaw. "I knew you'd appreciate that. Anyhow, that's how Lukin structured Krasnoport, since way back in the early 2000s. A bunch of foreign subsidiaries and offshoots that get dissolved and replaced by new ones."

"Shell corporations."

"Exactly."

Nolan felt a little thrill of vindication. Her instinct about an underlying coarseness to the polished man they'd spoken to in Holmby Hills hadn't been entirely capricious. "So Lukin is definitely dirty."

"Looks like it, but proving it is a different story. I haven't been able to find any history of compliance investigations, violations, or penalties, which means he keeps the company super sterile."

"It's possible he's behind Lindgren's murder."

"That wouldn't surprise me. He might be an immigrant living the American dream, but he's also ex-KGB. Fairly high up, he ran Lubyanka. The Soviets called it a prison, but it was really a torture facility. I don't think anybody got out of there alive."

Nolan grimaced. "What about Blake's work files?"

"Standard, boring international trade stuff. But what happens in Russia stays in Russia, so if I were you, I'd call the feds. Let them twist in the wind."

"The feds are already involved."

"Good call."

Nolan decided not to clarify that it hadn't been their call. She gestured to the stack of files on his desk. "Any of those for us?"

He passed a fat folder to Nolan. "The dope on everything I just told you, plus a list of companies Krasnoport deals with or has dealt with over the last ten years, and all the sketchy LLCs associated with it."

"Thanks, Ike. Can you run a facial recognition for us?"

"Sure."

Nolan passed him the Bel-Air file and a blowup of Dugard's driver's license. "This guy is using a stolen identity. Check out his Amex card, too."

Ike took another slug from his bottle. "You got it."

Chapter Forty-Four

PAUL'S HEART WAS STILL THRASHING FROM his conversation with Ivan. He stomped on the Jeep's accelerator and didn't let up. A hundred yards from the hotel, he hit a rock at high speed and the Jeep went momentarily airborne and almost flipped when it landed. He smashed down on the brakes and closed his eyes as it skidded wildly in the sand.

Son of a bitch. Ivan's *byki* and maybe Ivan himself were coming, there was no question about that now. He could feel him seething in his blood. Gregory had been right to warn him—he had to get Irina off the property. If Ivan found out she wasn't living out a happy retirement in Moscow, they would both be dead. But it was a long drive from LA to here and he figured he still had some time. What he needed to do wouldn't take long.

First things first: Marielle had started this whole fucking mess and she'd killed Gregory. The bitch was going to be sorry up until the moment she died. As much as he hated to do it, he was going to make Serena watch because it would destroy Marielle. His daughter was young, she'd get over it eventually.

Paul took the stairs three at a time and burst into the room where the women were, and where Glenn wasn't. That stupid fuck. If he was outside sneaking a smoke, he was going to kill him on sight. He had to get rid of him sooner or later anyhow.

He checked Marielle and then Serena. Both still out cold, their breathing slow and steady. Then he tried to raise Glenn on his Bear-Com.

"Where the *fuck* are you, Glenn?"

Nothing.

"Glenn, answer my goddamned call."

Still nothing.

He ran down the stairs and onto the porch. "Glenn!" he shouted. "You fuck, if you're out here smoking . . ." And then he noticed the blood. And the drag marks in the sand. Jesus Christ, what the hell was going on?

•

Sam was under a Pendleton blanket in the back of the Escalade, feeling the warmth of his breath against the wool. He'd gone through a gear check five times at the station, but he went through it again in his mind. Two sidearms, extra clips, check. Thermal camera, check. Night vision goggles, check. Phone charged and on mute, check. Auxiliary comm unit just in case cell coverage got sketchy. Remy was in place on the south fence line; Lenny was parked out of sight near the gate. Both were armed and ready to back him up.

Thanks to Remy's drone recon, he knew where all the buildings on the property were and where there were guards. They all agreed the women wouldn't be kept in the retreat center with the guests or in any of the buildings on the north side where they suspected there was contraband. That left the chapel, the hotel, and a cluster of cabins. He also knew where the mine entrance was, which was good cover if he needed it. What happened next was anybody's guess.

"We're almost to the gate, Sam. It's open. I don't see any guards."

"We were counting on that."

"Pulling through the gate now, the drive is well-lit. That wasn't on the footage."

"They're expecting you. They turned on the lights. Can you see the retreat center?"

"Up ahead, maybe a quarter click. That's well-lit, too. Lots of big windows."

Sam felt a quivering line of sweat trace down his cheek. "What else do you see?"

"A lot of dark desert everywhere. You just need to get away from the center and you'll be okay. There are no floodlights, so twenty yards and you're home free. Final approach up the drive to the portico. Building is on the passenger side. Emily and a woman are standing inside the doors of the lobby. Nobody else inside or outside that I can see."

"That's good."

"But there are cameras at the entrance. I'm parking right in front of the doors so the vehicle will give you cover on the driver's side, and I'll open the hatch before I get out. I'll be a distraction, so that would be your time to move. If something doesn't look right or feel right, I'll hit the door lock on the fob so it chirps. That means abort."

"Yes, sir. Colonel. Thank you."

"Good luck, son, and Godspeed."

Sam waited breathlessly, feeling the blast of chilled desert air as the hatch opened. The driver's door thunked closed, and the door locks didn't chirp, so Sam rolled out of the back of the Escalade as silently and stealthily as a cat. Twenty yards, home free. Godspeed.

Chapter Forty-Five

NOLAN WAS BOLTING A SLICE OF pizza at her desk while she flipped through her half of Ike's notes on Krasnoport. Matryoshka dolls had been a good analogy: there were dozens of companies associated with it and Lukin personally over the years, but the names meant nothing to her until she came across Hercules Mining—according to Dubnik's research, the company that leased the property to COD. Snug as bugs in a rug.

She turned to the final page and found another treasure: Loving Hearts, LLC; Irina Walters, president from 1996 until the dissolution in 2011. And Ivan Lukin, vice president from 1996 to 2004. A chill sank into her bones and made her skin prickle.

She waved at Crawford, who'd been derailed from his pizza by a phone call. He nodded, then held up a finger that conveyed: *Just a second, this is important.*

She gestured likewise: *Hurry up, this is important, too.*

He finally signed off and walked to her desk. "That was the lab."

"Sweet Genevieve?"

"It had to be an imposter, because this lady didn't chew my ass seven ways to Sunday before telling me to go fuck myself."

"She likes to work nights, it puts her in a better mood."

"Genevieve is a vicious harpy who doesn't like anything. If it really was her, she got a personality transplant. Anyhow, they found sand at Zoe Lindgren's place."

"She's a few blocks away from Santa Monica Beach."

"Not beach sand, Mags. Desert sand. Death Valley kind of sand. Circumstantial evidence that Children of the Desert is tangled up in this."

"I've got plenty of that myself."

"What?"

"Go ahead, finish. Did they find anything else?"

"Mixed in with all the cat hair were some human hairs on Zoe's body that didn't match hers. There was a follicle attached to one of them, so Genevieve is bumping it to the front of the DNA line. Don't ask me why she's doing us a favor, because I don't know."

"Any overlapping trace at Blake's scene?"

"There were animal hairs embedded in his suit."

"He would pick up cat hairs at Zoe's."

"There were also dog hairs. Brownish-black, medium length, like a German shepherd."

"Roan Donnelly has a shepherd. He said Blake loved it."

"There you go. You're up."

Nolan tried to clear her mental clutter and compartmentalize the new information. "Hercules Mining is a division of Krasnoport."

"Bingo."

"It gets better. Lukin was vice president of Loving Hearts from '96 to '04, and we already know it was a sketchy outfit. Michael was adopted in '97, and Blake was working for Krasnoport then." The prickles returned. "It's a big leap, but maybe Lukin was importing more than just agricultural products."

Crawford scowled until his forehead was a stack of fleshy ridges. "Not so big. I spent six months on a human trafficking task force before you ever took your detective's exam. There's a lot of money in black market babies. If they're blond and blue like Michael Lindgren was, the price goes up. Fifty grand a head or more, like they're cattle. Front the adoption behind a 'legitimate' agency like Loving Hearts and prospective parents like the Lindgrens just think they're paying a premium for express service on a custom baby."

Nolan felt physically ill. "That's horrific. Inhuman."

His face softened in sympathy. "There are worse things than dead bodies, Mags, as hard as it is to believe. But you called it. You said Lukin tripped your sleaze meter and your instincts are always good. If that's what Lukin was doing and Blake found out about it, that's enough for a death warrant. Zoe's, too."

Nolan pressed her fingers to her temple, trying to push away the horror of babies for sale to the highest bidder. "But Blake looks dirty, and if he was, he couldn't bury Krasnoport without burying himself. Why would he confront his boss and commit suicide?"

Crawford folded his lips together. Nolan thought it made him look like a sock puppet. "He wouldn't. So let's say he wasn't dirty, he was just a grieving father on a mission to find out more about his kid. He asks Lukin some innocent questions while he's looking for closure, gets a little too close for comfort, and nighty-night. And all of Zoe's calls to Lukin? Maybe she was asking innocent questions, too."

Nolan felt a faint, elusive wakening deep in a part of her brain. It lingered for the briefest moment, then receded. "Blake started looking for information on his kid six months ago. Six months after the divorce from a woman he suddenly hated after twenty years of marriage. It's bugging me."

Crawford sank heavily into a chair across from her. "Hate is cumulative. And big life events make people reflect on their lives and think about unfinished business."

Nolan didn't expect any great revelation by staring at the fingernails she'd chewed ragged over the past twelve hours. But the damage reminded her of the damaged children who may have been exploited by Loving Hearts; of the defaced photo of Zoe as Miss California Teen. "Death threats."

"Huh?"

"Remember what Dubnik said about that family getting death threats from their daughter?"

"Yeah."

"What if Michael Lindgren is still alive?"

Crawford seemed suspended in time for a long moment; unmoving, expressionless. He finally blinked. "If he is, how the hell are we going to find him? The feds' case on the kidnapping went cold when people were still listening to Britney Spears."

"They were looking for a dead child; we're looking for a living man. Laguna Beach has a book on the kidnapping that we can get with a phone call." She read the skepticism in his expression, which she always took as a personal challenge. "Don't give me that funny face, Al. We've got angles Laguna and the feds never had, maybe we can triangulate something."

"Funny face?"

"The one you give me when you think I'm off my nut."

"I never think you're off your nut, but you do get paranoid and defensive when you're exhausted."

Nolan appreciated the jibe for what it was—first of all, a distraction in the form of levity; secondly, advanced training to prepare her for working with a condescending, sexist asshole one day, which was bound to happen. She gave him a half-smile, too tired to execute a full one.

"It's a long shot, but a good idea, Mags. I'll get somebody out of bed down there."

"I'll go see where Ike's at."

•

Ike's lank face was pasty—a sharp contrast to his bloodshot eyes. Whether it was from Jack Daniel's, too much screen time, or lack of sleep, Nolan couldn't guess. The bottle was out of sight now and he was drinking coffee from an oversized Knott's Berry Farm mug. Maybe it was dosed, but she wasn't judging. Ike was his own country in LAPD's league of nations.

He glanced up wearily and passed her a few sheets of paper. "Facial recognition hasn't pinged your Florida phony yet, but that doesn't mean he isn't in the system somewhere. It just takes time."

"I know that, Ike, I'm not here to bust your balls. What else?"

"The Amex card he used was a pretty slick fraud, definitely not amateur hour. Already canceled, and the associated address doesn't exist, but he got his hands on a legitimate blank, because the chip and the CVC . . ."

"I trust you and believe you." She held up the papers he'd given her. "Details all here?"

"Everything I have so far."

"Thanks. You uncovered a bang-up connection between COD and Krasnoport with Hercules Mining. Way to go."

He brightened. "I've got one more. Mal was very thorough, but I did find a couple more things that weren't in his report. Probably because he wasn't looking for them." He waggled his brows. "It's good."

Nolan indulged in a brief moment of optimism. "What?"

"COD has received a lot of hefty charitable donations over the years from a Blue Orb Holdings, LLC. One of the companies . . ."

". . . associated with Lukin."

"It's a nice example of reverse money laundering. Basically, Children of the Desert is just one more division of Krasnoport. Really clever, hiding criminal activity behind a religious mission in the middle of the desert."

"What's the second thing?"

"I looked into COD's board of directors. For a nonprofit, there's a minimum of three to meet IRS guidelines, and currently, they have three listed: a Gregory and Paul Rybakov—a very Russian surname, by the way. Gregory checks out, he owns A-1 Auto Supply in Crenshaw. Paul checks out in all the ways that matter to the IRS, which is a Social Security number, an address, and a phone number. But he basically doesn't exist anywhere else, and that's not easy to do."

Just what Mal had said about Irina Walters. "Paul Rybakov. Father Paul."

"I don't think his work up there is very holy."

"Does the third board member check out?"

Ike's skeletal face lit up with a smile. "Sure does. Family lawyer in Inyo County named Keith Brandeis. He's been the sitting sheriff up there for six years. On top of everything else, looks like you've got a corrupt cop."

"I want to hug you, Ike. Thank you."

"You can hug me."

"That would be sexual harassment."

"I'm okay with that."

"You are a dog."

His previous brightness faded. "Seriously, don't step too deep into this, Maggie. Lean on the feds."

"We're going to nail our killer or killers, they can sort out the messy international crime syndicate stuff." Nolan had expected a genial snicker in response, but he remained morose and gulped his coffee with a wince. Definitely spiked.

"Be careful. Anything else?"

"Go home and get some rest. Al and I love and appreciate you. We don't want you to die at your desk."

He finally smiled.

Chapter Forty-Six

PAUL STARED IN SICKENED DISBELIEF AT Glenn's discarded body, partially concealed behind a cluster of mesquite. Some sick fuck had carved out his eyes, leaving dark, bloody holes. Who would do this? No one in the compound, no way in hell.

There was only one possible explanation and it made his stomach spasm: Ivan, sending a message. Jesus. That meant his *byki* were HERE and he had to get Irina the fuck out NOW. Unless they'd already found her. Then *he* had to get the fuck out. He started trembling from a toxic combination of revulsion, rage, and fear. After one last incredulous look at Glenn's sorry corpse, he ran for the Jeep. Marielle and Serena would have to wait.

•

Sam was creeping low to the ground as he approached the town, his night vision goggles illuminating it in a familiar, eerie green glow. He saw a grouping of cabins with dark windows, the steeple of the chapel, and a quintessential Old West structure with a broad porch. The hotel. There were lights on in the windows of both levels that showed as glowing white orbs—enough of them to indicate the building wasn't asleep.

His heart started to gallop as memories of crab-walking through another desert wearing night vision goggles began to infiltrate his mind.

Don't let this be a step back.

Good advice from York Nolan. This wasn't Afghanistan; he wasn't clearing a suspected enemy stronghold; and he wasn't going to get blown up. This wasn't war.

But his internal battle *was* war, and it was intensifying. What had seemed like the possibility of another step forward in his recovery was turning into a sharp retrograde and he felt himself tumbling into darkness as adrenaline sizzled through his system.

When he saw a Jeep careen around a building, its headlights sweeping in his direction, he launched himself flat into the sand. His heart was so loud in his ears, he could barely hear the roar of the engine as it sped north. For some reason, the action scattered the impending flashback and realigned his focus on the present. He took it as a tap on the shoulder from an unknown source, telling him to get his shit together for Remy's sister and her little girl. For himself.

He let the dust and his heart settle, spat grit from his mouth, then lifted his head and scanned the buildings of the ghostly town. As the sound of the engine faded, the silence was complete. No movement, no other vehicles, no signs of life. It was dark in the way only a desert could be, except for the riot of stars overhead and a sliver of moon. It was also as cold as a mausoleum and he hoped it wouldn't end up being his.

He heard sand shift behind him and his body turned into wire again. The sound was soft and quiet—the kind a small mammal or a slithering snake would make—but he had his Colt Python trained in the general direction as he flipped onto his back just in case.

It wasn't a small desert mammal or reptile, it was a slight, green-hued human figure standing a few yards away, arms slack at his sides. *Mike?* Christ, he'd really fallen down the rabbit hole now.

"Don't shoot me, Sam Eastwood. We're friends. Like you and Lenny."

He let out a shuddering breath and lowered his gun. "I won't shoot you, Mike, but you need to get down on the ground. Nobody can know we're here." *Don't fuck this up, kid.*

"They won't because there's nobody around."

"How do you know?"

"I've been here a long time."

Sam scanned the desert, the town. The retreat center was barely visible from here. He stood cautiously, every sense honed for impending disaster. But he'd been watching for a long time, too. The Jeep had been the only sign of life he'd seen and it was long gone. And they were far enough away from the town to be safe from any eyes searching the distant dark. "What are you doing here, Mike?"

"Hunting aliens. You're wearing a virtual reality headset."

He took the goggles off. "No, but it's kind of like it. Do you hunt aliens in video games?"

"Yeah, but I don't have a headset."

"Do you want to look through them?"

"Really?"

"Sure. But it's not the same as a video game, so don't be disappointed. This headset only shows you real things." He offered them to Mike as he approached tentatively, his gaze roving to avoid eye contact. His face looked dirty in the weak, milky moonlight.

"I can look?"

"Go ahead."

He held them reverently for a moment before he slipped them on. His mouth instantly formed an amazed O. "Everything is green and you look like an alien in the video games but this way better than at home."

"Pretty cool, right?"

Mike hummed in pleasure. "Is this what they use in your movies?"

Sam didn't waste any mental energy trying to figure out why Mike thought his favorite Clint Eastwood movies used virtual reality headsets before they'd even existed. "I'm not sure. Mike, you really shouldn't be here."

"You shouldn't be here, either, after what happened to you last time, but I can help you with aliens. I'm going to write a book about them."

He smiled weakly. "That's great. But I'm just looking for my friends right now. Did you drive here?"

"Yeah, in my truck. It's like Lenny's, but older."

"You need to go home. It's not safe here right now."

"I know that. But it's safer now for both of us, because I got one of them. It had a good disguise, but I knew right away what it was." He slipped off the goggles and returned them.

Sam noticed his hands were dirty, too. "You got an alien?"

He nodded. "The one who took the lady and the little girl."

His thoughts slammed into a wall of surreality. "How do you know about the lady and the girl?"

"Father Paul came into the station today asking about them."

So Father Paul was a lying son of a bitch and a kidnapper. Lenny had been right about that. The confirmation gave the place a more ominous tenor than it already had. "Did you see the lady and the little girl?"

"Yeah. Father Paul and the alien took them out of a van and carried them into that building."

Sam's pulse quickened as he followed his finger. "The hotel?"

He shrugged. "The one with the porch. We have a porch at home, but it's not that big."

"Are Father Paul and the alien still there?"

"I told you, I killed the alien. And Father Paul found the dead alien and got worried and left."

"Which direction did he go?"

"That way. In a Jeep. Fast."

North. Where the security was. He turned back to Mike and the moonlight hit him just right. The dirt on his face and hands looked an awful lot like dried blood. He squinted and his stomach lurched. No question it was dried blood. "Where is the alien you killed?"

He turned and pointed. "Over there somewhere."

Please, God, let it be an animal. "Will you show me?"

"Sure." He started shuffling through the sand toward town.

It was worse, so much worse than Sam could have imagined. He'd seen too many horrific things in war, but there was something about this atrocity that struck a different nerve. He glanced over at Mike, this murderous man-child smiling at his handiwork in approval. Sam didn't doubt that he really believed he'd killed an alien, which somehow made it seem even more terrifying.

Mike withdrew a screwdriver from his pants pocket and held it up. The gory shaft caught and reflected the moonlight. "You have to take out their eyes. Don't forget that."

Sam swallowed, ice sluicing through his veins. As repugnant as the thought was, this killer could help him. He would deal with the crisis of conscience later. "Mike, how did you get in?"

"There's a break in the fence."

"I need you to show me."

He turned and started walking away.

"No, Mike, not yet. I have to go save the lady and the little girl first. Then I have to get them out of here, the way you came in. Will you help me?"

"Okay."

"Thank you. Wait here for me. Don't move."

He frowned. "What if more aliens come?"

"Don't worry about that. Just sit tight, don't move, don't make a sound."

He nodded.

"And if you see another alien, don't kill it." For God's sake, don't kill it.

"But . . ."

"I'll be watching for them. I can take care of it."

"Do you have a screwdriver?"

Sam tasted salt from the nervous sweat dripping from his brow. "Sure I do, Mike."

He smiled, the moonlight glancing off his teeth. *"And if your eye causes you to sin, gouge it out."*

Sam swallowed. "Remember what I said: stay put."

"I promise."

Sam put some distance between himself and Mike, then ducked behind a creosote bush and pulled out his phone. It wasn't ideal to call, but Remy needed to know exactly what was going on, and a text wasn't going to cut it.

Chapter Forty-Seven

WHEN NOLAN HEARD HER PARENTS' DEDICATED ring tone—the official song of the Army—she scrambled for her phone in the messy pile of papers covering her desk. "Daddy. Are you with Mom?"

"We're on our way home. She's very tired and sleeping right now."

That wasn't at all like her nervy, hummingbird mother, especially after such high drama. But it was four in the morning, and they should all be so lucky. "Did Sam get in?"

"No trouble at all." His voice dropped in volume. "The preparation and plans were top notch, very impressive with such short notice. Exfil is the next challenge, but after spending time with Sam, I have a high level of confidence. Remy is also a solid man. Different skills, but an asset all the same. Let me know immediately when you get an update, whatever the hour."

"I will." Nolan was pleased by his crisply formal briefing and use of "exfil"—military argot for exfiltration. That was the old York Nolan, the one who'd existed before Max's death and her mother's decline. He sounded animated and engaged and she was amazed that Sam and this insane plan had brought him back to life. She would have been positively giddy if not for the darkness that had spawned it.

"Have you solved your case, Margaret?"

"Al and I are getting close to the end game. You haven't told Mom anything, have you?"

"I'll leave that to you."

Nolan heard soft mumbling in the background. "Is Mom waking up?"

More mumbling, no answer from her father.

"Daddy?"

He came back on the line. "Your mother would like to speak with you. Here she is."

"Margaret?"

She sounded very groggy, still half-asleep. "Hi, Mom. Are you okay?"

"Just fine, and glad to be on the way home. Are you okay, honey, dealing with your devil of a case? That's what your father called it."

Honey?

Nolan hadn't heard that childhood term of endearment for years, and it made her throat tighten. "I'm fine, too. Al and I are making good progress."

"That's wonderful news, and I certainly hope you can explain everything to me and your father once this is all over."

"I will." She heard her mother sigh, but it wasn't like the sharp, anxiety-fraught bursts she was used to. This sigh was soft; a gentle release of air.

"For some reason, I was thinking today about the time you fell off the swing set and knocked out a tooth. We were at the base in Germany, and Max carried you home. Do you remember that?"

Nolan felt a sharp sting behind her eyes. The emotion didn't come from the memory as much as from Emily Nolan finally uttering her dead son's name. "Max brought my tooth, too."

"He did. I think the Tooth Fairy gave you extra money for that one."

"He was the best brother."

"Yes, he was. And the best son."

"I miss him, Mom."

"I do, too, honey. I'm very tired, but I'll call you tomorrow. Be careful."

"I will. Good night, Mom." She hung up and brushed her eyes. She was hoping the gesture would go unnoticed, but Crawford was watching her.

"Everything okay?"

"Yeah. It's just that Mom . . . she sounds good. Really good. I'm a little freaked out."

"If your mom is good, that's all that matters. As Reverend Bandy says, the Lord works in mysterious ways."

"If Father Paul and Children of the Desert actually helped her, the Lord is really warped." She risked a look up at him and didn't start to cry, which was an outstanding achievement after the relentless emotional onslaught of the past fourteen hours. Or had it been more than fourteen hours? "Sam is in. He has the colonel's glowing endorsement."

"Mine, too. I hope he has your mom's luck up there. Mags, I've been frying my eyes on this kidnapping file and it isn't giving us squat. No witnesses, no suspicious vehicle reports, no suspects. The Lindgrens were put through the wringer, too."

"What about the database of the National Center for Missing and Exploited Children?"

"Nothing dovetailed there, either. Aside from Michael, there were only a handful of unsolved stranger abductions of children in Orange County and the Los Angeles metro area from 2000 to 2010."

"So no serial predator operating in that time frame that might connect some dots?"

"No. The other unsolveds were all at-risk youth, twelve to sixteen years old. It was a long time ago, Mags. Too long, and you know the stats. But it was worth a shot."

Nolan was disappointed, but not surprised. Ninety-nine percent of ideas hatched in a homicide case turned out to be dead ends. "So Lukin is the only ripe piece of fruit we have."

"He's a rotten piece of fruit. Let's go shake his tree and see if he splats onto the ground."

"He won't, Al. He's too slick."

"He doesn't fear us like he would the feds. We're just a couple of dumb cops trying to solve the murder of his employee of the year and his ex-wife. His guard will be down, then we start dropping little bombs of the stuff we know about his company. He'll start sweating it, and that's when people make mistakes. It's going to be great."

Chapter Forty-Eight

WHEN PAUL SAW DUANE BY THE north gate, he slammed on the brakes, straight-arming the steering wheel as the Jeep slithered and fishtailed in the sand. For a brief, harrowing moment, he thought this time it would flip. Duane looked comically alarmed, but nothing about this was comical. Not one fucking thing.

Paul jumped out and covered the short distance to Duane in a few strides. Now he looked more scared than alarmed.

"What's wrong, Father Paul?"

"Did anybody breach the fence or the gate?"

"No . . ."

"Are you sure?"

"Yeah . . ."

"Nothing on surveillance?"

"No, I . . ."

"The buildings?"

"It's been quiet all night."

"Are you SURE?" Spittle flew from his lips and Duane stepped back, bumping into the fence.

"I'm positive, Father Paul. I just got an all-clear from Karl ten minutes ago."

He released a trembling breath. If Ivan's goons weren't here, who the hell had killed Glenn?

"Why do you think . . ."

"I need you to do something for me," he snarled.

"S-sure. Anything."

Paul clawed for control, then forced a remorseful smile. "I'm sorry, Brother Duane, but it's been a very upsetting night. It's weak and sinful of me to take it out on you. I pray you'll forgive me."

"Nothing to forgive, Father Paul, we all have bad nights. How can I help?"

"I need you to go to the hotel. In one of the upstairs bedrooms, there is a very evil woman. A traitor to us all. Her daughter is with her and they're both sedated because Satan has ahold of them."

Duane's eyes were wide. "Satan? Here?"

"Yes, Brother Duane. Satan is everywhere. I need you to guard them while I take care of something."

"W-what if they wake up?"

"Keep them quiet until I get back."

•

Sam climbed the porch stairs and pressed himself against the side of the hotel, listening. Clearing a building was a progression of starts and stops; of waiting, watching, straining to hear while your pulse pounded in your ears. Stationary and motionless, you were relatively safe—moving was when it got dangerous. Soldiers knew this, cops knew this, and no matter how many times you'd done it before, fear was always there, spreading malevolent vines that petrified to wood in your heart and soul if you didn't keep moving.

He reached for the knob and turned slowly. The door creaked open onto a dimly lit lobby. Absolute quiet. After a minute frozen in place, he entered and methodically moved deeper into the space, hugging the wall. COD wasn't expecting interlopers—Mike had killed someone and he hadn't been detected—but that was no advantage now. Father Paul would be back for the body and the women and there might be others in the hotel right now. Sam had to proceed as if Hannibal's army was around the next corner. If you didn't anticipate the worst, it usually happened.

With painstaking care, he inched through the lobby, a sitting room with a poker table, a dining room and a kitchen that smelled faintly of bacon. Steady and stealthy. Clear the lower level before you go upstairs, and be prepared. If the women were there, somebody else might be, too, waiting for him.

•

It was torture to Marielle not to be able to touch her daughter, but Serena's breathing was steady and even. She was still alive, still oblivious to this nightmare. It was some consolation.

She had given an Oscar-worthy performance feigning unconsciousness, and that tiny bit of knowledge gave her a slight edge. Father Paul was looking for the man named Glenn, they'd been gone a long time, and she hadn't heard anything else since. This was her only window of opportunity and it was closing fast.

Her wrists were already raw from struggling against the zip ties, but she tried again. She couldn't stop trying. But they were unyielding and she couldn't work the gag out of her mouth, either. Tears of frustration and defeat leaked from the corners of her eyes. If Father Paul came back before she could find a way to escape, there would be no mercy. There was no question about that.

You did it before, you can do it again.

But the last time, she hadn't been bound and gagged. The tears came faster and she fought harder. Until she heard the creak of a stair riser.

Too late, too late, too late.

Her soul tore as she closed her eyes and resumed playing dead.

•

Mike heard the Jeep before he saw it, and scuttled behind the mesquite. It parked in front of the building where Sam Eastwood was, and he didn't have a good feeling about this. This man was dressed just like the dead alien next to him, so he must be one, too. But Sam Eastwood had told him to stay here, so he would. It was disappointing not to be able to kill another one, but he wanted to do the right thing. He took a piece of jerky out of the pouch in his pocket and gnawed on it, pretending he was watching a Clint Eastwood movie.

•

Sam had cleared two bedrooms, and his heart squeezed painfully when he entered the third bedroom. A table lamp illuminated the still figure of Marielle, bound to the bed frame and gagged; Serena was lying lifelessly next to her. There was an open leather case with syringes in it on the bedside table. Jesus God. He hoped he wasn't too late.

The room was small and there were no closets, but he dropped to the floor and shined his penlight under the bed. Nobody there. They were alone, at least for now. He felt some relief when he saw their chests rising and falling. Sedated but not in crisis. But he couldn't carry two of them. "Marielle?" he whispered. "Can you hear me?"

Nothing.

"My name is Sam Easton and I'm going to get you and Serena out of here. If you can hear me, please trust me."

Her eyes fluttered open and she recoiled. His face did that to some people, and after the trauma she'd already been through, he probably looked like another monster to her. "Hi, Marielle. It's going to be okay, but we have to hurry. I'm going to take off your gag and cut the ties on your wrists, it that okay?"

She looked at him with large, brown, liquid eyes. Beautiful eyes filled with ugly pain. She nodded.

"I'm going to have to use a knife on the ties, so don't be afraid."

She nodded again.

He worked the gag off first, then cut the ties. The minute he freed her, she scooped up her daughter and held her tightly while she rocked her and wept.

"Baby, baby, baby, are you okay?" she murmured into her hair. "Wake up, baby."

"Is Serena hurt?"

"No, he drugged us."

"Who is 'he'?"

"Father Paul." She glanced up, still guarded. "I know your name, but who are you?"

"A friend of Lenny's."

Her brows tipped poignantly It seemed to Sam she was someone unaccustomed to kindness. "He's looking for me?"

"Of course he is. He's waiting for you outside the fence and you'll see him when I get you out of here." Sam didn't know the situation with Remy, so he didn't mention that he was waiting, too. "Can you walk?"

"I think so." She slid her legs off the bed, tested them, then stood. She wobbled at first, but gained stability. "I'm a little woozy, but I can do it."

"You can lean on me and I'll carry Serena. There's a friend"—*who happens to be a killer*—"hiding by the hotel waiting to help us, but we have to get out of here now."

They both jumped when they heard a car door slam.

Chapter Forty-Nine

BY THE TIME NOLAN AND CRAWFORD arrived at Lukin's downscaled Russian palace, the Santa Anas had mostly blown themselves out, but they'd left plenty of debris. Crawford kicked away sacrificial vegetation as they walked through the open iron gate and up Lukin's flagstone drive. Lights burned in almost every window— Holmby Hills was still asleep, but the household of the self-appointed tsar certainly wasn't.

"Lukin's groundskeepers aren't up to Bel-Air standards," Crawford observed wryly. "Not very welcoming. I'm a little offended."

"You're doing a fair job cleaning up, Al. Mention it and maybe he'll make you an offer you can't refuse." She rang the bell and this time they weren't greeted by a pert, uniformed maid, but a hatchet-faced boulder of a man in a taut, shiny suit. There were plenty of bulges stretching the fabric, and at least one of them was a gun. A show of power? An attempt at intimidation? She wanted to tell him her gun was bigger than his, but there was no reason to be rude. Besides, it probably wasn't true.

He looked like a violent sociopath who ate puppies for breakfast, but he was surprisingly soft spoken and polite. "Good morning, Detectives. Please follow me. Mr. Lukin is waiting for you in his office."

Nolan again marveled at the vast expanse of polished marble floor and columns, the collection of gilt mirrors in the long hall, and the ornate Baroque furniture. She identified several oil paintings she hadn't noticed before as works by the old masters, certainly originals. If their suspicions about Krasnoport's legitimacy were true, they would all belong to the government soon.

Lukin stood when they entered. "Thank you, Sergei, that will be all." He offered a tight, disinterested smile; it was a very different vibe from the first time they'd met in his grand office. He was either annoyed or on guard. Either way, Nolan liked it. He was uncomfortable, not feeling totally in control, even though he appeared as collected and polished as he had during their initial interview.

"Please have a seat, Detectives." He gestured to a linen-covered table with a silver tea and coffee service and trays laden with fruit, pastries, caviar and blinis, black bread and herring. "A beverage perhaps? A bite to eat?"

All Nolan could think about was a single drop of nerve gas in a cup of tea, on a pastry or a piece of fruit. Or anywhere in this room. "That's very kind, but no, thank you. We're sorry to bother you this early . . ."

"Not at all. I've been up for hours. I don't sleep much as it is, but all this terrible news has made it even more difficult." He sat with a dispirited sigh and sipped from a delicate china cup, then eyed their rumpled clothing. "You've been working all night?"

"Yes."

"I'm grateful to you both for your devotion to Blake's case. And Zoe's. You must have made a determination about their deaths by now."

"They were both murdered."

His face sagged and his shoulders followed in sympathy. "It's impossible to believe. Inexplicable. I hope you're getting close to finding the killer."

"We believe we are."

"Thank God."

"We just have a few questions that we hope will get us there."

"What can I tell you?"

Crawford edged in. "Mr. Lindgren was looking for a woman named Irina Walters. Do you know her?"

His reaction was spontaneous and authentic. "Irina was an old friend from Russia. But I can't imagine why he would be looking for her. Are you sure about that?"

"Very sure. They adopted Michael through her agency Loving Hearts, correct?"

"That's correct."

"She was an old friend, so I guess you recommended her to the Lindgrens?"

"I did. But it was a lifetime ago."

"That puzzles us, too. I mean, what could he want from her after all these years?"

"I can't conceive of a reason."

"So Blake never came to you about this."

"Obviously not. But if he had, I couldn't have helped him. Irina and I had a falling out several years ago and she returned to Russia. I haven't spoken to her since."

"Arguments over the running of Loving Hearts?"

Nolan waited for a tell—a shifting of eyes; a barely discernible panic or an inappropriate fidget—but she was disappointed. Lukin was cool as a block of ice. Or else he was just being honest.

"I had nothing to do with running Loving Hearts."

"But you were vice president from . . ." He looked at Nolan, commencing the handoff.

"Ninety-six to two thousand four." Again, she waited for the ice to melt. And again, he disappointed her by waving a hand dismissively.

"It was an honorary position. I helped an old friend by investing in her business, but it wasn't a formal arrangement. We both agreed I should retain a legal stake until I was remunerated. And I was, in 2004. At that point, I resigned my position. But I never had any input on operations. There was no need for it, she did a brilliant job." He leaned forward on his elbows, his consistently stony face suddenly alive. "She saved hundreds of children from the horror of growing up in post-Soviet orphanages. You can't imagine the conditions; it would sicken the hardest heart. And in the process, she made the dreams of countless childless families in America come true. I was proud to be associated with Loving Hearts."

Nolan was taken aback by his impassioned testimonial, which also seemed genuine. And everything he'd said about his involvement with Loving Hearts so far made sense. Their bogeyman wasn't playing to type. It was time to toss in a little zinger and see how it played. "She did admirable work and you clearly respected her, Mr. Lukin. But back to the falling out. Was that around the time you quit the board, or when the litigation started?"

"Or when Loving Hearts filed bankruptcy in 2011 and Irina fled the country?" Crawford added.

Lukin gave him a sour look. "She didn't flee the country. When it became clear that Putin was going to put a moratorium on Russian adoptions in America, she returned home to continue her advocacy of these poor innocents brutalized by a cruel system."

"Right. So what happened between you two?"

"How could this ancient history possibly matter?"

"Everything matters in a homicide investigation, Mr. Lukin."

He let out an exasperated sigh. "Our disagreement had nothing to do with Blake's or Zoe's murders or Loving Hearts. It was . . . personal. It also precipitated my divorce."

Nolan believed she finally saw a tiny crack in the self-possessed façade. Possibly his first lie, but absolutely a sign that they were treading on thin ice. Crawford was pushing too hard and they couldn't afford to alienate him. She gave him a surreptitious warning look and said to Lukin, "I'm sorry we had to get personal, Mr. Lukin, but when information comes in that could be relevant to a homicide, we have to follow through. The only anomaly in Blake's behavior we could find was his search for Irina Walters, and since there was a connection to you, we needed to hear your perspective. Quite often people know things that seem insignificant to them, but are actually important."

He settled slightly and took a sip from his precious cup. "I understand, Detectives. I would be disappointed if you weren't pursuing these cases with the utmost vigor. Blake and Zoe deserve justice."

"That's our only goal," Crawford said earnestly, consulting his notebook. "With that in mind, just a few more questions if you don't mind?"

"Yes, go ahead."

"Do you know Gregory and Paul Rybakov?"

He lifted his brows with benign curiosity. "I'm acquainted with them and their work. Very impressive."

"At Children of the Desert?"

"Yes. I've made donations to them in the past."

"Through Blue Orb Holdings? Or would that be through Hercules Mining?" Crawford clucked his tongue and tapped his notebook apologetically. "Oh, my mistake. That company is leasing the property to the Rybakovs. You're very invested in the success of Children of the Desert."

"I believe philanthropy is a moral imperative to those who are fortunate enough to be able to give."

"There are a lot of companies under the umbrella of Krasnoport."

He leaned back in his chair and regarded them contemptuously. "You're very well-informed about my business activities, but perhaps not enough to understand that diversification is a key component to success at a certain level. There's nothing diabolical about it."

"We certainly aren't implying that," Nolan interjected. "But an avenue we're pursuing is that Blake had an enemy in one of the companies Krasnoport is associated with. That's the reason for our interest in your business." It was a lie, but it sounded good.

"Krasnoport has no enemies and neither did Blake, I told you that already. Perhaps it's time to pursue another avenue." He checked his large gold watch, which was code for "I'm lawyering up if you ask me one more question, bitches." She couldn't blame him.

"If there's nothing else, Detectives, I have some international phone calls to make."

Nolan knew the sweet spot for cooperation was over, so she decided to go for a Hail Mary and see if his face melted. "You didn't ask how Blake and Zoe Lindgren were murdered. It's all pretty horrible, so we'll be keeping it out of the press for as long as we can, but if that's something you'd like to know for your own closure, we can tell you in confidence."

He blinked reticently. "You told me Blake was drowned."

"Turns out he was dead when he hit the water. He was poisoned. With an organophosphate compound. Since you work with agricultural entities . . . well, that's why we were asking if he'd made any enemies in the course of his job."

"My answer is still no." He shook his head. "Poisoned. That truly is horrible."

"The coroner mentioned nerve gas."

He snuffled in disbelief. "That's ridiculous."

"He seems pretty sure about it. We're waiting for test results."

"Was Zoe also poisoned?"

"She was mutilated," Crawford said.

The color drained from Lukin's face. Even the most accomplished actor couldn't pull off such convincing shock. Nolan was positive he had copious amounts of blood on his hands; she was also positive that none of it belonged to Zoe Lindgren.

Lukin took a shaky breath. "Do you think Blake could have been responsible?"

"Do you?"

"I . . . I can't imagine it."

"Just one more thing, Mr. Lukin, and we'll be on our way." Nolan slid the printout of Dugard's license across his desk. "We believe this man may have had something to do with Blake's murder. Do you recognize him?"

He took the paper and studied it for a long time. It seemed to her that he was vamping for time. When he finally glanced up at them, he looked bewildered. "This picture is poor quality, so I can't be sure."

"But?"

"It looks very much like Paul Rybakov."

"Father Paul?"

"Yes. But he is a charitable man of God, not a murderer. It's just not possible, there's some mistake."

Nolan was tempted to march out the old cliché that anything was possible, but she didn't think the sarcasm would be appreciated. "Thank you very much for your time, Mr. Lukin. We'll leave you to your work."

Chapter Fifty

SAM DIDN'T FORMULATE A PLAN BECAUSE adrenaline and animal instinct took over the moment he heard the car door slam below. Survive or die. Do whatever it takes to save your people. It was the basest essence of human purity and his mind and body were suffused with it.

"Marielle, be still and pretend you're still out, can you do that?"

She gave him an empty, devastating look of terror that felt like a knife wound. Tears were streaming down her cheeks, but she finally nodded.

"Good. You're safe with me, do you believe that?"

She nodded again.

"Don't move, don't open your eyes, not until I say it's safe. Promise me."

"I promise," she whispered.

He hoped she kept her promises. She didn't need to witness another act of violence on top of the litany of nightmares she'd already lived through. Serena was still unconscious, which was a blessing. This would be quick, but it wouldn't be pretty; nothing a child should see. He grabbed a syringe from the bedside table and took his position behind the door, his breath and his heart pacing at the same furious speed.

His vision was preternaturally sharp and his ears were honed to every footstep, every creak of floorboard as he mentally tracked the progress of the unwelcome guest. Adrenaline amplified the sounds to the point of pain, and his coiled muscles screamed for release. He was battle-ready.

The Colt Python was solid and reassuring in his right hand, as was the syringe of sedative in his left. He didn't intend to kill, but an AR15 could be a problem. He had to wait and strike at the right moment, and do it fast.

Whatever it takes to save your people.

Sam held his breath when the footsteps slowed in front of the door. The knob turned, the hinges squeaked, and a man in desert camo carrying a big gun entered quietly. He stopped halfway between the door and bed and grunted, but he didn't seem to sense of presence behind him. As Sam shifted his weight, preparing to pounce, a floorboard creaked, giving away his position.

The man was pivoting as the Colt's butt collided with his skull—hard, but not hard enough for a kill. He dropped to the floor with a resounding thud. Sam counted seconds as he rolled him onto his back, disarmed him, and pocketed the AR's magazine. The man was surprisingly light, almost frail—the anorexic physique of a drug enthusiast. Sam didn't think he would be waking up anytime soon, but he shot the contents of a syringe beneath his tongue as a precaution, then shoved him under the bed.

Marielle was still on her back, her eyes pinched shut, her small body shaking fiercely. For a moment, his memories superimposed an Afghani mother and daughter cowering together on a filthy mattress after his team had liberated a village from a three-month Taliban siege. It was the same scene in the same play with different faces. Violence and trauma and heartbreak weren't bound by language or territory—pain was universal and ubiquitous. It always had been, and Sam knew it would only end when the world did.

"It's time to go, Marielle."

She opened her eyes slowly. "Did you kill him?"

"No."

"Are we safe?"

They had liberated that Afghan village, but a few surviving Taliban had still been lurking in the darkest corners, waiting. His unit had taken fire as they'd pulled out. This place was no different. Marielle needed to know that.

"We won't be safe until we're on the other side of the fence, but I've got your back."

•

Sam's uniform was soaked in sweat, even as the night chill numbed his hands and face. It was flop sweat; fear of failure sweat. He couldn't afford to fail. Fortunately, Serena weighed nothing, and even though Marielle was leaning heavily on him, it didn't slow him down.

As they approached the clump of mesquite where Mike was hiding, he stopped abruptly. No way was he going to let them near the carnage. He lowered Serena gently to the ground, easing Marielle down with her.

"Stay low and wait here," he whispered. "I'll get our friend, he's going to show us the way out. I'll be right back, will you be okay?"

She nodded and tried to smile, but he had the feeling a genuine smile would be a long time coming for her.

"Okay, good, you hang tight." He sent a quick text to Remy: *On the move M and S okay but drugged need medical attention.* Remy responded immediately: *Waiting for you.*

Mike was sitting cross-legged on the ground, looking as peaceful as the Dalai Lama in prayer, even though he was next to the eyeless corpse he'd created. "I didn't move, Sam Eastwood, even when I saw the other alien. I got worried when he went into the building, but you said you'd take care of him."

"You did good, Mike."

"Did you take care of him?"

"He won't be bothering you anymore. Did you see anybody else while you were waiting? More aliens maybe?"

"Uh-uh, nobody else." He gestured to the body next to him. "When I killed him, it made the rest of them weak."

"We need to leave now while they're weak. Can you show us the way out?"

"Yeah."

"But don't mention anything about aliens, okay? We don't want to scare the woman and the little girl."

"I won't."

Chapter Fifty-One

NOLAN AND CRAWFORD WERE INSTINCTIVELY
SILENT as they walked down the drive to their car. The meeting
with Lukin had aroused paranoia in both of them. It was easy to
imagine that the entire property was bugged like a foreign embassy
in Moscow and there were assassins and canisters of nerve gas behind every tree.

As they approached the gate, another beefy man leading a mon-
strous creature that looked part wolf, part bear, part lion, walked
through. If the vicious warning growls were any indication, the beast
didn't appreciate strangers. He dropped the leash, and said sharply,
"Angel, heel!"

But Angel wasn't heeling. Angel was an inappropriately named
maniac hell hound, fighting the leash hard as it lunged, snarled, and
foamed at the mouth with sinister intent.

The handler gave them a disingenuous smile. "I think I have her
under control, go ahead and pass, I'll close the gate behind you."

"You *think* you have her under control?" Crawford snapped, his
face ashen.

"Just walk slowly and don't look at her. She takes that as a challenge."

"What kind of dog is that?" Nolan asked, wincing at Crawford's elbow in her side.

"Let's get out of here, Mags."

The man lifted his chin proudly. "Ovcharka. You might know the breed as Caucasian shepherd. They're very loyal. She is Mr. Lukin's pride and joy."

Her mind was sharply focused on the new vision gelling there. "I suppose patting her is out of the question."

"I don't advise it."

Crawford pulled her away impatiently, and they gave dog and man wide berth. If anything, their passage inflamed Angel's blood-lust. Nolan never wanted to kill an animal, but her hand was firmly on the butt of her Beretta and she suspected Crawford's was on his, too. A methed-out gangbanger was more predictable than a vicious watchdog, and Angel was definitely a working animal, not a pet.

As the gate closed behind them, the handler very deliberately dropped the leash. Angel vaulted down the drive and launched herself against the iron spindles with a resounding crash. Unharmed by the collision, she continued a snarling assault on the gate.

"Asshole," Crawford shouted.

The handler laughed, whistled, and Angel turned away from her intended prey reluctantly and trotted up to him, tail wagging.

Once they were safely in the sedan, Crawford started fuming. "Did you see that? He did that on purpose. Goddammit, that was a message from Lukin, what do you bet?"

"No, I just think Dog Boy is a sadistic cop hater."

"And you're insane, asking to pat a man-eating whatever-the-hell it's called. What was that about?"

"The dog hairs in Blake's suit. I wanted some fur to match up with what Genevieve found so we can search Lukin's car."

Crawford cocked a brow at her. "You think he drove Lindgren to the Bel-Air."

"Lukin or Zoe would be the only two people who could convince Blake to leave his house and she's out of the running. The Bel-Air housekeeper said there was always a big man at the door of the Swan Lake suite, the kind of employees Lukin clearly favors. And he didn't sell Paul Rybakov very well."

Crawford considered. "He did stare at that license for a long time, like he was working out a problem."

"Right. It doesn't make sense that Lukin would ask his pet preacher to come down from Death Valley to kill a man when there are so many candidates available here. I think he threw him under the bus."

"I'm sold on Lukin, but don't count out the pet preacher. They're all one big, nasty family. Goddammit, it really frosts my nuggets that we don't have anything to justify hauling in either of them." Crawford let out a dejected sigh. "Organized crime is a bitch. They work the system better than the system works itself."

Organized crime *was* a bitch. They were up against the same infuriating blockade that Remy had hit with COD. But he had found an illicit solution and was willing to risk his career and Sam Easton's life to execute it. Sam had offered—of course he would—but did consent make it right?

She reeled a little from a sudden wave of queasiness that had nothing to do with pepperoni pizza and everything to do with her intense attraction to a lawman with a wanton disregard for the law when it suited his purpose. She'd put herself in Remy's position when he'd told her about the plan; had fully empathized with him. But when the rubber met the road, would she *really* let Sam risk his life for Max?

Did you forget your own father gladly aided and abetted? Think about that one. Think about right and wrong and how it's not always black-and-white. Or maybe you're just looking for an excuse to keep Remy at arm's length.

She lowered her head and pressed her temples, trying to squeeze away the impending existential crisis. Fucking hell, she was tired.

"Mags, are you okay?"

"Just a headache." She was her mother's daughter, God help her. Time to table the internal ethics dialogue. "We need something we can use. There are two Rybakovs in the stew. Gregory is here in LA. Get an address while I drive. And call Crenshaw division, see if A-1 Auto Supply is on their radar."

Crawford worked his phone while Nolan picked her way through Holmby Hills, dodging more foliage. At a stop sign, a soccer ball rolled slowly across the street in front of them. It reminded her of an eerie telegraphic scene from a horror movie, which seemed appropriate, since they were living in one. As she was about to merge onto the 405, Crawford sighed and pocketed his phone.

"Gregory Rybakov was found dead in his shop two hours ago. Piece of metal in his neck. The detective in charge said it looked like a slaughterhouse. He was also shot in the head. Why am I not surprised?"

"Somebody wanted to leave a strong message."

"Yeah. It definitely wasn't a robbery. They found guns and drugs and stolen vehicles. Shit, at this rate, we're not going to have anybody left to throw in prison."

"We have Lukin and we'll get him." Nolan's phone played Tannhäuser again. Another missed call from Remy, which wreaked havoc with her stomach again. But she wasn't going to stop the car on the 405 to puke. Besides, this was business, and she genuinely cared about what was happening with his sister and niece. She stoically dialed him back and put him on Bluetooth. His voice sounded strange coming out of the car speakers, like he was inside the engine compartment. It also sounded strange because she didn't know if she could trust him anymore. "Do you have news on Marielle and Serena?"

"Sam found them. They're alright and he's working on bringing them out."

Nolan thought he sounded breathless. "That's great. Is everything else okay?"

"Sam found a dead body on the compound with the eyes gouged out. He's with the killer."

"*What?* Who?"

"A local kid who thinks he killed an alien. I figured you'd want to get up here."

"What do you mean Sam's with the killer? Isn't he in custody?"

"He's helping Sam. I'll call Inyo County to handle the homicide once Marielle and Serena are safe. It's a damn long story."

"Listen, Remy, be careful with Inyo County," Crawford warned. "The sheriff is on the board of Children of the Desert. In bed with them, and Father Paul is definitely in bed with Lukin. One or both of them are good for Blake Lindgren's murder, but we can't touch either of them with what we've got."

"Then get on a helicopter. Once Inyo County gets here, this whole place is going to belong to law enforcement. That's your golden hour to corner Father Paul, but if what you say is true, I have a feeling hell is going to break loose here soon. I have to go, but keep me posted and I'll do the same."

Nolan listened to the dead air of an ended call and eased her grip on the steering wheel. For now, she and Remy were on the same side. She glanced at Crawford. "I think it's time to call SAC Daley and read in the feds."

Chapter Fifty-Two

PAUL SLAM-PARKED THE JEEP IN FRONT of the small, windowless warehouse and pounded furiously on the metal door. "Irina! Wake up! Wake the fuck up!"

He finally heard the padding of feet and the click of the lock. She yanked open the door and faced him with a ferocious glare—a tiny dog with a nasty temper. She was swaddled in a Turkish bathrobe and her gray hair was done in a long braid that bristled with wiry strays.

"Calm down and be quiet, you'll wake them," she hissed.

"You have to leave now. The wolves are coming."

She stepped away from the door and gestured him into the anteroom, lit by a single floor lamp. "You've always been too paranoid about Ivan. He doesn't know anything, how could he?"

Paul leaned down until he was almost nose to nose with her. "You have no idea what the fuck has been going on!" he hissed back. "Ivan is suspicious, Gregory is dead, and we will be, too, if you don't *move*!"

She withdrew, shrinking into her robe. "Grisha is dead?"

"*Yes,* Irina. He's dead, dead, dead."

The ferocious glare was back. "Did you kill him?"

"No, Irina, I put him out of his misery after somebody else stuck him in the neck and left him to die like a pig in a slaughterhouse!"

"Who? Ivan didn't do it. He wouldn't—"

"It doesn't matter who did it! I'll help you load the van, then you get the fuck out!" Paul heard an infant begin to fuss and cry, then another. A chain reaction was starting, and an apocalyptic vision began forming in his mind.

"Where are we supposed to go?"

"Get on the road to LA and I'll call you later with a location."

Her gaze hardened. "You're coming with me. There are eight of them, I can't do this alone."

Two more babies started wailing, and Paul felt his last tether to control unraveling. He grabbed her by the neck and shook her hard before dropping his hands and stepping back. It wouldn't do any good to kill her; not now. "I'm not going anywhere. This is *my* place, *my* kingdom. Drug the brats and throw them all in a trash bag, I don't care. Just get them off the property and deliver them."

She swatted at him angrily. "You bastard. Have some compassion."

Volcanic rage welled up from his core and spread like magma through his body. "*Compassion?* I know what you did, Irina. Gregory told me you gave me back to Ivan when that evil bitch Zoe wanted to get rid of me. What kind of compassion was that? What kind of compassion do you think Ivan will have if he finds out you're back here, selling children for us instead of him, you stupid bitch?"

Tears made her eyes sparkle in the dim light. "I've always cared about you, Misha. I always will."

"SHUT UP! I'm not Misha anymore! You made sure of that, so fuck you, Irina."

He watched in incredulity as she pulled a small .38 from the pocket of her robe and waved it at him. "Everything Gregory and I did was for your own good. Look at you now, so rich and successful. You wouldn't have survived if we hadn't made you strong. But you won't survive Ivan. Forget about Children of the Desert. You've lived a dream, but it's time to save what you can and start over."

"I'm not starting over!" he screamed, lunging for the gun.

•

Remy stood at the break in the fence, watching the desert through night vision binoculars, his chest tight, his breathing shallow. He couldn't anticipate how the reunion would go or what eight years away had done to her mind. She hadn't sought him out, so he could only assume she still hated him. Or maybe she didn't even remember him. He had to prepare for the worst.

Lenny had just arrived from his position at the south gate, blissfully unaware of anything except the fact that Marielle and Serena were safe and Sam was bringing them out. He was standing next to him, looking through his own binoculars. "It's going to be okay. They're going to be okay. Goddamn, this worked. I wasn't sure it would."

"I wasn't sure it would, either. They were drugged, so I called an ambulance. How far away is the hospital?"

"Probably coming from Southern Inyo Hospital, which isn't far. They should be here soon. Did you call the police, too?"

"On their way."

"Good. They might take a little longer, depending on where they are this time of night. It's a huge county."

Remy suddenly felt an immense sadness for this gentle, reassuring man. He didn't know Inyo County couldn't be trusted, or that there was a dead body inside and Mike was responsible, but he'd find out soon enough. God, things were a mess. He gritted his teeth against the bitter words he had to say. "Lenny, Mike is in there, too. He's showing them the way out."

The old man's face worked through a catalog of emotions before settling on bewilderment. "That can't be. Why would Mike be in there?"

"He told Sam he was hunting aliens."

"I guess that makes sense. He's obsessed with them."

"There are some serious things going down and I've got a lot to deal with here that can't wait. Will you follow them to the hospital?"

"Of course I will."

"Take Mike with you."

"I can drop him at home."

"No. I want both of you far away from here for a while."

Lenny shoved his hands in his jacket pockets and looked at him anxiously. "There's plenty you're not telling me, Detective Beaudreau."

"That's true, and I'm sorry for that. But it's better this way for now. Will you trust me?"

"I trust you."

They both froze when a gunshot rang in the still night air. Small arms fire, coming from the north side. After long minutes of breathless waiting without another report, Lenny finally spoke.

"I don't know what all is going on here, but I'm going to be happy to get out of here."

"I will be, too."

They both resumed their silent vigil and after what seemed like a millennium, Remy finally saw them, a collection of specks growing closer. He held his breath as they gradually came into focus. A frail man was leading the way—obviously Mike, the implausible, confirmed killer of one by mutilation. Possibly the killer of Zoe Lindgren. Behind him was Sam, carrying a little girl. His niece. And Charlotte, leaning on him for support; thinner than he'd ever seen her but still beautiful. He remembered to breathe and felt something inside come apart. The only thing holding him together was the screaming tension in his muscles.

He didn't realize his feet were moving, but he was suddenly at the fence. Charlotte's face was haggard with worry, her empty eyes darting in every direction—the look of someone who was acquainted with horror—and a trembling rage shuddered through his body.

But when her eyes finally lighted on him, her expression smoothed.

She stopped a few feet from the fence and stared at him uncertainly as tears began running down her cheeks. "Remy?"

He swallowed the boulder in his throat. "I never stopped looking for you, Charlotte."

Sam's face was tight, eyes downcast, relinquishing his right to witness this moment. He helped her through the fence and Remy wrapped his arms around her tightly without a single thought that she might recoil. She softened in his embrace and collapsed against his chest, her slight body and tears warming him. He had no idea how he'd managed to keep himself from breaking into a million shards, but he did, even when she looked up at him with a faint smile; even when she reached out her hand to Lenny.

Chapter Fifty-Three

ALL THE BABIES WERE WAILING NOW, but Paul could only hear the roar of uncontrollable fury in his ears. He was standing over Irina, pressing her own gun to her temple. "Don't you ever point a gun at me."

"You broke my arm."

"Shut up and consider yourself lucky." He slammed his hand over her mouth and smashed the gun against her arm, relishing the sound of her muffled, agonized scream. "Maybe next time I'll hold your hands to a hot frying pan until they smell like roast pork, you fucking bitch, see how you like it. I'm taking my hand off your mouth now. If you scream, you're dead."

She whimpered, but didn't scream. "I didn't do that . . ."

"But you watched."

"You wouldn't stop starting fires, we had to teach you—"

"Shut UP!"

She curled into a defensive ball. "You were a monster. If Zoe hadn't given you back to us, you would have rotted in an institution."

"Better than what I had. But you couldn't risk that because the adoption papers would be scrutinized. I know how this works." He delighted in smacking her arm again. "You are an evil woman, like Zoe. I think you should share her fate. God would like that."

"What did you do?"

"I threw her away, just like she threw me away, and it was rapture. After all these years, she recognized me, Irina. I walked right into her house and she recognized me. I wish you could have been there to see the shock and fear in her eyes. It was glorious, but eventually I had to remove them." His lips writhed into a cruel smile. "'*And if your eye causes you to sin, gouge it out.*' Matthew said that. Now get up and do what I told you. Shut them up, get them into the van, and leave so I can go to the chapel and pray."

As Irina scrambled to her feet, his phone chirped and he snatched it from his pocket. Probably Sister Carina with something else to whine about. The sheriff's name on the caller ID gave him pause, but he didn't answer. Whatever he wanted, it could wait.

Paul spun around when he heard the Jeep, his heart battering the inside of his chest. He pocketed the gun and walked into the wash of headlights, slamming the door behind him. It was Karl Hetson, the dumbest in his army.

"Father Paul? Are you okay? I heard a gunshot." The confusion on his face made him look even more brainless. "Do I hear babies?"

"Yes, Brother Karl," he said with impressive serenity gilded with just the right amount of distress. "Some of the residents have some very sick children. I'm bringing them for medical attention."

"Oh. The gunshot?"

"A careless accident. Where are the rest of the men?"

"I'm the only one on besides Glenn and Duane and I don't know where they are. We're shorthanded, you know." His small, furtive eyes swept over the building. "Are you sure you don't need help?"

"Yes, I'm sure. Go back to your post."

"Sure thing." He took one last, troubled look around before he drove away.

•

It was agony to watch the ambulance drive away. Remy felt like his heart was chained to the bumper and with each revolution of the tires, it ripped a little more. After eight years, a few minutes hadn't been enough. He should have been grateful Charlotte recognized him and hadn't spit in his face, but that would have made this easier. All the questions, all the unspoken words that gorged his brain would have to wait. But he had to let it go for now. They were finally safe, and that's what mattered.

Sam stood quietly next to him—a solid, consoling presence. "She's in shock now, but they're both going to be okay," he finally said.

"God, I hope so."

"It's going to be a process, but you'll untangle things and find your way. I know about having patience when things go to shit. It's the hardest thing in the world, but don't give up. Jesus, I sound like my shrink. Sorry."

"Don't be." Remy took a deep breath and turned to look at him. "I owe you a hell of a lot more than a bottle of whiskey. It's overwhelming."

"You don't owe me anything. Just get the fucker who took them."

"There's a lot more happening here, Sam. Dangerous things."

"We figured it was a pit of vipers coming in. I guess there's some consolation in being right."

"We can't trust the sheriff, either. He's up to his neck in this."

"What can I do to help?"

"We support Maggie and Al, they're on their way in a chopper. I don't know the half of it or how this is going to shake out, but be prepared for anything."

"What are you going to tell the sheriff when he gets here?"

"Enough to scare the shit out of him. Once I'm finished, that dead body is going to be the last thing on his mind. He'll be thinking about the dangerous people on this property and the possibility of doing prison time himself. When they show up, get in my Porsche and stay put, I'm keeping you out of this."

"You can't forever."

"I can't do any of this forever, but it's what needs to be done now. When I get Sheriff Brandeis squared away, you and I will lead a few squads and go to the north gate to make sure no one gets out from that end. I'll brief you on everything I know on the way."

Sam looked around at the vista spread before him. He came here to run because it was a safe analogue to Afghanistan, but not tonight. "It's too quiet."

"I don't like it, either."

•

When Karl saw the flashing police bars by the gate, he slammed on the brakes, killed the headlights, and backed the Jeep into the shadow of one of the warehouses. A gunshot, crying babies, and now the cops. Maybe he wasn't the brightest boy Ma Hetson had raised, but he was smart enough to know this was big trouble. Time to get the hell out of here. Father Paul was an asshole anyway. Let him deal with his own shit.

Chapter Fifty-Four

NOLAN WATCHED THE CHOPPER'S SPOTLIGHT WASH over the desert, exposing the desolate landscape in ghostly magnesium white. The silhouette of mountains lifted from the rocky ground, looking like a giant's pile of stones. The steady thump of the rotors had penetrated her bones and her entire body felt like it was coupled with the frequency. She wondered if she'd ever stop vibrating.

In the distance, she finally saw pinpricks of light punctuate the incessant darkness, then felt the bird gently arc toward them.

"Seven minutes out." The pilot's voice came through the headphones. "Check two o'clock. Looks like you'll have a ride."

She and Crawford both saw the pulsing red and blue lights, barely discernible but growing in size quickly as they sliced through the air. Their presence would be audible now and she wondered what Father Paul would think of that.

•

Remy watched through the borrowed squad's window as Maggie and Al disembarked and crouched, buffeted by the wash of the rotors and sand as they scuttled out of range of the blades. He jogged to meet them as the bird lifted back up into the fading stars. "Good to see you two." He pointed to the east, where the horizon was just barely beginning to show pale pink. "Just in time for a desert sunrise."

In spite of her exhaustion and rattled bones, Nolan smiled. "I hope that's the most exciting thing that happens here. What's the status?"

Remy took a deep breath and tried to keep his voice steady and regular. "Marielle and Serena are okay. They're on their way to the hospital to get checked out. Sam is at the north gate with three squads. All is quiet and it bothers us that nobody has shown themselves yet. Inyo came in silent but somebody had to have seen the lights by now. And if they didn't, the helicopter would have pricked up their ears."

"No sign of Father Paul, then?"

"No sign of anybody."

"If he was smart, he'd go hide in the retreat center. He knows we won't touch that because of the guests."

"Or he'll bolt. He has five miles of perimeter to choose from. We can't cover it all. We can't cover a thousandth of it."

"Where's our killer?"

"At the hospital with Marielle and Serena and Lenny."

"He's hurt?"

"I got him out of the hornets' nest for now. There's too much going on and he's not going anywhere. He's very mentally impaired. He genuinely believes he killed an alien."

"If he's so impaired, how would he have gotten to LA to kill Zoe Lindgren?"

"He can drive. And if he thought she was an alien, then it would have been a serious mission. You'll see for yourself." He offered Maggie the front seat while Al climbed in behind the cage. "Sheriff Brandeis is here. I had a conversation with him. He's scared, so keep an eye on him. He might not be the only one who bolts."

As they approached the small grouping of squads, they saw headlights from inside the fence. A few moments later, they could all make out a speeding brown van, shimmying in the sand as it barreled toward them. It stopped abruptly but no one got out.

"Oh, shit," Crawford muttered. "Might be showtime."

Remy stomped on the accelerator. By the time they reached the gate, Sam and the officers were crouched behind open car doors, their weapons drawn. Floodlights were trained on the van and one of the officers was calling on a bullhorn. "Let us see your hands!"

No movement. Then a shrill, muffled scream. Remy grabbed the shotgun from the rack and clambered out; Nolan and Crawford followed and took positions of safety.

The bullhorn split the silence again, but no response this time.

Sam turned and gestured to them, then pointed to the fence. *Should I go in?*

Remy shook his head. *Wait.*

The bullhorn.

The wait.

Another high, thin scream.

•

Nolan was staring down the sight of her gun, her eyes aching from not blinking. An inky corona started to bleed into her peripheral vision, like the aperture of a camera slowly closing. Exhaustion and tension. Fear. She shook her head and rebooted her vision.

She was thinking of Beverly Hills, it was impossible not to. And Sam was thinking of Afghanistan, she knew it. When he'd turned toward them, his face was transmuted into something she'd never seen before. Maybe that's exactly what her face looked like.

Rocks were digging into her knees, but the pain kept her sharp. Even in the chill of the desert, her hands were slimy with sweat. She was vaguely aware of a sharp orange line tracing the tops of the mountains. *Just in time for a desert sunrise. Please God, don't let it be my last one. Don't let it be anybody's.*

But this *was* somebody's last stand and they would fight for it. The captain always went down with the ship and . . .

. . . *if he was smart, he'd go hide in the retreat center.*

The last stand. The retreat center. The guests. Holy Mary, Mother of God, that's what cult leaders did . . .

She spun in her crouch like a dervish. "Nerve gas," she hissed at Remy and Crawford. "What if he's going to take everybody down with him?"

Abject shock registered on their faces; they were frozen in a horrific moment. Then the bullhorn bellowed again and they all jumped.

"PLEASE STEP OUT OF THE VEHICLE AND KEEP YOUR HANDS IN THE AIR!"

Nolan watched breathlessly as two trembling hands emerged from the driver's side window. It all came out in a rush when she saw a tiny old woman in a bathrobe step out of the van and into the sand. Agonized wails, no longer muffled, followed her.

"I'm injured and I have sick children," she called weakly, dropping to her knees.

"Irina Walters," Nolan whispered.

Chapter Fifty-Five

PAUL USED TO DREAM OF A cliff above an angry, churning ocean. The jagged, frothy swells were voracious teeth, waiting to devour him. Always, the cliff would start to crumble beneath his feet, sending a shower of rocks into the ravenous maw. Finally, the last piece of earth would give way and he would plummet down, down, down. But he always woke up before he hit the water. He'd always wondered what would happen if he didn't wake up. Would he die?

As he stared at the empty bed, he thought he might find out.

He snatched Duane's discarded AR15 and smashed a lamp with such fury, splinters of amber glass sprayed across the full length of the room and ticked against a far window. Then he saw the combat boot and part of a camouflage-clad leg protruding from beneath the bed.

He dragged out Duane's limp body and slapped him over and over. "WHERE ARE THEY? WHO DID THIS?"

But that was a stupid question. He knew. The *byki* were fucking with him. He was their entertainment for the night.

He propped Duane up against the bed for a better angle and slapped harder, but his head was dead weight and just lolled back and forth with the force of the blows. He let him drop to the floor when a faint thump-thump-thump entered the outer fringes of his hearing. A helicopter. Ivan. Ivan, you motherfucker . . .

Suddenly, an internal switch snapped and the rage leached from him. He was too exhausted to sustain it any longer. A numbness replaced it and he sat down on the bed, staring at the broken glass sparkling on the floor. The prisms of light seemed to glow and pulse and he took this as an augury of lucidity and truth. He prayed for it until it was revealed to him in a single, breathtaking moment. Ivan wouldn't come *ever*; certainly not when his *byki* were already here. He had planes, but not a helicopter. No, it wasn't Ivan swooping in. That left only one other possibility: *bitch cop daughter.*

He felt the laughter bubble up slowly, break from his lips, then rise to a hysterical, howling crescendo that brought tears to his eyes. It was a heartbreaking tragedy that Emily wasn't still here, that would have been so beautiful. But any one of his lambs would do. He fumbled for his phone.

"Sister Carina, I need you to come to the chapel immediately and pray with me."

•

Boxes of babies. Screaming babies. Jesus Christ.

Nolan wanted to retch, but she didn't. Another cop was doing that for all of them. Sam, Remy, and Crawford were stone-faced as they lifted pairs of flailing infants and held them close as they carried them to squads that would take them to the hospital. No time to wait for ambulances.

A young Inyo County officer who wasn't puking took the last two. Tears rained down his cheeks. She hoped he didn't feel like an idiot for crying. The kids always got you. They'd all been there before getting used to ugly; probably Sam most of all. Which begged a deeply troubling question: how did you get used to ugly? Did you have to lose part of your humanity to cross the Rubicon?

The hideous monster cloaked in the small body of an old woman was still crumpled on the ground, weeping now. The missing cog in a convoluted gear. Maybe not the key to everything, but she was definitely a key to something.

"Irina Walters?"

She nodded and wiped her face. "I was a prisoner here."

Bullshit. "I know who you are and what you are. I know about Lukin and Loving Hearts and Children of the Desert. You sell children. Traffic them. That's a federal offense and it should carry the death penalty as far as I'm concerned."

"I save them from worse," she mewled.

Nolan knew she was showboating and felt a depth of violence that sickened her. "Ivan Lukin gave me the same line. He actually stood up for you. Was your falling out because you decided to line Father Paul's pockets instead of his? Did he give you a bigger cut?"

She blinked and remained mute.

"You can stop acting. Tell me where Father Paul is."

The red, rheumy eyes sharpened. They were calculating; doing damage assessment. "I won't tell you anything. Why should I?"

"Because things aren't going to go well for you, but I can make them worse. You belong to the feds now. Maybe you know enough to cut a deal. Or maybe you'll rot in prison. I really don't care, you're not my problem. But if you cooperate, I can make a recommendation." Even if she did, it wouldn't matter. Hopefully, Irina Walters didn't know that.

"You need me."

"And you need me. Father Paul. Paul Rybakov. Where is he?"

Her face registered mild surprise even as her shoulders slumped in defeat. "He told me he was going to the chapel to pray."

"Was Gregory Rybakov his father?"

"He would very much hate to hear that."

"Why?"

"Gregory was an adoptive father. He raised him in Russia. Paul didn't appreciate his parenting skills."

"So he killed him?"

She averted her eyes. "I wouldn't know."

"Blake Lindgren was looking for you. Did you know that?"

She looked genuinely puzzled. "No."

"You placed Michael with the Lindgrens."

"So?"

"So, they were both murdered. Do you know why?"

She looked away again.

"Did Ivan Lukin kill them?"

"I don't know. Am I under arrest?"

"You will be."

"Then I want an attorney."

"You don't have a right to one yet. Is Michael Lindgren still alive?"

Her face cleared and Nolan thought she saw a hint of amusement in her eyes. "You don't know as much as you think you do."

"Then edify me."

The corner of her mouth trembled. A smile? A *fucking* smile? Nolan fumed inside, where there was a piece of tinder waiting to ignite.

"You'd better go find Father Paul. He's not very stable right now, so I would be very cautious how you approach him. He broke my arm, but you? He would do worse."

"The feds are on their way. They don't show mercy to people like you. Are you going to take your chances with them or are you going to tell me what I want to know? I'm driving the bargain right now, so think carefully."

Her face hardened. "You'll help me?"

"I'll do what I can, you have my word."

"What do you want to know?"

"Is Michael Lindgren alive?"

That glimmer of a smile again. Nolan wanted to take it off her face with the butt of her Beretta.

"He's in the chapel."

"With Father Paul?"

"Michael Lindgren *is* Father Paul."

Nolan tried to keep her expression impassive, but her brain was in full chaos; a riot of shattered fragments reforming into something new. Crawford tensed next to her, his expression fixed in stunned disbelief. "Blake found out he was alive. That's why he was looking for you," she finally said.

Irina's eyes widened. "Zoe must have finally confessed after all these years. He would have gone to Ivan first for answers, and that was his death warrant."

"Confessed what?" Crawford barked.

"The kidnapping."

"Tell us."

She released a heavy sigh of resignation. "It was Ivan's idea, I had nothing to do with it. Zoe didn't know what to do with Misha, he was a terrible, hopeless case. So violent. Dangerous, even as a ten-year-old boy. I'm sure he would have killed them eventually. Zoe called him when Blake was out of town. They made arrangements to get him out of the country."

Nolan's mouth was as dry as the sand beneath her feet. "Why kidnap him, for God's sake? He could have been institutionalized and rehabilitated, or placed in another home."

"That would have brought up inconvenient questions about the adoption. Ivan couldn't risk the papers being scrutinized. It was big business for him."

"Jesus Christ." Crawford spat.

Irina looked at him impassively before continuing. "And Blake loved that boy, he couldn't know Zoe wanted to discard him like a piece of trash. Ivan is a fiend," she said venomously. "He had the revolutionary idea that he would be able to use Misha if he had the proper discipline and instruction. He was right."

Everything came crashing together: the rampant alcoholism, the sudden divorce, the hatred Blake had for Zoe, according to Roan Donnelly. The guilt was killing her, so she confessed and started this madness. And then her son found her. "Did Michael know his own mother arranged for the kidnapping?"

"Gregory told him at some point, I don't know when. I didn't know that until tonight."

"Did he kill Zoe Lindgren?"

She blanched and shivered. "Yes. He told me how, then quoted the Bible: 'And if your eye causes you to sin, gouge it out.'"

Nolan took a startled breath. Who the hell was the other killer at the hospital? She pulled the fake driver's license photo from her pocket and showed it to Irina. "Is this Father Paul?"

"No. I don't know who that is, but he looks like one of Ivan's."

"One of Ivan's what?"

Irina's eyes flared in anger. "Misha was Ivan's first experiment, but he wasn't the last."

•

Paul was kneeling at the altar, praying over a line of cocaine. The tools of the Lord were spread before him on the chancel floor: a handgun, an AR15, a pyramid of desert-dried wood, and a perfume bottle filled with VX. He hoped bitch cop daughter would like the scent.

Sister Carina was kneeling next to him, eagerly awaiting her turn at the straw. "Why are they persecuting us, Father Paul?"

"True servants of God have always been persecuted, for all time. The unholy, the blasphemers, the goats of Satan fear us, so they try to destroy us. But the Lord will not forsake us. We will inherit the Kingdom of Heaven, and they will inherit a lake of fire. 'I will strew your flesh upon the mountains and fill the valleys with your carcass.'"

"Ezekiel."

"Very good."

His little lamb frowned in consternation. "Ezekiel prophesied great slaughter and conflagrations before the second coming."

"It's the Word. Things must be torn down before they can be rebuilt; all sinners scorched from the face of the Earth before Heaven can reign again. The righteous will survive the trials to rise from the ashes and remake the world in God's image."

Her eyes darted nervously to the pyre he'd gathered near the altar.

"The Lord gave us free will, Sister Carina," he explained patiently. "Sometimes we have to nudge things along."

"Is this the end of days, Father Paul? The Consummation?"

"No one knows the hour of Christ's coming, Sister Carina," he said, setting up a line and passing her the straw.

Chapter Fifty-Six

NOLAN, CRAWFORD, REMY, AND SAM WATCHED in dull, mute shock as Irina Walters was taken into custody. There were a million words in their minds and on their tongues, but they weren't ready for voices yet.

One of the Inyo deputies approached. Nolan recognized him as the man who'd cried while carrying the babies. "We're short a few squads now, Detectives, so I'll give you all a ride to the compound. Ready when you are."

"Thank you, Officer," she said dully.

Remy gestured to his Porsche. "Sam and I will take my car. Follow us, we know where the chapel is."

Sam didn't hear him. He was too consumed with pulling together pieces from his recent memory that formed a chilling possibility.

"Sam?" Nolan's hand on his arm startled him back to the present. "Are you okay?"

"I don't think so. That Bible verse Irina quoted, about the eyes?"

"What about it?"

"Mike, the man who killed the soldier here, said the same thing when he was showing me the body. But the way he is, he wouldn't know that quote unless someone had taught him. He's obsessed with aliens, but I don't think killing anything by gouging out their eyes

with a screwdriver would cross his mind, either, not without instruction." Sam looked at the horrified faces of people he now considered
friends. "He was adopted, too, and his mother didn't know his history, but she told Lenny he was always scrambled. That's the way she
put it. He knows Father Paul. Mike didn't kill Zoe Lindgren, but . . ."
His words trailed away and died.

Nolan felt all the blood drain from her face. "Ivan might not be
the only who was training vulnerables to kill."

Crawford revived and twirled a finger in the air urgently "Come
on, let's go get this bastard."

Sam fought nausea as he buckled himself into the Porsche and felt
the familiar pressure of the seat belt against his chest as the powerful
engine launched them forward. "This is worse than I thought, Remy.
Worse than I could have imagined."

"We're all a little shell-shocked," Remy said grimly. "No offense."

"I was wrong, thinking you had to experience combat to see
atrocities. But that's short-term, you've made a career of it. How do
you cope?"

"Same way as you, Sam. I muddle through the best I can. Me? I
drink too much, I don't let people in, and I fly my drones. I visualize
them carrying the bad away. Sounds mawkish, but they help more
than martinis."

He sighed heavily, trying to let some things go. "Maybe I should
give it a shot."

"Anytime, Sam."

"Father Paul isn't going to go quietly."

"I don't think he will."

"When we get there, I'll recon the chapel. You're going to need
as much information as possible before you decide on an approach."

"You've done enough, Sam. Too much. We all want you out of
harm's way."

"That's not going to happen and you know it. Besides, I don't take
orders from civilians."

"I figured that out. You're so goddamned stubborn, but I'm

grateful for it." Remy punched the accelerator and let the Porsche fly faster.

•

The sun was a smooth, orange disk rising in the sky by the time they'd all arrived at the chapel. Now, a half-hour later, the day's new light warmed Nolan's face and glanced off the stained-glass windows, shooting rainbows that vied with the multihued sky. Desert sunrises were indeed something to behold, as were glowing, stained-glass panels, but there was nothing holy about these. She would never look at a church the same way again. This job didn't just follow you home, it dogged you for the rest of your life, chipping away at beauty and small pleasures along the way. Something they didn't mention at the academy. If they did, the washout rate would be higher.

Next to the chapel was the hotel where Marielle and Serena had been held, and beyond that, the crime scene, where Remy was having a discussion with Sheriff Brandeis, a square man carrying a heavy gut. His world was crumbling around him, and she wondered if he knew it yet. His slumped posture indicated that he might. Scumbag.

A fresh fleet of squads had arrived, courtesy of Scumbag. Some had been dispatched to the retreat center to make sure the guests stayed safely inside; some were patrolling the five-mile perimeter, watching for rats fleeing a sinking ship. The rest had positioned themselves around the chapel, attentive to Crawford as he made his rounds and briefed them on their hastily conceived plan.

Sam appeared from behind a corner of the chapel and headed toward her, his gait purposeful. He was in his element, she realized. Possibly even happy. She now understood what Remy had been up against, and why he'd committed the unpardonable violation of putting a civilian in harm's way. Sam didn't consider himself a civilian, and he didn't give a damn about regulations or their continued exhortations to stand down. He didn't even give a damn about the possibility of nerve gas. Taking him out of the picture would have required disarming him and locking him up in the back of a patrol car, which wouldn't have held him long, even without a gun, as he'd blithely pointed out. She also knew why her father had been complicit in the rescue plan. He understood a man like Sam. He *was* a man like Sam.

"There are no windows in the chapel except for the stained glass, but there's a side entrance. I found a camera there and disabled it, Detective, but I'm sure there are more. I couldn't hear anything through the door, but that doesn't mean anything. If there are hostages, they're going to be quiet. If it comes to a confrontation, I could breach that door while Father Paul is focused on you at the front. If he's armed, and I assume he is, he won't know where to shoot first."

"That's an absolute last resort. We called the feds and a critical response team is on the way here."

"What's their ETA?"

"They're an hour out, but we don't have that kind of time if there are hostages. We'll make initial contact and assess the situation from there. This is a seat-of-the-pants operation. Fluid, you'd call it?"

"I think your description is more accurate." He nodded toward the crime scene. "Looks like Brandeis is on his way over. I'll make myself scarce."

"You stay right where you are, you're a part of this."

Sheriff Brandeis's gait was unsteady. He'd just spent some time with a body and he probably wasn't used to that. "Detective Nolan, your colleague briefed me on everything. Hell of a situation we have here. And I'll tell you as I told him—no offense intended—but I really can't see Father Paul being a danger to anyone."

Nolan was unreasonably fixated on the pearls of sweat clinging on his upper lip. "And I'm sure my colleague told you, Father Paul is not who you think he is, Sheriff. Consider him armed and very dangerous."

Brandeis looked like he wanted to crawl out of his large skin.

"Thank you for calling up more officers."

"We'll offer you every courtesy we can," he said stiffly.

"And we appreciate that. Did my colleague also tell you that federal agents are on the way?"

His florid face went gray. "Is that really necessary?"

"Father Paul is a killer, Sheriff, and he may be holding hostages in that chapel. We will attempt to resolve this without incident, but I think backup is very necessary. We need to borrow tac gear. I'm sure that won't be a problem."

"Detective, there has to be a misunderstanding. Let me call Father Paul first. If he's in there, I'm sure he'll come out of his own accord."

"Please do." She waved Remy and Crawford over while Brandeis fumbled with his phone. "Put it on speaker, Sheriff."

The phone rang and rang, but finally a deep voice answered. "Good morning, Sheriff. I see from my cameras that weren't destroyed that there are a lot of police in my compound, which is private property. Is there a problem? Should I call my attorney?"

Brandeis was sweating copiously now. "I just want to talk to you, Father Paul. Where are you?"

"I'm in the chapel praying. At least I was until you interrupted me."

"Come on out, let's have a chat."

A low chuckle emanated from the phone. "I'm really not in the mood for a chat." The phone clicked. Dead air. The silence of the desert.

Chapter Fifty-Seven

NOLAN FELT AN ADRENALINE FRISSON HUMMING through her body as she took her position at one side of the chapel's double doors, Crawford on the other. His warm, likable face was now taut and severe. Remy was a few feet back, gun drawn; Sam was at the side entrance he'd reconned earlier, waiting for a signal to enter if it came to that, which she prayed it wouldn't. Inyo County officers and squads were in place around the chapel, but Sheriff Brandeis was notably absent—an outrage. He'd deserted his men and women at the most critical moment of an Old West showdown, probably to take care of some dirty laundry before the entire compound became a federal crime scene. He was worse than a scumbag.

Nolan squelched her thoughts, focused, then nodded at Crawford. Go-time. She reached out and rapped hard on the big redwood door, keeping her body clear of the shooting zone if things were going to go down that way. "Paul Rybakov?"

No response. She rapped again.

"Paul Rybakov, LAPD! We need to speak with you."

"Ah, Detective Nolan. I recognize your voice from the recording of your conversation with your mother. So does Sister Carina. You spoke with her earlier."

She could hear him clearly, but his voice was distant. Technically, it didn't matter—bullets traveled a long way—but there was something reassuring about knowing he wasn't right on the other side of the door. "Sister Carina, are you in there?"

"Say hello to the detective, Sister."

"Hello, Detective," she parroted.

Nolan shivered at their cool, detached voices; at the image of a gun pressed into Sister Carina's temple. "Are you in danger?"

"No, but you are."

The voice wasn't cool anymore, but young and petulant. A bratty child defending her twisted deacon.

"It seems your family emergency was very short-lived, Detective. I'm glad for that. But I was very sorry to see your mother leave. We had some meaningful time together. She had a lot to say about you and Max."

Nolan recognized the blatant manipulation and ground her teeth together to keep the anger inside. "Irina had a lot to say about you, too, Father Paul. Or would you prefer Misha?"

Another moment of silence. She imagined he was momentarily stunned. "Misha is dead. And reborn."

"Your father Gregory is dead, too, but there's no rebirth in his future."

"HE'S NOT MY FATHER!"

A very sore spot. Irina had made herself useful. "How about your other father, Blake Lindgren? He's also dead. Nerve gas, the coroner told us. Ivan Lukin said you did it and I can't blame you, him tossing you out like a rotten piece of meat and sending you back to Russia."

"Blake didn't have anything to do with that!"

He was unraveling as she baited him, forcing access to realities that probably hadn't been in his psychological repertory for years. Dangerous. Productive? Hopefully.

"Is nerve gas something you keep on hand in your warehouses along with guns and drugs and babies?"

"I didn't kill him! Ivan is a lying goat of Satan."

"But you killed Zoe. Gouged her eyes out. There's a Bible verse for that. Irina quoted it."

"Zoe was a sow of Satan. So is Irina. Evil women."

Nolan couldn't argue with that, although it was stultifying that he didn't recognize evil in himself. But then, sociopaths never did.

"Were Marielle and Serena evil, too? Is that why you kidnapped them?"

"I didn't kidnap them, I brought them home."

The calm conviction in his voice was chilling. "And drugged them and tied them to a bed. Nice homecoming. I know you'll be happy to hear they're alright and at the hospital now. I'm sure they'll have a lot to say, but frankly, Father Paul, you're screwed no matter what they say."

"You know, Detective, this really isn't going anywhere."

"No, it's not. And neither are you. If you have weapons, lay them down and get on the floor facedown, both of you. We're coming in."

She heard a strange cackling. "I wouldn't do that if I were you, Detective Nolan. I don't want to kill Sister Carina, but I will."

There was a whimpering protest that was silenced immediately. "What do you want?"

"I want my kingdom."

"You never had a kingdom. This belongs to Ivan Lukin. It always has. You're just an employee."

"IT BELONGS TO ME! I CREATED IT OUT OF NOTHING!"

"Let Sister Carina go and we'll talk."

"In good faith, I'm sure. On second thought, you're welcome to come in. Do you like perfume, Detective Nolan?"

"Very amusing. A woman named Dawn Sturgess died the same way Blake Lindgren did after someone gave her a perfume bottle."

"You certainly do your research. You also have a very active fantasy life. Children of the Desert is here to do God's work, not kill people. Unlike you and your law enforcement friends."

"Then why did you ask me if I liked perfume?"

"You're done, Father Paul, it's over!" Crawford exploded, startling her. "Drop your weapons and get down on the floor NOW."

"Alright, if you insist. Please come in." He chuckled. "Of course, how would you know if I did put down my weapons?"

They couldn't know, and that was a problem. Nolan looked at Crawford, then at Remy, and nodded toward the side of the building where Sam was waiting. Maybe Father Paul was delusional enough to think his trap would work, but he wouldn't be expecting theirs.

•

Sam was crouched on the ground, parallel to the door when Remy gave him the signal. He'd been listening to the dialogue, and Father Paul scared him. This time, there *was* an enemy combatant inside—an unstable, unpredictable megalomaniac, decompensating in a spectacular way—exactly like the fervid maniacs he'd pursued in another life.

As he aimed his Colt at the door's lock assembly, he caught a faint whiff of smoke. *He's burning down his temple. Dying for a cause. And he'll take as many people with him as he can. Go. Go now.*

Go now! Shaggy and Wilson flanking him; Rondo and Kev taking up the rear. Let's toast these sons of bitches . . .

Sam gasped and swallowed the distant memories so they stayed deep inside. He watched the orange flash bloom at the end of his Colt as it shattered the lock and splintered the door. When he kicked it down, he saw flames licking at the altar where a tall man in a white robe and a young woman stood, facing the front. They both spun as Sam shouted, "GET DOWN!"

Father Paul lifted an AR15 and Sam fired twice, shattering his forearm, just as he'd planned to do. The gun dropped to the ground, followed by the man, his wide eyes staring in fearful disbelief. "The man with the melted face. Who are you?"

Your worst nightmare and every other cliché you ever thought of. Go ahead. Make my day. This one's for you, Mike.

The flames were spreading fast; too fast. "Fire!" Sam shouted, and the woman named Sister Carina howled and bolted toward the front doors as they burst open. Nolan and Crawford charged in, Remy behind them.

"DOWN ON THE GROUND!" Nolan screamed—an ethereal, banshee call.

The girl dropped to her knees, and Crawford half-dragged, half-carried her out while Nolan stood her ground, gun aimed at Father Paul. Remy covered her from the side, and Sam knew he wanted to take a shot and end this, just like he did. But it was Nolan's gambit, so they waited.

Father Paul rose unsteadily. His ruined arm had stained his robe red, but his face was placid—there was no indication of the excruciating agony he should have been feeling. Flames at the altar were growing, rising toward the ceiling, feeding off the desiccated redwood beams above. Then Sam saw Father Paul's good arm lob a small, cut glass bottle into the air; the trajectory was straight and true, heading directly toward Detective Nolan.

He launched himself into space and he was in college again, leaping to catch a hard drive to left field before it hit the ground. *Get it get it get it don't fuck up this time.* Then fast-forward in time, Wilson shouting, *"Incoming!"*

Sam screamed above the voice of memory—"RUN, MAGGIE!"— then landed hard on his elbows, palms still upturned.

Pray for us sinners now . . .

Nolan was frozen in place.

And at the hour of our death . . .

He felt the bottle land softly in his outstretched hands.

Amen.

Chapter Fifty-Eight

NOLAN, CRAWFORD, REMY, AND SAM WATCHED the flames ravage the chapel. They swirled and writhed with fury and sent columns of smoke and sparks toward the peaceful cerulean sky. Heaven and Hell. Appropriate, Nolan thought.

There weren't enough tanker trucks to save it, and there was nothing anybody could have done to save Father Paul—and they had all desperately wanted him to live so he could die an old man in prison. When Sam had caught the bottle, Father Paul had turned and walked directly into the inferno like a mad zealot, his arms outstretched as if to embrace it. Nolan wondered if he'd seen the fires of Hell or divine light before he'd been consumed. Or maybe he hadn't seen anything but escape. Whatever he professed, he was no man of God, although he may have come to believe his own proselytizing in order to justify his vile existence—the absolute pinnacle of cognitive dissonance.

She turned away, her soul sickened by everything she'd seen here. More things that would follow her to her grave. Sam caught her eye, and she saw equivalent devastation in his. Another horrible, shared experience between them. Half-insane with exhaustion and black emotions, she giddily thought they had to stop meeting like this. "Thank you," she mouthed, which seemed so pathetically inadequate. He'd saved Marielle and Serena, and then he'd saved her and probably a lot of other people. He would make a better cop than any of them.

Sam acknowledged her with a barely perceptible nod, then looked up at the FBI chopper setting down in the distance. Nolan followed his gaze and wondered what kind of memories a helicopter landing in the desert brought back to him.

This was an end for all of them, but in many ways, it was only the beginning.

•

Remy was sitting in a stiff chair in the hospital waiting room, considering the pattern of beige and seafoam-green squares and circles on the institutional upholstery. Somebody somewhere had been hired to choose it, but the selection made no sense to him. Had it made sense to them?

His body was throbbing with physical and psychic aches more intense than any he'd felt before. An unopened can of Coke sat on the table next to him, but he couldn't marshal the energy or will to pick it up. Lenny was sitting across from him, chin in hand, eyes remote and fixed on the far wall. Mike was stretched out on a love seat between them, sound asleep. The sleep of the innocent. He was a killer, but he didn't know it.

"Thank you for being here, Lenny."

His face was weary and hangdog, but he mustered a smile. "You couldn't have stopped me. I'm thanking the good Lord they're going to be okay."

"I'm with you there."

"Some rest and fluids and they'll be good as new. Amazing. Lucky." He tipped his head. "You both have a lot to process."

He didn't know the half of it. "We do."

"You'll do it together, one step at a time. You look exhausted and dehydrated yourself. What happened back there after I left, Detective? By the smell of you, there was a fire."

Remy dragged his hands through the tangle of his hair. "I'll tell you the full story, but I don't think I'm up to it just now."

He nodded solemnly. "Mike talked to me on the way here about the alien. He told me there were bodies in that old mine, too. Some old, like mummies. Others not so old."

Jesus. Mike's kills or somebody else's? At least it was a guarantee that Mike would be forthright about it. "Thanks for letting me know, Lenny. We'll get a forensics team up there."

"Mike really believes he killed an alien, Detective. He's always been this way. What's going to happen to him?"

"The police will be here soon, and he'll have to go through the process like any murderer. But I don't think any judge will find him competent to stand trial, so he won't go to prison."

"Then a mental hospital?"

"A place where he can get some help. I know you'll be there for him, and he'll need it. And appreciate it."

A sweet-faced, matronly woman in a white coat entered the waiting room and offered her hand with a smile. "You must be Detective Beaudreau. I'm Dr. Singh and I'm very happy to tell you that your sister and niece are doing well and responding to IV fluids. They were severely dehydrated, but they're out of danger now."

Remy let out a breath he didn't know he'd been holding. "They were drugged and there were cuts and abrasions . . ."

"Mr. Jesperson told me a little about what they've been through, and I'm so sorry. Thankfully, neither of them sustained major injuries and the sedatives are wearing off. They just need plenty of rest and a little TLC for a few days. This is a happy ending."

Remy hoped so. "I'd like to bring them home today."

"That won't be a problem. Marielle is still groggy, but she's been asking about you. You, too, Mr. Jesperson. And a man named Sam. Is he here?"

"No. But I'll call him." Remy pushed himself up out of the chair, feeling a hundred years old. He glanced at Lenny. "Come on."

"Thanks, but this is your time, Detective. I won't interrupt."

He extended his hand to the man who looked as old as he felt. "You have as much right to be there as I do. Maybe more."

"Then so does Sam. Go on ahead, I'll call him. He's going to need a ride. Wait, hang on a second." He dug into his jeans pocket and pulled out Charlotte's necklace.

"You give it to her when you come back, Lenny. That's between the two of you."

He nodded gruffly and left.

Remy followed Dr. Singh down the hall. He hated the smell of antiseptic, the squeak of shoes on the polished floor, the rattle of rings on a metal rod as a privacy curtain was opened onto a hospital room—it reminded him of visiting Louis right before he'd died of his injuries. But from now on, he thought he might associate the sounds and smells of a hospital as a start to something, not an end.

Charlotte look so small, so helpless, but her eyes weren't empty and terrorized anymore as she met his gaze. Tears sprang from them and tracked down her cheeks. "Remy."

He went to her and took her outstretched hands. "God, Charlotte. It's good to have you back."

She sniffled. "Were you really looking for me all these years?"

"Of course I was. So were Mom and Dad. Why didn't you come to me once you escaped?"

"I can never forgive myself, so I didn't expect you to forgive me, either. I thought it was better if everybody thought I was dead."

He took her in his arms again and held her as sobs wracked her body. "Don't say that, Charlotte, it's not true. Don't say anything right now. We'll have plenty of time to talk. For now, let's get to know each other again." He looked at the bed next to them, where Serena was stirring. "I think my niece is waking up."

Charlotte looked up and her trembling lips formed a smile. "Serena, are you awake, baby?"

The girl's eyelashes fluttered and blue eyes opened briefly. "Momma? Where are we?"

"We're in the hospital but we're going to be okay."

"I'm tired."

"Go back to sleep, baby. When you wake up, you can meet your uncle Remy."

She curled small fists under her chin and rolled over. "I have an uncle?" she mumbled before she started snoring softly.

Chapter Fifty-Nine

IVAN LUKIN STARED OUT THE WINDOW of his Gulfstream G650 as it taxied down the runway at Hollywood Burbank Airport. Angel was sleeping on the sofa across from him; his Fabergé egg was in a Halliburton case at his feet. There was $20 million in various currencies in the hold, along with some of his other valued personal possessions and marketable product. It was a good day for a business trip; he had several stops planned before Kaliningrad.

As he sipped vodka and lime, he pondered all the people he should have killed a long time ago. The list was long, but Zoe was at the top. If he'd taken care of her the night of the kidnapping, none of this would be happening now. Come to think of it, he should have killed Misha, too—he'd been a dismally failed experiment. And Irina and Gregory. But now wasn't the time for regrets; now was a time to look ahead. This was a minor setback and he would emerge victorious, just like he always did. Like any great international corporation, he was simply too big to fail.

Retirement was a possibility. A man should take time later in his life to enjoy the vast bounty of his labors and achievements. As the Chinese saying went, contentment was knowing when you had enough.

When his phone rang, he smiled down at the screen. "Detective Nolan. Do you have news for me?"

"Some sad new for you, I'm sorry to say. Father Paul is dead."

"I'm stunned."

"He took his own life."

"Terrible." *Wonderful.*

"Fortunately, Irina Walters is still alive. We found her at Children of the Desert. Turns out she wasn't out of the adoption business after all. Well, it's not really adoption, it's human trafficking. Good thing you cut ties with Loving Hearts a long time ago, or else you would be in serious trouble."

Ivan felt prickles of sweat crawl beneath his Brioni shirt. Those *fucking* traitors. "Yes, it is a good thing. Although I'm very displeased that I was giving donations to an organization involved in such a hideous thing."

"I didn't say Children of the Desert was involved. Of course, I implied it, didn't I?"

"You absolutely did." Ivan tried to keep the irritation out of his voice.

"We still haven't figured out why somebody would poison Blake at the Bel-Air, though. I think you said that would be stupid, didn't you?"

"Yes, very stupid. Do you have any ideas?"

"My partner and I believe that because the place had sentimental meaning to the Lindgrens, the killer was hoping to frame it as an encounter gone terribly wrong. But Zoe was dead a day before Blake ever showed up there, which kind of blew that out of the water. No pun intended."

"A murder-suicide, perhaps? As you mentioned, the Bel-Air had sentimental meaning. The Swan Lake suite was a favorite of theirs."

"Funny you should mention it. That's where we think he was poisoned and where he died. Then thrown into the lake to disperse the nerve agent that killed him. Did you know many of them are water-soluble?"

"No, I didn't."

"Not very useful information, I suppose. Anyhow, Blake obviously wasn't a suicide, autopsies don't lie. So we're trying to come up with a motive."

Ivan smiled in satisfaction. To her credit, the detective was clever. But he would be long gone before they could unravel anything. Not that they possibly could. He had little confidence in the competency of law enforcement because he'd been able to successfully evade it for so many years. "I was wrong about Children of the Desert, so perhaps I was also wrong about one of the companies we work with. International trade can be a prickly business. There is a lot at stake."

"I imagine there is. We'd like to speak with you about Michael Lindgren's kidnapping as soon as we get back to LA. I hope you don't have any travel plans."

"Nothing planned, no."

"That's good. We'll be speaking soon, then."

"Yes. Good day, Detective." Ivan finished his vodka and hung up as the plane slowed, then stopped. A few moments later, Sergei exited the cockpit.

"I'm sorry, Mr. Lukin, but the captain says there's been a ground hold. He hopes the delay won't be long."

Ivan looked out the window again and saw flashing lights as a formation of police cars drove across the tarmac. Detective Nolan had an excellent sense of humor. He liked her for that. "Sergei, another drink, please."

While Sergei busied himself in the galley, Ivan moved to the sofa, sat next to Angel, and stroked her great head. She snuffled, lashed his hand with her long pink tongue, then sighed and laid her head back down on her massive paws.

No regrets, he thought again as he pulled his favorite pistol from his shoulder holster: a Makarov. So many memories. Such a good life. He'd finally gotten that fucking egg from Viktor, things didn't get much better than that.

Chapter Sixty

THREE DAYS LATER, NOLAN'S PHONE JOLTED her out of a dead sleep. She rolled over in her bed, groped for it, and was shocked to see the clock read almost noon. She couldn't even remember falling into bed last night. It was a miracle she'd even made it this far. "Hello?"

"Margaret, did I wake you?"

People always lied about being wakened by the phone, as if it was something to be ashamed of. She was guilty of it just like everybody else, but this morning she told the truth. "Yes, but I'm glad to hear your voice, Mom."

"You poor dear, you've had such a time, go back to sleep."

"No, no, I have to get up." She pulled herself out of bed and slipped on a robe. "How are you and Daddy?"

"We're good. We'd like to come for a visit when you're recovered from your horrible case. We saw your press conference, you were wonderful. Is everything all wrapped up?"

Wonderful? Who was she talking to? She stumbled into the kitchen and started filling the coffee carafe with water. "We found our killers, so our part is, yes. We're just waiting for some DNA and toxicology reports so we can tie up some loose ends. But the overall scope of it is so vast, it will probably take a year for the feds to sort out the rest."

"We've been reading about it; there have been so many arrests. They say this was a blow to Russian organized crime. And to certain politicians."

"Heads are going to roll, and not just in this country. When can you and Daddy come? I'll tell you all about it."

"You pick a day and let us know."

"How about tomorrow?"

"We'll be there, text us a time." She paused for a long moment and took a fortifying breath. "Your father and I went through the box of Max's medals last night."

Nolan almost dropped the carafe.

"We want you to have one."

"I . . . I . . . I couldn't . . ."

"No, it's all decided. Max would want you to have one. We want you to have one."

She sagged into a chair and didn't speak until she could trust her voice. "That means a lot, Mom."

"I had a dreadful experience at Children of the Desert, and what happened after I left is unthinkable. But it did make me realize that life is too short to run from the things that hurt you, or the things you're afraid might hurt you. Remember that, Margaret."

Epilogue

CHARLOTTE HADN'T BEEN IN A LEGITIMATE church in over a decade. It was hard to think of herself as Charlotte Beaudreau again, but it was well past time to reclaim her real life; the one before Father Paul and Children of the Desert and all the bad things.

She stood at the doors, terrified that once she stepped inside, her greatest sin would be revealed. That a bolt of lightning would strike her dead.

"Are we going in, Momma?"

She stroked Serena's hair, done up in an elaborate French braid woven by Remy's housekeeper. "I can't decide."

"This is a way better church than Father Paul's. But you said we don't ever have to talk about him again."

"That's right."

"What are Grandma and Grandpa like?"

"I'm not sure what they're like now, but they're so excited to meet you."

"I'm going to miss Uncle Remy."

"He'll miss you, too, but he'll visit us soon."

"I'll miss Lenny, too. Do you think he'll come to see us in New Orleans?"

"I know he will. He probably already has a plane ticket." Should she tell her that Lenny was driving down just to ride with them to the airport and say good-bye? No, she'd let it be a surprise.

"Let's go inside, Momma. It's kind of weird standing outside doing nothing."

"You're right." She took a deep breath and pushed the door open. The church was empty and quiet and smelled like wood and hymnals and flowers. A shaft of morning light from the round, stained-glass window behind the altar striped the polished pews.

Charlotte reflexively dipped her hand into the font of holy water and crossed herself. No lightning bolts. Not yet. Her eyes drifted to the row of confessional booths with their clover-shaped lattice.

Forgive me, Father, for I have sinned. I haven't been to confession since I was fifteen. I hurt my family. I almost ruined my daughter's life. I killed a man. God will never forgive me. I don't deserve to be forgiven.

"Let's go pray, Serena."

"Who should I pray for?"

"Everybody you love."

Me. Pray for me.

•

Sam pulled the Mustang into the lot of Braemar Country Club and parked next to York Nolan's Escalade. He knew he was going to get his ass kicked—he hadn't golfed in years—but the environment and the company would be good.

Melody called as he pulled his clubs out of the trunk. "Hey, Mel."

"Hey, you. What's going on there?"

"Not much."

"That's funny. LA is still all over the news. I swear I saw you with Detectives Nolan and Crawford at a press conference."

"Must have been some other guy with a wrecked face."

Her laugh chimed on the other end of the line, and Sam realized how much he'd missed it. "What's up with you?"

"I'm coming home."

Some of the heaviness suffocating his heart lifted. "Chicago didn't do it for you?"

"It's okay, but I miss So Cal. Besides, you obviously need a keeper."

She was absolutely right about that. "When?"

"I fly in tomorrow night."

"My sofa happens to be available."

"I kept my apartment, you know that."

"Yeah, but I figure you'll want to get together for drinks so we can swap crazy stories. And I have this bottle of Jefferson's Ocean, so there's a possibility it will end up being a late, drunken night."

"Sounds good to me," she said breezily.

"Send me your flight information."

"You'll pick me up?"

"Of course, what kind of a question is that?"

"In the Mustang?"

"Absolutely."

"Actually, I don't really miss So Cal that much."

"No?"

"No. I miss you, Sam."

•

Nolan was luxuriating in the hot sun and the cold martini, practicing her new skill of living in the moment. Tomorrow wasn't guaranteed, so why waste a single, precious second of life? It was incredibly liberating to abandon the rigid structure of her routine and personal expectations. The term *reckless abandonment* came to mind, and she almost giggled.

The surface of Remy's swimming pool glittered temptingly and she imagined what the cool water would feel like on her baking skin. God, it was good to be here in Bel Air doing absolutely nothing. She looked over at him on the chaise next to her. His sunglasses were wraparounds, so she couldn't tell if his eyes were closed.

"What are you thinking about, Maggie?"

Nope, not closed. "Jumping in the pool."

"Be my guest."

"I didn't bring a suit."

"That shouldn't stop you."

"Another martini, and it won't."

He pushed his glasses to his forehead and gave her a look that made her feel naked already. "Then I'll mix a new batch."

"No complaints from me. But first tell me what's in that big box by the diving board."

"It's a drone. I thought we'd set it up and give it a test run."

"Don't you already have a thousand of them?"

"You're close, Maggie," he smirked. "I have ten. But this one is for Sam. He expressed an interest."

She thought of Sam and her father on the golf course. They were probably finished by now and having drinks in the club. Colonel York Nolan hadn't played a game of golf since Max had died, and thinking of him back out on the greens tightened her throat. It was a bizarre turn of fortune that Sam had entered all of their lives as a murder suspect, and ultimately had either saved them or made them better. But she would never say it out loud, it was too weird and maudlin. "That's nice. I'm sure he'll love it, Remy."

"I know we said no shop talk, but I'm curious if there's been any progress on the bodies in the mines."

"They're still working on identifying all of them. A lot are over a century old, from back in the mining days. But there are more recent ones, and a few have matched with missing persons through dental or prison records. Two of them have damage to the eye sockets. With DNA, we might eventually know who was responsible."

The following silence was long, punctuated by birdsong and the distant sound of traffic.

"Are Charlotte and Serena going to be alright?" she finally asked.

"Eventually. They've been through a lot."

"Will you be going to New Orleans?"

"Soon." He gave her a roguish smile, dispelling the darkness that had seeped into their conversation. "So what do you think, Maggie? Drone or more martinis?"

She stood and began to unbutton the bodice of her dress. Her mother was right. Life was too short to run from anything. "I'm jumping in that pool."

Acknowledgments

MUCH GRATITUDE TO THE STELLAR TEAM at St. Martin's Minotaur, for their brilliant work and support: Kelley Ragland, Hector DeJean, Danielle Prielipp, Madeline Houpt, the superb art department, and many other alchemists who magically turn manuscripts into books and send them out into the world. It's a joy to work with you.

Ellen Geiger and Matt McGowan of Frances Goldin Literary Agency—you are keystones and friends, and I thank you both from the bottom of my heart for being there for me all these years.

Family and friends—I am always humbled by your love and support and cheerleading, whatever I do.

In memory of the real Irina Walters, who was an academic mentor and a truly wonderful person. *Pokoysya s miron.*

In memory of Phillip Lambrecht ("Doggy Daddy"), who taught me how to ride a motorcycle, oil paint, play chess, and swear at computers. You weren't ready to go, and we weren't ready to let you.

Dearest PJ—I miss you so much. Death leaves a heartache no one can heal; love leaves a memory no one can steal.